The Silver Crown

Iris ran her tongue over his lips again and then sat back and pushed one finger into his mouth – thinking about his jaws. Those jaws that had nearly savaged her more than once. It turned her on. The things about him that tore him apart just made her wet. 'Bite me, werewolf,' she whispered.

Alfie closed his teeth around her finger.

'Harder.'

Alfie bit harder. Iris closed her eyes and felt it. It felt so real. She thought of everything. She thought about the Beast the night everything changed, ripping into her brother, tearing Alfie's flesh. She thought about her old colleague Jude who the Beast had killed in front of her. She thought of Alfie attacking her in his wolf form. She thought of her wedding night with Blake when he'd handcuffed her to the bed and fucked her, saying, 'Sometimes I think you *want* the Beast to kill you. Go the same way as your brother. Maybe that's why it won't do it.' Iris hadn't replied, just looked away, rolling her face into her arm – her lean muscular arms pulled taut in the cuffs. 'Oh my God,' Blake had said, not breaking the rhythm of his fucking. 'Is that true? Do you want the Beast to kill you?'

The Silver Crown
Mathilde Madden

BLACK LACE

Black Lace books contain sexual fantasies.
In real life, always practise safe sex.

First published in 2007 by
Black Lace
Thames Wharf Studios
Rainville Rd
London W6 9HA

A catalogue record for this book is available from the British Library.

www.black-lace-books.com

http://lustbites.blogspot.com/

Typeset by SetSystems Ltd, Saffron Walden, Essex

Printed and bound in Great Britain by CPI Bookmarque,
Croydon, CR0 4TD

The paper used in this book is a natural, recyclable product made
from wood grown in sustainable forests. The manufacturing process
conforms to the regulations of the country of origin.

ISBN 978 0 352 34157 0

Distributed in the USA by Holtzbrinck Publishers, LLC, 175 Fifth Avenue,
New York, NY 10010, USA

For Ewan who knows about trilogies.

1

Far, far away, on the most south-western tip of the British Isles was a small wooden cabin. It was a simple place. One room. Perfectly situated just off a dirt track on the edge of some woodland. The cabin's previous owner, a middle-aged man, had died the full moon before last. Now, in this solitary spot, a werewolf lived alone.

The werewolf was very happy. Finally free. He found work where he could. Manual labour mostly, on the farms and conservation centres. He'd be raping the earth with pesticides one week and saving the planet the next. This was the kind of thing that amused him. And if work was hard to come by he knew the land. He trapped rabbits and game birds. Once he broke into a farm and stole a goat, but that was far more trouble than it was worth.

He never got lonely. If you are a werewolf there is always the company of women.

This particular night, the werewolf had brought home a woman called Sabrina. He had found her in the pub in the nearest village – looking totally out of place amongst the tangled, tousled surfer girlfriends and lithe, hardy farmer's wives.

Sabrina was one of the most beautiful women the werewolf had ever seen, with perfectly curved hips under her dark-indigo jeans and a tight pink sweater that even the werewolf could tell was very, very expensive. She had golden skin that spoke of warm places and soft breezes and a dark cloud of wavy hair. Her white teeth glittered too. One of her front teeth glittered more than the others.

It was silver. A silver tooth. When the werewolf looked at it – when he imagined it scraping across his skin – he got scared and hard.

He'd already asked her back in the pub if it was real silver. She'd laughed. 'No. I don't think so. Some kind of special alloy, I think. And when she said that, the way she'd looked at him, it was almost like she'd known.

The werewolf's cabin was all wooden floor and warm rugs. There was a stove for heating but it wasn't much of a match for the January cold. It had been a hard winter. The werewolf pulled Sabrina into his bed, covering her with soft blankets and his own paranormal warmth before he started to strip her.

Her body was amazing. Firm and toned, shaped like his fantasies. He used his tongue everywhere. Werewolves love to use their tongues. Every inch of skin got anointed as he revealed it. Her stomach as he pushed up her sweater, her legs as he drew down her jeans, her breasts, her hips, her back. He dropped onto the floor in front of her and kissed the tops of her elegantly arched feet. He worshiped her. He was an arrogant creature usually, cocksure and confident, but Sabrina unnerved him just a little. Too beautiful. Too beautiful for him.

She smiled down at him and normally a smile from a girl like Sabrina would make him preen inside, but she still had him on edge. There was something about her. He was scared. Like this must be some kind of trick. Like there had to be a catch. Like she would suddenly stop and laugh at him for thinking he could land a woman like her.

She slipped off the bed onto the rug next to him. They were both naked. It crossed his mind that she ought to be cold, but she didn't seem to notice it. He gave off a lot of heat. Werewolves do. Maybe he was giving off enough to keep her warm too.

She pushed him flat onto his back and got on top, her

whole body pressing itself along the length of him. She put her mouth to his. They kissed closed mouthed for a little, and then slowly she worked her tongue between his lips. He opened his mouth like he belonged to her.

Some werewolves have a particular affinity for metal. All werewolves can sense mercury and silver. But he could do more than that. When he ran his tongue over her tooth he only had to graze it twice with the tip before he muttered, 'Chromium alloy,' and Sabrina laughed darkly into his mouth.

When she moved down his body, she used her chromium alloy tooth to pluck his nipples to hardness and then let her hot mouth cover his cock. He writhed on the floor.

The chromium alloy didn't hurt him. It tingled but it was not an unpleasant feeling, even when it was nipping at the head of his cock. It was nothing like silver or mercury. Those could sting. He'd been with a girl once who had every one of her back teeth filled. The mercury amalgam against his cock had left him sore with the memory of her for weeks.

Her mouth was hot and damp and spiked with sensation. He bucked his hips and Sabrina pulled back. She sat up and sucked on her bottom lip as if savouring the taste of him. Then she smiled that unnerving smile again, hitched forwards and slipped herself onto his needy twitching cock. He looked up at her, curves and dark hair and chromium tooth. She was like something from a fairy story. She was like the reward that good werewolves got.

When the werewolf woke up the next morning and saw her puffy cloud of dark hair on the pillow he almost felt sad. Sad that he was going to have to say goodbye to her. Sad that he never did more than one night with anyone. It was better that way. Now that he didn't have a pack he preferred to keep his ties as loose as possible.

He blew lightly in Sabrina's ear and she opened her eyes. 'Hi, tiger,' she said, smiling.

The werewolf nodded. 'Hey, baby. Listen, I've got to work today. Sorry.'

'That's OK,' Sabrina said. She climbed over him and out of the bed, picked up her jeans and started shimmying into them. Then she grabbed her sweater and pulled it over her head as she walked across the cabin to the chair by the door and picked up her handbag. The werewolf had a small mirror on the wall by the front door. Sabrina turned to it and started rooting in her bag.

'So,' said the werewolf, looking at her reflection. 'I guess I'll see you around.'

Sabrina caught his eye in the mirror and smiled. She turned slowly, drawing something from her bag at the same time. 'Oh you won't be seeing me, baby. You won't be seeing anyone.'

The werewolf ran his tongue over his suddenly dry lips. 'What?'

Sabrina was pointing a gun at him. She winked. 'That's right, Leon. Silver bullets.'

Leon pushed back his shoulders. 'Oh, what? You're a Vix? What's going on? Vix don't come this far west. They staking out new territory?' He sniffed. 'And using new tactics?'

'Tell you what,' said Sabrina, 'when you're holding the gun you can ask the questions.'

Leon let his eyes slide down her body and up again. He couldn't decide whether the fact she was so eerily beautiful made this easier or harder.

It certainly made something harder. He slid his legs out from under the bed clothes and stood up naked in front of her. His erection bobbing against his scarred belly.

'Stay where you are.'

Leon stopped still. 'I just have one more question.'

'What?'

'Why is it that you pointing that gun at me is making me so horny, sweetheart?'

'Really? It's making you horny? Well you'll love this, then.' Sabrina laughed. She tipped the nose of the gun and fired straight into Leon's shin.

Almost before he heard the shot Leon crashed onto the floorboards, crying out. He grabbed his wounded leg, squeezing tight, trying to push out the pain. He looked up at Sabrina with tears in his eyes. 'What did you do that for, you crazy bitch?'

'What? Didn't that make you horny? *Sweetheart*?'

'Of course it fucking didn't.'

'Well isn't that a shame.' Sabrina walked across the cabin, until she was close enough to bend over and press the gun against Leon's chest. 'But now perhaps you understand why it's important not to piss me off.'

Leon looked up at her. He only been this scared of one other person his whole life. 'What do you want?' he choked.

'I want your sire, Leon. I want Alfie Friday.'

2

Friday, 18 January 2008

Iris knew that Blake had kept the old office. So, as far as the feel of the place went, nothing much had changed. Except now Blake had a bright new plaque for his door that said *Blake Tabernacle, Director*.

Iris – dressed in her full and freshly pressed uniform of dark-red army fatigues – planted her fist just below the shining brass and knocked so hard her knuckles stung.

'Come in.'

Blake's office looked the same. Iris wasn't sure what she'd been expecting. Desk in the same place, wall of books, door to the lab half ajar. And there was Blake, sat at the desk looking the same as ever – dirty lab coat over his own red fatigues, sharp little face and far, far too much unmanageable dark hair in a style that made it look as if the top of his head had just exploded.

As casually as possible, Iris crossed the room to Blake's desk and stood in front of it. There was no chair there. Blake stopped typing, leaned back and looked at her. 'Ah, Iris. Pleasant break?' he said, sounding different. Sounding, rather worryingly, like Doctor Tobias.

'Fine thanks.'

'How many times did you do it?'

'How many times did I do what?'

Blake smiled the slowest, creepiest smile Iris had ever seen. Outclassing all his previous records.

'Fuck off, Blake.' Iris said angrily, noticing at the same

time that she had fallen into a militaristic at-ease position, with her legs hip width apart and her hands clasped behind her back. She coughed and purposely started to fidget with her ear lobe, pushing her weight onto one hip and cocking her head to give Blake a wearisome look. 'This is not how it's going to be with us, you know.'

'It isn't?' Blake shucked his chair back a little on its castors and leaned right back in it, spreading his legs wider and taking up space. It was like a game already. Her move. His move. 'Don't you think I get to decide how it's going to be between us? And in future that really ought to be "Fuck off, sir". I outrank you now, Iris. And just because you're my wife I'm not going to be giving you special treatment, you know. Not good for morale.'

Iris paused. She sucked her bottom lip for a second then said, 'Look. Blake – and, God, I am not going to start calling you "sir". But, OK, have your little power trip if you want. Seriously, have a ball. You're my boss now. You always acted like you were anyway and now its official. I bet your dick's hard under that desk just thinking about it. But don't start pissing me around and asking me questions about my sex life. Me and Alfie – that's private. If you think it's cute, well, it's not cute. You are not cute.'

'Oh, Iris, don't be so mean, you'll make me cry!' Blake stayed in his semi-reclined position and swung the chair back and forth a little. 'But, well, at least you know I'm the boss, right? You know I'm in charge now?' He raised his eyebrows at her.

Iris's move. She leaned forwards, placing her palms on the desk and putting her face in Blake's space. 'And you do know I'm the best werewolf hunter you've got? If I hadn't taken time out from my leave and come out with you on the last sweep on Christmas Eve you'd be dead. I saved your damn life, Blake, so if you think you can talk to me like . . .'

'Iris, we've both saved each other's lives on sweeps a thousand times. We don't keep score on that.'

'And you do remember the prophecies, don't you? I'm the one. The Warrior Wolf who will kill all the Ancient Beasts. So you do get the not pissing me around thing?'

Blake rolled his eyes. 'God, Iris, two seconds you've known about that prophecy and already you're strutting around like cock of the walk – just because of that and the fact that you've now got Fido for a pet with his licky-licky tongue. I've known you for ten years, Iris. You're not fooling me. Nothing's changed. Your brother's still dead, Alfie's still a werewolf and you're still a fuck up.'

Iris shook her head. 'You don't know shit about me, Blake.'

Blake smiled like his moment had arrived. 'I'm your husband, Iris.'

'Not for very much longer.'

'Oh, that old riff, well that's great, Iris. You get your lawyer to send me some paperwork and we'll talk, until then, we're still married.'

Iris sat down on the edge of his desk and leaned back towards him. 'Blake,' she said, softly, darkly, 'you need to move on.'

'Yeah,' said Blake, 'I know, baby. It's such a tragedy. How can I ever get over you?' He reached over Iris's legs and pressed a button on the intercom on his desk. 'Aurelia, could you bring in those coffees, please.'

Iris looked at Blake. 'Aurelia? Yeah, I knew she was still working here even though she'd been bitten. She lives with Alfie now that she's his cub. She's your, what? Your secretary?'

Aurelia was already standing in the open doorway with a small tray holding two steaming cups. She smiled. 'Not secretary, personal assistant,' she said in her familiar cut-glass voice, as she strode into the room. Still so beautiful. Aurelia had always been startling even as one of Iris's team of werewolf killing soldiers in dark-red fatigues with her hair scraped back. Right now she looked phenomenal. Iris couldn't decide what it was that made Aurelia so extra-specially breathtaking. The natural overtly sexual glow that followed a werewolf bite or the fact that she was now dressed in kinky-secretary chic: tight white shirt, short black skirt, high black heels. Her long blonde hair was loose around her shoulders and the way she was looking at Blake, Iris was horrified to find herself actually slightly jealous.

When Aurelia got to Blake's desk she set down the tray and stood in front of it expectantly, with her hand on her hip like a cheesecake pin-up. She gave Iris, still perched on the edge of the desk, a slightly odd look. Blake smiled. 'That's great, Aurelia, and could you come back in when Mrs Tabernacle leaves.' He winked, so slow and deliberate it was like a parody of a wink.

'When Mrs . . .' Aurelia narrowed her eyes. Then followed Blake's gaze to look at Iris, who shifted on the desk, annoyed. 'Oh, oh right. Iris.' Aurelia turned away – without giving the slightest impression she thought any of this was odd – and did the whole look-how-beautiful-I-am walk in reverse.

When the door closed Iris said, 'So, that was subtle. And yes, I get it, you got your WXX in the end.'

'Yeah. Tell your boyfriend thanks. Funny, I never thought of asking a human-loving lyc to just *make* me one.'

'Don't, Blake. Alfie's really cut up about it. Biting Aurelia . . .' Iris's voice trailed away. What to say?

'Is he? Is he? A blot on the horizon, is it? Not quite the happy little set up you would have wanted if he's got a new pup to take care of.'

Iris felt her jaw tighten. 'It's fine. She lives with him in the old pack house. It doesn't bother me.'

'Really? Even with you living there too. I know you are. Your lights are never on in your flat.'

'God, Blake, you haven't been to my flat.'

'Only twice. Just to see if you'd got bored of werewolf dick yet.'

Iris rolled her eyes. 'Oh God.'

'Actually, Iris, I need to know these things. If you're living in that pack house you need security. I had Cate put the cloaking spell on it.'

'You had Cate do what?'

'The cloaking. Like we have here. It's also on my flat and yours, Tobias's old house and now that pack place. We need to be careful, Iris. If lycs find us . . .'

'So the pack house is cloaked from lycs? Damn it, Blake, the whole reason Alfie kept that place was so his old pack would be able to find him if they came back.'

'Well, they will be able to. The cloaking has a loophole in it. If it didn't, Alfie and Aurelia wouldn't be able to find their way home, would they? The spell has a hitch in it so if a werewolf has been to a place before he'll find it fine, but otherwise – no dice.'

'Oh, you really did go the extra mile,' Iris said, half sarcastic, half genuine admiration.

'Not really. All the cloaking we use has that hitch in it. Always has done.'

'Really? Why?'

'Think about Iris. What sort of creature did our boss turn out to be?'

Iris could barely believe Blake's nerve. Bringing up the way their boss had turned out to be Iris's werewolf nemesis as if Blake had had no involvement in that whatsoever. 'Turn out to be! *You* knew all along. But, yeah, I see. Tobias had to have that fix so he could find his own way here.'

'Or to his own house. Or your place. Damn that Beast was clever. He'd read that prophecy. He was so certain a werewolf would kill him. So he had everywhere he went cloaked from lycs who hadn't been there before. The only time he ran any kind of risk was full moon when he was out in his wolf form.'

'And that's when he had us out there, keeping lycs away from Oxford.'

'You've got to admire him really,' Blake said.

Iris pulled a face.

Blake coughed. 'Just on that level, I mean.'

Iris nodded. 'Well, just be careful. With Aurelia, I mean, like I said, Alfie's very sensitive about it. If you hurt her...'

'Oh, yeah, yeah. I know. In fact I've only been *comforting* her because he's been neglecting her. The big bad wolf. Spending too much time with you. She's jealous.'

Iris felt herself shiver. 'Blake you haven't been...'

'Been what? Been sleeping with her? Sorry, is that a problem because I thought we might have changed from The Institute of Paraphysiology into The Institute of Sleeping with Werewolves and I just missed a memo.'

'Blake. It's not like that. Alfie's...'

'Different?'

'Yes.'

'No. No, he isn't. He's just the same. He's nearly killed you twice and he will turn on you in the end.' Blake smiled, shaking his head. Both of them were silent for a minute and then Blake said, 'But enough banter. We need to talk about you. About your job. About your, well, destiny. You're right, I'm sorry to say. This Warrior Wolf thing does interest me. You interest me. If you're going to be killing Ancient Beasts I want you doing it on my watch, no matter how compromised you might be.'

'Compromised?'

'OK, when I say *compromised* that's just my shorthand for someone who has been sucking a werewolf's dick anytime in the last twenty-four hours.'

'And you and Aurelia?'

'Actually, she doesn't have a dick.'

Iris raised her eyebrows.

'OK, fine. The difference is I am not in love with *Aurelia*.'

'So, your problem is what, Blake? That Alfie's a were-wolf, or that I'm in love with Alfie, or that I'm not in love with you?'

Blake didn't reply.

Iris hopped off the edge of his desk. 'And, God, would you get some chairs in here. What is wrong with you?'

'I do have some chairs. I put them in the lab. I wanted to make you stand.'

Iris made a face and went over to the door to the lab.

As she did Blake called after her back, 'I just wanted to see how long it would be before you started whinging about it.' Just inside the half-ajar door of the lab were two hard backed chairs. 'And "not very long at all", turned out to be the answer.'

Iris carried one chair back and set it in front of the desk. She took her cup from the desk and sat back with one ankle propped on the opposite knee. She took a sip of the coffee. 'Wow,' she said, after she had swallowed the first mouthful of wonderfully smooth rich blackness, 'this is certainly a cut above that instant stuff you used to make in the world's most repulsive kettle over there.' Iris pointed to where Blake's horrible electric kettle and dirty mugs used to be, not really surprised to see them gone.

Blake tutted. He clasped his hands in front of him and leaned forwards, extending both his middle fingers and pointing at Iris, 'Look, can we talk about work? Can we talk about what I see as your main job here from now on: the killing or, if possible, capturing of Ancient Beasts.'

'Yeah, sure, I mean if any Ancient Beasts show up on sweeps, I'll be sure and whack them.'

'Yeah. It's actually not as simple as that, Iris? Look, do you know what The Silver Crown is?'

'Is that like the Silver Collar?'

'Not really, well, not at all, actually. The Silver Crown is a werewolf organisation. Secret. Covert. I think even a lot of lycs don't know about them. They're the werewolf police. Secret police. Werewolf Gestapo.'

Iris drank some more coffee. 'They sound cuddly.'

'Oh, yeah. About as cuddly as grenades covered in broken glass. Now I have these documents about The Silver Crown, here . . .' Blake broke off and opened his top drawer. He took out his spectacles and put them firmly and lopsidedly on his nose. Then he opened his bottom drawer and slapped a mouldering stack of yellowish paper on the table.

Iris glanced at the top sheet. As usual for documents Blake showed her it looked like unintelligible squiggles. 'Ri – ight?'

'Oh, yes,' said Blake, 'and I got the translation done. Done by some other drippy milk-skinned gimp rather than migraining my way through it myself for a change.' Blake fished out some more paper. This time white and neat. He offered the documents to Iris but as she went to take them snatched them back out of reach. 'Maybe I should keep these. Dangerous information for one with such dubious motives as you. I'll just give you a précis.'

'Blake . . .'

'Now look, about these papers. I got them from the doc's house.'

'You broke into the doc's house!' Even though she knew Blake was not above a little breaking and entering, she was slightly surprised that he'd be so brazen.

Blake looked a little shifty for a second. 'Not exactly. He, er, well, he left it to me.'

'He left you his house!'

'He had to leave it to someone.'

'He left you that enormous house in Summertown. That must be worth ... oh my God.' Iris sat back and whistled through her teeth.

'Well I don't know exactly. But I'm sure once your hot shot lawyers are on the case they'll make sure you get half in the ...'

'God's sake, Blake. I didn't mean that. It's just, well, it's weird. Don't you think it's weird that the doc left you his house?'

'Maybe. Slightly. But look property prices are really not what we are talking about right now. Don't you want to know what the translation said? Of the papers?'

Iris nodded.

'They're all about The Silver Crown. How it's made up of twelve powerful werewolves. Well, except it's eleven now. Because you killed one of them.'

Iris leaned forwards. 'Dr Tobias was one of them?'

'Yeah. It clearly says so. All those meetings he was always rushing off to. I reckon that was because he was part of this. The Silver Crown are all about maintaining the werewolf status quo. Keeping humans out of it. Enforcing laws. It all makes sense. I think The Silver Crown *are* the Ancient Beasts. No one's made that link before – but if Tobias was one. Well The Silver Crown are twelve powerful lycs. Maybe they are the twelve children of the She Wolf. The Ancient Beasts. '

Iris looked down. 'Right. Well I'm meant to kill the Ancient Beasts. That's what the prophecy said about me, right? So where do I find them?'

'Well, thing is, maybe you won't have to. They're going to be pretty upset about you destroying one of their number. Upsetting their power base. Maybe they'll find you.'

'Great. Save me a job.'

'Iris, this is serious. Twelve Ancient Beasts, well eleven, that's no easy stroll, even for you.'

'Well how will they even find me? You've done all that cloaking, remember. Alfie's the only lyc who ever found us and that was because he scented me.'

Blake actually looked a bit pale. 'They'll find a way. They know an awful lot about lyc business. And you're compromised. Alfie could be your weak spot.'

'No. Alfie would never . . .'

'Iris, this is serious. You can't trust anyone right now. Least of all a lyc. If The Silver Crown are coming for you . . .'

'I'll kill them. All of them. Isn't that the point?'

Just as Iris said that she looked up and standing right beside Blake, was the figure of someone long dead. Matthew. Her brother. Iris was a little surprised. She'd thought he wasn't haunting her anymore.

After Iris had gone, Blake pressed the button on his intercom and called Aurelia into the office. He didn't speak to her, just nodded at his crotch as he scooted his chair away from the desk.

As she dropped to her knees between his spread legs, she looked up at him and said, 'And afterwards, another lesson about werewolves?'

'Of course, baby. You know how it works.'

Aurelia got his dick out and took it easy and deep into her mouth. Blake sighed. He looked up at the office door – imagined Iris's retreating back. She really hated him now. He could feel it boiling off her. It turned him on.

He stroked the top of Aurelia's blonde head. She was so good at this. All the legends about female werewolves seem to be true. About werewolves and sex and their mouths. He thought of Iris's slight blush when he had made that crack about Fido being 'licky'.

Thinking about them together, Iris and Alfie, made his heart burn and ache. The strength of his feelings combined with the glorious sensations of what Aurelia was doing to him with her teeth and tongue and soft palette was so intense. He could barely tell the pain from the pleasure as his world turned upside down.

3

As Iris walked through the door of her office on the floor below, Alfie came at her from one side, whirling her around and forcing her back up against the wall. He held her firm with one arm while he reached out and slammed the door shut. 'Hi, Iris, just like old times, eh?' he said, moving back to hold her with both hands tight around her wrists as he lifted her arms up over her head. Iris gasped as he stretched her body, forcing her up onto her toes.

'Alfie,' she hissed, twisting in his strong grip, 'what the fuck are you doing here? Blake will go nuts if he knows there's a werewolf...'

But Alfie slipped both her wrists into one hand and clapped the other over her mouth, 'What? I just thought I'd celebrate your return to work by re-enacting a few treasured memories. We had a lot of fun here, as I recall.' He came close and nipped the side of her face with his teeth. She moaned behind his hand. 'But no mentioning the ex. Don't say that name. "Blake". You do that far too much, you know.'

Iris struggled a little in his big hands. But there was no way she was shifting either the grip on her wrists or the one on her mouth. However, she managed to twist her head a little and bite the fleshy ridge at the top of his palm. Alfie yelped and drew his hand away, but he didn't free her wrists. 'Alfie, how can I not mention Blake? He's just upstairs. He's my boss. And he's not exactly your biggest fan.'

'Really,' Alfie snarled as he spun Iris around in his

arms and slammed her face first into the wall, twisting her arms up into the small of her back. He reached down with the hand that wasn't holding hers and slipped it past the back of her waistband and into her underwear. He teased his way past her arsehole and round, dipping his fingers into the hot seam of her cunt.

Iris knew she was wet. All for him. He made her wet. Alfie. The scent of his body. The feel of it. Iris was tough and mean and strong, the Warrior Wolf, and yet he – Alfie, werewolf, Beast cub – could make her feel small and even girlish. Alfie licked the back of her neck and rubbed her clit at the same time. Iris moaned again.

He had her hands tight, but she twisted in his grip a little to make contact with the wall with her right shoulder then pushed back. The surprise was enough for her to get her wrists suddenly loose and she turned, bringing up her left knee and slamming it into Alfie's groin. Then she used her foot skilfully in the tiny space between their bodies to hit Alfie just below the knee on his dominant right leg, sending him over backwards before he recovered himself. He went down with such a loud bang that it seemed to shake the entire building. Iris sprang forwards and plonked herself on Alfie's big chest. 'Well it seems like both of us are a fountain of good ideas,' Iris said, battling a little to get his arms pinned under her knees.

Alfie gasped. 'And nice moves. New?'

Iris made a face. 'No. Old as the proverbial. I just never really used them on you before, because you screwed my concentration too much.'

'And now I don't?'

'No, not now I know I can have you anytime I want. And that I know I'm the only person who can work that magical werewolf-controlling collar around your neck. Oh, and that I'm your spooky werewolf life mate I reckon I'm pretty secure.'

'If you like, Iris, but I'm still not sure I believe in that stuff.'

Iris snorted.

'But I'm glad if it helps you understand how I feel about you. And there's the fact you're in a prophecy – destined to slaughter all the Ancient Beasts. That must feel good.'

'Mmm.' Iris knew she should tell Alfie what Blake had said about The Silver Crown. About the nasty werewolf secret police that could be coming for her right now, ready to take revenge for her killing the Beast. But she didn't. She just said, 'Yeah that, oh and you know what makes me feel most secure of all?'

'I think I do.'

'Can I do it now?'

Alfie smiled at her. The smile of a man who had just been made an offer he couldn't refuse.

Iris lifted herself off his chest a little so Alfie could roll onto his stomach underneath her.

He raised himself up on his elbows and unbuttoned his shirt then shucked it down his arms. Iris barely gave him time to get the fabric out of the way before she ducked her head down and ran her tongue over the bite scar on his shoulder. She'd done this before. She knew what would happen when she licked his scar but, even so, when she felt Alfie weaken – melt under her tongue like chocolate – it was an amazing feeling.

The first time she had done this – sometime during that glorious first week they had spent shut up in Alfie's attic bedroom trying out every sexual position they could think of and trying desperately, greedily to make up for eleven years apart – they had both been shocked by how much the touch of Iris's tongue on his scar had dismantled him.

When he had been able to speak he had said, 'It feels ... oh God, Iris, I can't describe. Look, you know when I do this?' As he spoke, Alfie had rolled over underneath her and pulled himself up so he was sitting with her straddling his lap. He leaned in and rubbed his stubbled chin against Iris's jawline in a move that always made her starry-eyed and wet.

Iris nodded, 'Uh huh.'

'Well, believe me, what you feel when I do that is nothing compared to what you licking my bite does.'

'So when other people have done that to you it hasn't felt the same?' Iris had said.

'No. The only time I felt that is during claiming.'

'What's claiming?'

'It's a cub-sire thing. I'd have thought Blake would know about it. When your sire comes to you, at that first change, he does that. Puts his mouth right where he bit you and the pleasure is so intense – it's like he wipes away all the trauma and pain of the attack. It makes you forgive him. It's incredible. That's claiming. Intense indescribable bliss. Beyond anything. A supernova of an orgasm, but instant and lasting as long as he keeps his mouth there. Your sire's mouth on your bite. That's the biggest thing really that binds you to your sire. Keeps you enthralled. Just the knowledge he can give you that amount of pleasure can be enough to ... sometimes, with sire and cubs who have sex with each other there's a lot of claiming involved.'

'Right. Except I'm not your sire. So what's happening? Maybe it's a life mate thing.'

Alfie shook his head. 'Yeah, well, who knows what it is. Maybe something to do with your new status as a wolf-killing super bitch.'

'I could ask Blake about it.'

'Oh, Iris,' Alfie had rolled his eyes, 'will you stop always bringing up Blake when we're in bed.'

Iris had laughed but then licked his bite scar again until he was up on his hands and knees on the bed in front of her unable to speak.

Later, Iris had said, 'You never did it, though. In that way. Sex and claiming. I mean, with Leon or Misty.'

Alfie made a strange face. 'Um. Once, with Misty. Um, I was fucked up one night. I had the chains then but the girl I'd picked up had totally freaked out at the mention of them. Left. Practically ran out the door. I was a bit wound up, drunk and horny, possibly it was close to the full moon. So I wanted Misty to come to bed with me instead. It was a bad time. I did something bad. I tried to persuade Misty with claiming.'

'And?'

'She didn't speak to me for a week.'

Ever since that night in the attic when they had discovered it, claiming had become a staple of Iris and Alfie's sex life. Iris found being able to turn Alfie – her big strong wolf – into a keening needing little puppy dog was something of a rush. And Alfie, Alfie was just powerless to say no.

On the floor of her office, Iris played with Alfie's scar tissue with her tongue for a little while longer as he moaned and gasped beneath her, then leaned close to his ear and said, 'Let's get up on the desk.' She wanted sex and she didn't fancy lying next to him on the industrial lino tiles somehow. Her office floor looked even less clean than usual.

Iris moved her in-tray and her computer keyboard out of the way and sat down, letting her legs fall apart idly. Alfie stood up, slotted his big body between them and kissed her first on the nose, then deeply and languidly on the mouth, before moving down her throat in little kisses and delicate soft bites. Iris sighed, tipping her head back. Alfie's mouth – wolf fangs – on her skin felt so real, so right. She couldn't believe she had felt any other way for so long.

All that time she'd thought she wanted to kill werewolves. She hadn't. She'd wanted this. Alfie. Werewolf.

That bone-snapping, bloodthirsty danger. He could change. The collar held him stable. But the potential was still there. Throbbing under his skin. That adrenaline she'd felt in the park the night Matthew was killed. She'd been searching for that feeling ever since. And here it was.

Alfie started unbuttoning her shirt. 'Have you got any of those handcuffs in here?' he said, looking up and raising his eyebrows.

'Ha ha. No. Basement or Blake's office, I'm afraid.'

'Shame.' Alfie dipped his head and kissed her nipple. 'You know, you just said his name again.' Alfie swirled his tongue and then finished his sentence with a firm bite.

Iris yelped out, 'What?'

'You said his name. Wasn't I meant to be putting a stop to that? You seem to have distracted me by being incredibly, sexily good at fighting and being able to turn my scar inside out with your tongue.'

Iris rolled her eyes. 'What are you talking about, Alfie?'

'I want you to stop saying his name. Blake's that is. In fact, if you say it more than three times during sex, I want you to pay a forfeit.'

'What sort of forfeit?'

Alfie scooted his head across to Iris's other breast and bit the other nipple too so she yelped again. 'A forfeit of my choice. Come on now.' He pulled away from her and replaced her keyboard. Having lifted it down from where Iris had put it on top of her ancient monitor, he switched on her computer.

'What? Come on now and do what?' Iris said, shuffling her body around to face him and gathering her shirt together.

'Oh, I want you to type it up.'

'Type what up?' Really very bemused, Iris slipped off the desk and started fastening up her shirt properly.

'No,' Alfie said, 'don't do that. Leave it. Leave it open. I like you like that. You have my absolute favourite kind of tits; did I ever tell you that? Little and pointy and ...' His voice disappeared into thickened arousal. He took a breath. 'Leave your shirt open.'

Oh, OK, he's in that *mood. He wants some Alpha time.* With her shirt still unfastened, Iris sat down in her chair. Wondering how much she was going to humour her bossy boss man. Wolf. Big bad wolf. Alfie stood behind her. The computer finished firing up and Iris opened up a word processing programme and waited for further instructions.

'OK,' Alfie said, 'Write *I, Iris Instasi-Fox Tabernacle Friday.*'

Iris looked up and over her shoulder, 'Alfie I am not calling myself that. I told Blake and I'm telling you, my name is enough of a mouthful without me adding even more syllables on the end ...' His expression stopped her, 'OK, OK.' She started to type and, as she did, Alfie reached up and under her arms, took one of her breasts in each hand and ran a thumb over each nipple. Iris bit her lip to stop herself moaning. She stopped typing. She hadn't even finished the word 'Iris'. 'Alfie,' she said, 'are you going to do that all the time I'm typing.'

'I think so,' Alfie said. 'Unless you'd prefer this. He used his forefingers with his thumbs then and rolled both of Iris's nipples in a firm pinch, making them tighten until she was breathless.

'Uh, that'll make it quite hard to concentrate.'

'OK, well maybe we'll keep that in case you make any typos. Come on now, *I, Iris Instasi-Fox Tabernacle Friday, do solemnly swear that I will stop saying the bloody name of my damn idiot ex-husband every time I make love to my gorgeous werewolf boyfriend Mr Alfie Friday, and if I do it three more times I will perform a forfeit of his choice.* And make a little place where you can sign and date it.'

'Oh fuck,' breathed Iris, trying to ignore Alfie's thumbs caressing her nipples and type perfectly. She only had to back space twice but both times Alfie tweaked her so hard that she yelped and giggled and desperately wanted him to fuck her instead of playing silly games.

But he didn't let her go after that. Of course he didn't – not in his Alpha mode. He spun her chair around and slid onto the floor between her legs and started to remove her trousers. When they, along with her underwear, were dragged down and off onto the floor, Alfie pressed the flat of his big tongue against the softly closed lips of her cunt. Iris squeezed her eyes shut. He always did this. She loved this. This tease. This little gesture that said, here's my tongue, it's right here, and I'm not doing anything with it until you ask me nicely. Iris looked down at him, watching her. He pulled his tongue away and then licked her quickly. Not close enough, not intimate enough to send her spiralling, but it still made her moan, 'Please, Alfie.'

Alfie's eyebrows flickered. She knew he wanted more than that. He liked her to ask. Blake had liked that too. But she'd never told Alfie that.

'Please, Alfie. Use your tongue. Lick me. Lick my cunt. Make me come with your mouth. Come in your mouth.'

Alfie laughed and while he was laughing he slipped his tongue into her, brought up both his hands, held her open and moved even closer.

Iris lost it so quickly. He was so damn good. Along with his tongue, he used his stubble-spiked chin, his teeth, the pad of his thumb. He turned Iris inside out.

He stopped just as she was on the edge of orgasm, made her whimper for a moment and then, lifted her right off her chair. He turned, holding her, her legs wrapped around his waist, and leaned over to press print on her computer. Then he set her down on the floor, turned her over and pulled her towards him with a big hand on each hip.

He slammed into her hard. It was always hard with Alfie and, really, he got her so damn wet it never mattered. Iris was strong but her arms were shaking as she tried to lock her elbows to support herself on all fours, fighting the urge to let herself buckle and rest her chin on the floor like a conquered bitch. She turned her head to look at him over her shoulder. His shirt was off now and his jeans and underwear were pushed down to his knees. His big hands were mostly holding her steady, but every now and then yanked her backwards, impaling her on him. She thought about him as a wolf. How he would feel covering her. Furry belly. That hard alien prick. And then she shook herself. He'd hate if she was thinking of him that way. Wolfman. Wolf. Man. Forbidden.

She reached back with one hand, bracing her left arm to keep her upright. As her right hand found its way into her cunt, her left arm shook even harder. She found herself thinking of a push up competition she'd once had with Blake. One armed, he'd said. Left arm. They must have done a hundred each – sweating and screaming.

She'd won. He'd gone down first. His left arm crumpling as he landed nose first on the asphalt of the yard, swearing. She'd laughed and sprung on top of him. His forfeit had been to make her come three times before he got his turn. Hand, then mouth, then cock. They'd done it in the back of the truck.

Alfie would hate her thinking about that, too. Reliving that dirty, diesel-scented sex with Blake, But she was gasping now, on the edge of orgasm.

The document was sliding smoothly off the printer. Alfie reached up and pulled the piece of paper down. Then he leaned right over and placed it and a pen on the floor in front of Iris, without his cock missing a single strong smooth stroke inside her. 'So you really expect me to sign this?' Iris gasped. Still drawing circles over her clit, supplementing Alfie's thrusts.

'Oh yes. Come on, I'll do that for you,' Alfie said breathlessly, pulling at her wrist and replacing her hand with his own.

Iris picked up the pen and put it on the paper. Alfie's relentless rhythm was making it slide all over the place. She could barely keep the pen in one place and she needed to come so much she could barely think of anything else. 'Alfie, I don't know if I can write like this.'

'Well you better try. I could stop, you know...' Alfie drew right back, almost drew his cock completely out of her and froze, his fingers still on her clit.

Iris almost screamed with sudden frustration. 'OK, OK,' she said, using the still moment to scrawl her name across the bottom of the page.

As she did so, Alfie drove back into her, his fingers twisted. He pinched her clit gently. In just the way he always had. Iris was coming – so hard – and, as she finished scrawling her name, her arms collapsed underneath her, bringing her nose down firmly on Alfie's kinky little contract.

After a short hard panting recovery she rolled over. Alfie was lying next to her, holding the piece of paper. 'So,' Iris cooed in his ear, 'you got some kind of secretary kink?'

Alfie laughed.

'And, you know, after what I saw downstairs I reckon Blake has too. You need to take a little more care of Aurelia, Alfie. It can't be good if she's going to Blake for guidance.'

Alfie looked sideways at Iris. 'I can't believe it. The contract is still warm from your printer and you're breaking the rules.'

'Oh,' said Iris, realising what she'd just said. 'But that doesn't count, does it? We'd finished.'

'Iris, my come isn't dry yet. It counts. Now you know the rules. You say that name three times during sex and you do a forfeit. Anything I ask.'

Iris laughed. 'OK, OK, we will never speak of him again.' She sat up and began to fumble her clothes back to respectability. And there, standing behind Alfie, was Matthew again. Matthew's ghost. Just Matthew looking at her. No emotion. She squeezed her eyes shut and the next moment he had gone.

Why was he still here?

4

Zac had never once thought about what being a werewolf pack Alpha would be like. They weren't even a big pack. There were only three of them. Just him, Pearly and Pure. And Pure wasn't even a werewolf. Still it seemed like an awful lot of responsibility just ensuring that they were safe and housed and fed.

Zac knew Oxford wasn't safe. Full of Vix. But where *was* safe? All Zac could feel when he thought about safety was the overwhelming pull of home. Home meant his old Alpha, Alfie; meant his sire, Leon; but most of all, to Zac, home meant *Home* – Texas.

After they'd escaped from the Institute in November they had gone back to the old pack house.

The November full moon had only been a day away and the house they returned to was dark and empty. Full of ghosts. The overly soft armchair poor Misty had liked to sit in to watch TV, Leon's cupboard in the kitchen which was still full of his chocolate bars, Alfie's chains on his bed in the attic. They couldn't stay here long – it wasn't safe for werewolves in Oxford – but that wasn't the reason they couldn't stay.

But the moon, the moon was coming. So they had to stay at least one night. They had to Lock Down. Couldn't run wild in Oxford. Not with the Vix everywhere.

Zac had got Pure to lock him and Pearly down in the cellar for that one last night. When he got down there, the sight of the four cages belonging to his old pack had made his eyes prickle and his throat ache.

Alfie's enormous cage, Misty's small one, Leon's hated

prison that Alfie practically had to wrestle him into every time, and Zac's own, the one that looked so shiny and new. The cages, those four cages, were his pack.

His pack. How could he ever replace them? How could he ever be happy any other way? He knew that nothing he built in its place could rival that structure. Pearl with her tall curvy frame, her wide hips and wide mouth, her hair the colour of oatmeal, was sweet and kind and dazzlingly beautiful but she couldn't replace Misty or Alfie or Leon. And as for Pure, Pure wasn't even a werewolf.

Pearl looked around the cellar and said, 'Do we need to be in the cages?'

'No, sugar. Don't see why. With the old pack we did it because there were three males in a confined space. But I think we'll be OK together. In fact, because of the sire-cub thing on the first change – claiming – it's probably better if we don't Lock Down fully.'

Pearl frowned. 'How come it works here? If we're underground?'

'Oh yeah, well, the cellar isn't totally light proof. We only need the tiniest chink. It's not so much the moonlight itself that makes us change as the moonlight kicks off a chain reaction in us. Leon's more of an expert in how it all works. But you'll feel it and you'll know. Those gaps in the door, the vent up there that opens onto the pavement: they're enough. We might have a slight delay before the moon hits us, but it won't stop us changing.'

'Oh good,' said Pearl with a sparkling grin, 'I can't wait.'

Zac shucked of his black leather jacket and started to unbutton his black silk shirt. 'You're really not scared at all, are you?'

'No. Why? Should I be? Does it hurt?' said Pearl, snapping open the poppers that ran all the way down the front of her lilac-coloured nurse's uniform. Zac had suggested to her a few times that they should maybe get her some other clothes. They had even looked through Misty's stuff once but it was all far too small and, as Pearl had pointed out, 'All her gear is way more out there than my boring utility uniform, baby.'

Pearl shimmied out of her underwear and Zac did the same, sliding his satiny black boxers down over his satiny black legs.

Pearl straightened and smiled, 'So, you ever done it as a wolf?'

'Never got the chance. Locked Down every time.' Zac said, knowing that wasn't what she was asking.

'So you've never done it *while* you were changing?'

Zac shook his head and felt his cock pulse. Pearl was naked. He was already getting hard.

Pearl loved werewolves. Had wanted to be one ever since she found out they were real. Pearl had stuck her arm into his cage a month ago with sheer excitement gleaming in her eyes. Pearl buzzed with it. Loved it. Made it sexual. Made it about sex. Made him excited, aroused by what he was. By what they were about to do. Embrace the moon and change their bodies. Be animals. Be savage. Be wolves.

Pearl smiled. She crossed the tiny cellar in a couple of strides and pressed her warm body against Zac's. Sex in November in an unheated cellar would be an unattractive proposition to most people. But things were different for a couple of werewolves. High metabolism, very hot blooded. Sometimes Zac thought lycanthropy was a bit like permanently running a slight fever. And with Pearl draped around him, moving to kiss him, the Vix on the move, his new status as a pack Alpha and the moon rising outside, coursing through his blood, he felt the delirium more than ever.

Zac was six foot one, but Pearl was only a few inches

shorter. She was a big well-proportioned woman, made of generosity and curves. Zac liked that. He liked the way his long angular body folded and softened into the lushness of her. Pearl was amazing. She wasn't ashamed of the space she took up. She revelled in it. She leaned back in seats and stretched out her arms. She let her legs fall apart. She was cartoonishly voluptuous and larger than life. And Zac realised as he kissed her that he couldn't wait to see what her wolf looked like.

He kissed his way down her body, wanting to cover every inch. He licked her tits and then kissed his way sideways to make her laugh as he kissed her armpits, biting at the small tufts of blonde hair. Fur. Her fur. She turned around and he licked her spine. Flat and human. He kissed each vertebrae as he got onto his knees. Pearl leaned up against the wall as Zac pushed his tongue into the soft groove just below her spine, where her arse began.

He slipped his tongue down, deeper and deeper. Pearl gasped as he flipped over her arsehole. Tight and tiny. He ran his tongue over it again. And then again. And he felt it soften. Melt beneath his slow, wet licks.

He pushed his tongue into her. Into her *there*. She moaned loudly, moving away from him as her arms shifted a little and she moved closer to the wall. 'Yes, Zac,' she whispered. 'Yes, Zac, God. Fuck me there. There.'

Zac stood, his cock heavy between his legs – jutting out. He reached around and pushed three fingers into Pearl's mouth. She sucked at them furiously, while he moved in, pressing close so she could feel his skin coating her. She gasped into his hand when she felt his cock nudging between her legs.

'Come on, werewolf,' Zac murmured. 'She wolf. Get them wet for me.'

He pulled his fingers slickly from Pearl's mouth and

teased the tip of one around her arsehole. He felt her soften in his arms. He pushed one finger inside, then all three, lubricated by Pearl's salvia. She wolf.

With his free hand he found his cock. Hard and dripping precome like he'd never known it do before. He slicked the wetness down its length.

The moon was coming. He started to fuck her.

He held her with one hand as he moved inside her, then reached around and worked two of his fingers inside her vagina. She was so wet. He found one of her hands there too, working her clit.

'God,' he whispered, 'you're so tight. This is so hot. The moon. Can't last . . .'

'Come then. Come in me,' Pearl said, her voice hitching. She was close too.

As Zac began to come he felt the ripples of Pearl's orgasm pulsating through him at the same time. He threw his head back and cried out. Opening his eyes, he could just see out the tiny vent. Nothing but dark sky. How long did they have? He wanted to fuck her again.

By the time Zac felt the stretch in his muscles he was inside Pearl on the dirty floor, with her splayed beneath him. Her legs and mouth open and welcoming.

He couldn't stay fucking her for the change. The way a werewolf's body ripped apart and rebuilt was too violent, even though he knew Pearl would probably want that. He pulled out of her and rolled over, letting the fizzing electricity of the change rush over his body, using his last piece of consciousness to look over and see the beautiful pure white wolf Pearl was becoming.

In the morning they ransacked the house for money or anything else useful, but found very little. The month before Misty had been paid very well for doing a secret underground transformation show for a human/werewolf 'special interest' broker called Omega. But most of that had been spent.

They found Zac's passport in the kitchen drawer but they didn't have Pure's or Pearl's. Zac's plan of going to Texas and summoning Leon seemed to be receding fast. Zac felt sick. This was all wrong. He couldn't really be Alpha while his sire was alive. That was what summoning was for. But how to get his sire back? He had to go to Texas. To where he was bitten.

Could I go on my own? His heart beat a little harder at the thought.

Zac was sitting on the sofa, explaining his panic to Pearl – who was cross-legged on the floor – when Pure strolled in and asked what the problem was? And when Zac explained, Pure smiled and mentioned that he still had contacts in the military.

Not only could Pure fly a plane, but he knew just how to get the clearance they needed for him to fly one all the way to the US.

'Seriously, dude?' Zac had said. 'You can sort it so we can just fly to Texas? Even with all the crazy security they have now?'

Pure had laughed. 'Zac, mate, we'll be *part* of the crazy security they have now. All we need, to make it happen, is money.'

Pure looked a lot like Pearl, but in a harder, more masculine kind of way. Hard where she was soft. Pure's beauty was slightly cruel, slightly unnerving. And the fact that he now had a livid scar right down his sculpted face, wasn't helping those nasty associations any.

And, well, money, was exactly what they didn't have. Werewolves never have any money. Werewolves are not good at earning money, at working, at holding down jobs. Werewolves are all about hierarchy and power and obedience – Zac had heard Leon call it The Line – and werewolves found submitting to humans almost impossible, abhorrent. Working for humans never went well. So, really, Zac only knew of one sure way for werewolves to make money.

It meant getting in touch with Omega. It meant staying in Oxford. It meant putting Pearl in the situation that had killed Misty a month before – shot by the Vix as she transformed in front of an audience of enraptured men. It meant waiting for another moon. It was every kind of bad idea. But it was the only way.

But Zac wasn't letting himself think too much about what he was doing. No good Alpha would risk his pack like this. Putting them all in danger from the Vix. Practically selling Pearl.

It was called the downwards tide, or the backwards pull, the agonising choice between your cubs and your sire. Choosing your cub over your sire was meant to be the mark of a truly strong wolf. Zac knew he wasn't that strong. He wanted Leon back more than he wanted to keep his pack safe.

Zac thought about Alfie. How agonised he had been about coming to Oxford to find the collar. What he'd said when Misty had told him how they could fund the trip. Omega. 'Sleazy,' Alfie had called it. He'd paced the floor for hours then stopped and punched the wall of their Miami hotel room hard enough to make his knuckles bleed. And then, very late that night he'd told Zac that they were going to go and that Zac was the only one Alfie trusted to kill him if anything went wrong during this trip.

The next morning, after Zac had sworn he'd do it if Alfie asked, they'd started making arrangements to fly to England.

But Alfie hadn't been choosing between his cubs and his sire then. He'd been choosing between his cubs and himself.

* * *

When Zac called Omega, she was delighted with the proposition. She understood Zac's fears after what had happened with Misty and assured him that nothing like that would ever happen again. When pressed, she offered to move them a safe house straight away that they could stay in until full moon – possibly because of how taken she was with the prospect of Pearl.

'Well, no offence, darling,' she had said, when Zac had gone to meet her in her over-stuffed office – as she blew sweetly noxious cigar smoke casually in Zac's face as a kind of punctuation – 'I mean, maybe I shouldn't say this to you, what with you being such a glorious, gorgeous ebony beauty yourself, but in this business the money's always on the white girl, especially a blonde – she's all natural, right?'

Zac nodded. Barely understanding the question.

'Well if she isn't we can always shave her, that's nice too, punters love that look. But, yeah, you know, darling, a good-looking young white girl with a white wolf inside her...' Omega stopped and gave a dirty chuckle that Zac forced himself not to think about. 'Well,' she went on, 'that's going to be top dollar. Very nice. I can get you all the work you want. And because I like you, handsome, you can name your price.'

'One show only,' Zac had said, coughing and waving another plume of cigar smoke away. 'One show and we're gone.' And he named his price. More than twenty times what Misty had earned. Enough to grease all the palms they needed to get a plane and clearance to fly to Texas.

That December moon had fallen on Christmas Eve. The special night had made the show a huge sell out. Zac was slightly surprised no one seemed bothered about the police raid that had happened during the last show. When he found a moment to ask Omega about this in a low voice she had tapped the side of her skull and said,

'Amazing what a little witchcraft can do to combat bad publicity.'

And there was no doubt that Omega could afford witchcraft. Zac had seen what she had been charging for tickets and quickly realised he could have asked for three times as much money and still left Omega with a hefty profit.

By this point Zac had completely managed to convince himself that Pearl doing this public transformation show was the best thing for everyone. But Pure, it turned out, hadn't been so happy. Normally Pure agreed with whatever Pearl wanted and, as Zac was Pearl's sire, that meant that despite being human Pure fitted into the pack hierarchy quite well. But once Pearl was preparing in Omega's basement, Pure took Zac aside into a corridor off the main viewing room. His cruelly beautiful face was hard and set.

Zac squared up to Pure, facing him across the tight small space. 'It was the only way.'

Pure bristled. 'You could have just forgotten about it. We could have just gone to London or something. Why do we need to go to America so badly?'

'We just do. And anyway wasn't this all your idea? Your contacts.'

Pure shifted and scratched the short dark hair on his head. Zac noticed then that Pure had grown out his shaved head into a close dark crop that was exactly the same as Zac's own sharp haircut. 'It's not right,' Pure said. 'I told you I could get you to America if we could get enough money together. I never knew you'd do something like this. Sell *her*. Pimp her out.'

'She agreed to it.'

'She has to agree. You're her sire. She's does whatever you say. I know how your system works. Vix trained me for months. I know more about your sort that you do yourself.'

Zac had thought then, and not for the first time, how weird and wrong it was to have a human in the pack. He didn't know what Pure's game was, why he was hanging around. Why they were letting him. Like he'd just said – he'd been a Vix. How could they be sure he wasn't a Vix now? He'd got them out of the Vix HQ, helped them escape – and, sure, it was useful to have a human around who could keep an eye on things at full moon. Times like tonight where, while Zac was going to have to go off and change in the cage Omega had provided for him in a secure room, Pure would be able to stay and watch. But despite all that Zac still vowed to himself that next full moon he'd make things right with Pure. Even though Pure claimed not to want a bite, Zac knew that if Pure was one of them it would all be much simpler. That he'd understand that things between sire and cub were so much more complex than Pearl just doing whatever he said. That having a cub was more emotionally tangled and bittersweet than having a child. That he looked at Pearl and he saw everything he was. That Zac looked at her face and felt certain this was the face that would finally kill him. That his need to protect her ripped at his insides. That choosing between risking her and reuniting with Leon was like choosing between losing a leg and losing an arm.

Everything would be better if Pure were a wolf too. Not least explaining it to Leon. Leon wouldn't like this current arrangement at all.

After the show Pure had been true to his word and arranged everything so they could fly to Texas.

Although, what with the world grinding to a halt for Christmas and then New Year, once the money had been collected and Pure had made all the arrangements it was nearly mid-January, but they still had enough time to summon Leon before the January moon.

*   *   *

Finally, in Austin, they booked a room in a nasty cheap motel with two nasty cheap double beds. Zac and Pearl made love quietly in one of them, when Pure was asleep in the other. Zac wished he had got another room for Pure to sleep in, but Pure was just making him more and more nervous. He couldn't bear to have him out of his sight.

One night, the second night they were there, as Zac moved silently inside Pearl, hushing her mouth with kisses and making orgasmic shapes with his finger between her legs, he looked over at Pure. And his eyes were wide open looking back at him.

Neither man spoke. Zac was sure Pure was stroking his cock as he watched them. Zac leaned down and licked Pearl's neck, keeping his eyes locked with Pure's.

Pure's lips moved, as if in a silenced groan. Zac started to fuck Pearl harder, covering her face with a kiss whenever she started to look in Pure's direction.

Zac arched. Thinking about how they must look to Pure. His dark sleek shape covering Pearl's generous ivory curves. He pictured himself as Pure, watching, stroking. It made him so hard, so horny, to think about being watcher and watched. Pearl was coming, squirming under him, touching her own clit. Zac looked back at Pure, who was mesmerised by Pearl's climax. Zac watched Pure starting to come, to arch and buck into his own hand, before he stifled his own orgasmic moans in Pearl's shoulder.

5

Security had been a vital part of Blake's new order at the Institute. Not only was he taking the threat of The Silver Crown very seriously, there had been too many escapes under Dr Tobias. CCTV cameras in all the rooms was simple enough to justify. They should have had it installed when they moved in to this building a year ago.

And it wasn't that he'd kept the new security measures a secret from Iris. He just hadn't had a chance to tell her yet.

Blake had rewound the tape. As he watched Iris half-dressed on her hands and knees, with Alfie pistoning his big body over her, he worked his own cock in his fist. He was glad he hadn't missed this while he was showing Aurelia some books from his library.

They'd be long gone now. Fido probably leaping through the window again. Shame, or he could have dashed downstairs and caught them in the act. It was that thought that started to tip him over, beginning the point of no return, the slippery slope to bliss. He gripped the edge of his workbench with his free hand as he worked his dick, gasping, watching Iris. 'Iris.'

A moment later, as Iris and Alfie were getting dressed on screen, Blake readjusted his own clothing. On his lab computer was a copy of the document Alfie had had Iris type up – which Blake had recreated using the key stroke logger he had installed on Iris's machine. He smiled as he read it over again, before reaching down to the ancient VHS machine under the desk. He pressed eject and the top loading maw sprang open presenting him with a clunky cassette. DVD hadn't been around so very long, and yet already, VHS cassettes seemed like something from the glorious age of steam. He picked up a marker pen and wrote on the spine of the tape *Iris 2: w/ Fido 18/ 01/08*. Then sighed and put the tape on a shelf. He picked up another tape which was lying on its side. This one said *Iris 1: w/ B 25/12/07*. He slammed it into the machine.

Christmas Day. The day after the December moon. The picture that appeared on his screen after some spooling and static was of Iris in his office. The lights were on and, through the high window, dawn was lighting the sky. Iris was standing with one hand on her hip. Her shirt was untucked. Most of her hair had fallen out of her pony-tail. There was a smear of blood across her left cheekbone. She looked utterly stunning, but it was her eyes Blake really noticed. Glittering fire.

She had saved his life that night, just as she'd said. She'd stabbed a lyc he hadn't spotted, a scrappy hound that had dived on him from some tree cover. She'd thrown herself between the two of them. A move he was sure no one else would have risked. It had knocked him unconscious for a second, his head hitting a stone. He came round a few seconds later trapped under Iris and the dead creature.

The moment he had captured on screen was the two of them laughing about it. Just like they had so many times before. Go out, look death in the eye, come back and laugh in its face. Iris had taught him that. Taught him to laugh at it all.

Iris was made to kill monsters.

He'd seen it bring her to life over and over. Back in the day, before most lycs had fled the city during full moon he'd seen Iris do amazing things. He seen her throw a dagger and hit a lyc fifty yards away right between the eyes. He'd seen her jump into the weir and drown a swimming lyc with what looked like her bare hands, although she had later said she had stabbed it under the water. He'd seen her practically riding on the Beast's back as she fought to get her gun into its mouth – another theory she'd had about how to kill the creature that hadn't quite panned out.

Iris was made to kill monsters and Blake was made to admire the way she did it.

Blake watched himself, on the screen, walking over to Iris. He looked dishevelled too. His sleeves were rolled up and his arms were bloody. He had a large red gash across his forehead where Iris's boot had caught him. He crossed the room fast, took Iris in his arms and kissed her.

Even now, watching it happen on screen, he felt like he could taste her still in his mouth.

They kissed for barely a full second, before Iris pulled her leg back and kneed him in the balls so hard he winced every time he rewatched the tape. And then she slapped his face so viciously he nearly went over backwards.

But Blake had watched this tape many, many times and there was something in Iris's eyes as she turned away from him and stormed out of the room. Something new, and yet familiar. Something he couldn't quite place.

In a dusty strange little book store, Zac grinned a huge grin. The old black woman behind the counter grinned back. 'Hey, ma'am.' Zac leaned right over the counter to take the old woman in an embrace.

'Zachariah,' said the old woman. She nodded her head, still smiling broadly at him. 'My wolfen boy. You're looking good on it, that's for sure. And you have some cubs, I see.' She looked over Zac's shoulder at Pearl and Pure.

'Yeah, man. Well, one.' He gestured to Pearl. 'This is Pearly, my girlfriend. And, yeah, my cub. And this is Pure. He's human – just along for the ride. He's Pearl's cousin.'

The woman narrowed her eyes at Pure, only very slightly, but Zac picked up on it straight away. 'So what are you here for, darlin'?' said the woman, coming out from around the shop counter and catching Pearl and then a bemused Pure in easy soft embraces.

'I here for summoning, Jin. I lost my sire. This is where I was bit, isn't it? This is where I need to be to put it all back together.'

Jin nodded sweetly. No questions – a light understanding. 'Sure. I'll go and get you a silver blade from out back, honey.'

After she had disappeared into the backroom and Pure had wandered off to examine the store's books on werewolves, Pearl leaned close to Zac, 'Um, babe, before we do this, there's something I always wanted to ask you. About Leon.'

'Sure, sweetcakes.' Zac said easily, but something deep inside him tightened. *Leon.*

'It's just, well, you know that time I told you about. The first time I came to the pack house. That stuff with him and Alfie. Well, what was that? What's the deal with those two?'

'Alfie's his sire, hon, didn't you know?'

'Oh yeah, I knew that, but, I mean, is there any more than that? I mean, is there anything else to their relationship?'

Zac turned and scrutinised Pearl. She was frowning. He knew what she was talking about. He said, 'Nah, babe. I know what you mean, but it's just Alpha tension stuff. Leon can't kill Alfie because he has, like, mega strong thrall 'cause of the Beast. But also they're two macho arrogant guys who really shouldn't have to spend too much time in the same city, let alone the same pack house. Hey, you know that song, "This town ain't big enough for the both of us"? Well that's Leon and Alfie.' Pearl laughed and Zac gave her a little squeeze. He'd never done a summoning before and he was nervous as fuck.

Summoning was ... complex. Zac couldn't exactly explain it to Pearl, but he thought that somewhere inside her she knew how to do it too – would be able to do it if she had to. If one day she found herself in the cellar of the pack house in Oxford, thinking of calling him to her from wherever he was, she'd feel this way. Summoning was the one piece of pure simple untainted power that one werewolf could hold over another. And it ran the wrong way – like stroking a cat from the tail to head – it ran from cub to sire.

Everything about summoning felt sickeningly wrong.

6

In his cabin Leon stared at Sabrina. Then at his blood still pooling on the floor of the cabin around his damaged leg. It was starting to be quite a big pool. Leon – who was a werewolf, a hunter and a trapper, a man who had seen lots of blood before – was starting to feel slightly faint at the sight of it.

'There are eight pints of blood in the human body.' Sabrina said. 'I imagine even your paranormal body will conform to that standard. How much do you reckon is on the outside now?'

'Wha – ?' Leon shook his head at her.

'Of course,' Sabrina went on, brightly, 'for someone in your situation, one would naturally be asking the question, how much of that blood can one lose and still live to tell the tale? Well, in actual fact it isn't as simple as that, you see it's not about volume per se, it's about pressure. Blood pressure. Just like the doctor measures, if creatures like you see doctors. Although, actually, isn't our Mr Friday a doctor, himself? If there could ever be such a thing as a werewolf doctor.'

Leon shook his head. 'He never qualified.'

'Really? Even so, it's shame he's not here now. He could explain this blood stuff far better than me. But I'll try.' Sabrina paused thoughtfully and twirled the gun in her fingers. 'Right now what we're worried about isn't high blood pressure. It's low blood pressure. And your blood pressure is getting dangerously low.'

'So call me an ambulance, you deranged harpy.'

Sabrina smiled. 'I haven't finished. Now, imagine you

cut off a person's arms and legs – or in your case, let's say tore them off, ripped them off with your big butch fangs – that would deprive that person of a lot of blood. What is it? One pint equals an armful? So both arms would be two pints gone and both legs, that must mean four more. That's six pints, but if you did that, ripped off the limbs and then cauterised the wounds, the blood pressure to the brain wouldn't drop and the person would be OK. Like in that film, where he cuts off her arms and her legs.'

Leon was starting to feel light-headed. 'What are you talking about? Have you gone fucking mad? Madder?'

'Your problem is your wound hasn't been cauterised, you're losing a lot of blood. So all I need to do is wait here until you pass out from lack of blood to the brain. Then you're done for. I can kill you just by watching. Good, eh? I don't even need to waste another bullet on you.'

'You sick fucking Vix bitch.'

Sabrina stalked across the wooden floor and hit Leon on the side of the head with the hilt of the gun. 'I'm not a Vix.' She moved the gun down and ran it over Leon's chest, tracing his heart. 'But maybe werewolves don't bleed to death. Not even if the wound was made by silver. I just don't know. Interesting. But, on balance, I think the best thing for you would be if you started co-operating.'

'I've told you, I don't know where Alfie Friday is.'

'You could summon him?'

'Forget it, sister, you know the deal doesn't work like that. I can't betray him.' Leon looked down, inhaling through his nose. 'I'm thralled.'

'Who says you'd be betraying him? Maybe we just want to talk to him. Maybe you'd be doing him a favour. Maybe daddy wolf would pat you on the back and forgive you whatever you did that meant you got exiled from your pack.'

'OK, first, he didn't kick me out – I *chose* to come and live out here. Second, look, I'm not an idiot, if you want Alfie for some benevolent reason something tells me there'd be more gentle persuasion and less shooting me in the leg and telling me how long before I bleed to death. I can't betray him. I can't help you. And even if you were telling me the truth, my sire is the last person I want to see right now.'

'Aww. Family fall out?'

'I don't see why you can't find him yourself. If you found me.'

'Ah, well, that's the funny thing. Be assured the people I work for are very powerful. We have a team of seers that keep us in touch with every werewolf on earth. But we know Friday is with the Vix – the same ones you keep bringing up. And all their hideouts are seriously cloaked. Well, naturally, they don't want werewolves to be able to walk in through the front door. Unless ... you haven't ever been to their HQ have you? With Friday maybe?'

'No. Of course not. Why would I go there. Any were-wolf that went there would end up dead soon enough.'

'Yes. I thought not. Which means the only way we can get to Friday is to summon him.' Sabrina was still stand-ing over him. She swung the gun around carelessly in her hand, but it was always out of his reach. 'And you're Alfie's first sired cub. You'll have the strongest pull. That's why we came to you.'

Leon frowned and shook his head. 'I'm not. I'm not his first sired. That's Misty, she ...'

'Oh, right, I meant first sired living cub.'

'What?'

Sabrina frowned as if she was unsure of something, then she turned away and went back to her handbag sitting on the chair. She pulled out a black notebook. 'See, now, I told you we have a lot of power, well, not quite as much as we had until recently, but it's enough to run some pretty good seers. We keep very detailed records. Look, Alfie Friday, sired by Malcolm Tobias, aka the Beast, 1 June 1996. Misty Sun, sired by Alfie Friday, 20 August 2003, died 26 October 2007.'

'What? Misty, what?' Leon said, but Sabrina just kept talking.

'Leon Whitesnake, sired by Alfie Friday, 19 September 2003. Aurelia Toto, sired by Alfie Friday, 23 November 2007. Then we have Zachariah Booth, sired by Leon Whitesnake, 13 April 2006. Pearl White, sired by Zachariah Booth, 26 October 2007. And that's your whole family.'

Leon frowned. He couldn't take all this in. Couldn't process. 'How, how do you know all this?'

'We keep the records, Mr Whitesnake. To protect everyone. It's what we do.'

'Misty's *dead*?'

Sabrina looked back at the notebook, trailing her finger down the list of details. 'Yes.'

'Who? How? Was it Alfie? Did he flip on her?' Leon felt hot and cold at once. The pain in his leg had faded. It was like his rising vicious anger was now the only thing stopping him from passing out.

'Well,' said Sabrina, 'that's an interesting question. Why don't you summon Alfie for me and we can ask him.'

Leon looked at her. He could feel his mouth opening to say something and he wasn't even sure what it was going to be. But he never found out. He never said anything because at that same moment he started to speak there was an enormous rushing howling sound like a gale had sprung from nowhere and then Leon felt himself lifted right out of space and time by something that could only be a powerful primal magic.

Leon had never been summoned before. But he knew what this must be. Nothing else could feel like this.

He heard Zac's voice, screaming for him, wailing. The

sense that his cub needed him overwhelmed every part of him. He found himself – even through the spiralling blackness – trying to reach out to Zac with his hands, with his heart.

And then he was standing in a bookshop. At least he was standing for a moment or two before his injured leg crumpled under him.

Slinging her handbag over her shoulder, Sabrina stomped out of the cabin, cursing. She walked across the grassland outside and over a rough unfinished road. Beyond the road was a thick copse. Sabrina rooted in her bag and drew out a circular tangle of silver wire, which she placed on her head. Then she slipped between the trees, moving deftly through the undergrowth.

Two young, coltish men – one dark, one blond – appeared from between the trees and approached her. Their eager expressions did not stay eager for long.

'Where is he?' said the blond.

Sabrina rolled her eyes. 'You won't believe it.'

Both men looked at her, clearly ready for unbelievable news.

'Summoned,' said Sabrina. 'Ripped right out of there by his damn cub.' She paused and fished in her bag for the notebook. She flicked through the pages. 'Got to be by Zachariah Booth, that's his only progeny.'

'And where's Zachariah Booth? Can we trace him? Get the seers on it?'

'Maybe. I'm not absolutely sure that Leon Whitesnake can be any help to us. Not when he knows what we want Friday for. He's uncontrollable. Clearly deeply thralled. Desperate for his sire. Screaming for it. It was coming off him in waves. I could smell it on him when I fucked him.'

'There's got to be a way,' said dark hair.

'Oh, there's always a way. I told him Friday was in

Oxford. I reckon all we need to do is go there and wait for him to come to us.'

Zac looked around. The room went awfully quiet. And then there was a sickening crunching thump from behind the nearest bookcase. Zac rushed around it and saw Leon, naked, collapsed on the floor holding his bleeding shin. Zac didn't know whether to laugh or cry.

He rushed over and dropped into a crouch. 'Sire. What's wrong with your leg? Did I do that?'

Leon let go of his wound and grabbed Zac by the collar of his black silk shirt, pulling him close and then slapping his face hard. 'Summoning. Damn it, this better be serious, cub.' Tears were pricking behind Zac's eyes. This close he could see Leon was rather dazed and glazed himself. Zac swallowed hard. Leon stared at him for a moment more and then pulled him down into a close hard back-slapping embrace.

Inside him, Zac's heart soared so high and so hard he thought it might burst right out of his body.

7

Ten minutes after she woke up the next morning, Iris was on top of Alfie. With him inside her and her mind full of wolves. When she was anxious, Iris liked to fuck. She still hadn't told Alfie about what Blake had said about The Silver Crown coming for her.

She looked down at Alfie's body. He was so damn big and so damn strong. He looked as if he was built of everything in the universe that could be hard and soft at the same time. He was a werewolf. That turned her on. Fear. Beasts. They were coming for her. 'You know how sex makes you change?'

'Orgasm makes me change. Unless I have the collar.' Alfie reached up and tapped the magical piece of metal around his neck, hissing a little as the silver stung his fingers.

'So if you didn't have the collar on, and we had sex, you would change when you came?'

'Yeah, or possibly even sooner. Why are you asking? This is why the collar is a good thing, right?' He reached up and put his big hand at the top of her thigh. She ground her pelvis on him a little, enough to make him moan.

'The collar comes off,' Iris said darkly, her voice wobbling a little as she kept moving on Alfie's cock. 'I mean, we could take it off. Take it off and have sex.' Alfie moaned again; she couldn't tell if it was the friction or what she was saying. 'I could take it off you,' Iris said.

'That's how you used to do it right. Get chained down for sex? Give the girl some kind of memory wipe afterwards?'

Iris was squirming around on Alfie's cock now. Alfie reached up and slipped his hand between her legs so he could rub her clit at the same time. The fat rough pad of his thumb right there. Perfect. 'Yeah,' he breathed, 'yeah, that's what I had to do. I had no choice really. It was still dangerous. I never hurt anyone – but I could've.'

'It's just,' Iris panted, Alfie's thumb was so well placed, driving her over the edge – almost too quickly – 'I'd like to see that. I'd like to see you come from having sex. I mean, uh, *change*, change from having sex.'

'But why, I . . .' Alfie lost his words. He closed his eyes.

Iris rolled her hips and ground against the soft, napped, perfect texture of Alfie's thumb. 'I, oh, yeah, so beautiful, your body. I love your body. I want to see it . . . want to see all of it.' Iris started to come. She was still talking as she arched her back and felt her nipples pinch tight all by themselves. Her words turned into moans and the juddering spasms deep inside her grabbed at Alfie's cock and pulled him with her over into orgasm.

Iris cried out, louder, as she felt Alfie start to jerk and come inside her. His strength and desire in orgasm making him fuck her harder, bucking up off the bed. Iris moaned. The first wave of her orgasm receded just before an unexpected second wave came. So strong this time. Screaming, twisting, she fell forwards, holding herself against the wall behind the bed, aware of nothing beyond the hard sweet wholeness of being filled by Alfie's cock.

When, still panting, she rolled over and off him, and nestled into the gap under his arm, he said, 'That was good. And you didn't say it.'

'Hmm?'

'You didn't say Blake's name. You have to be careful now you know, you only have two chances left.'

Iris shook her sex-addled head. 'Two more? It's not cumulative.'

Alfie laughed. 'Big words won't save you Iris.'

'No, look, OK I did say Blake's name once in the office. But that doesn't mean I get the forfeit if I say it twice more. I have to say it three times in one go. It resets back to zero after we, um, finish. And, you know, I still think we had finished then, anyway.' Iris rolled over to face away from Alfie

Alfie gave a little purring noise and spooned up close behind Iris. He said, 'It resets to zero? I really don't know what gave you that idea.'

'So if I say Blake's name twice more during sex? Ever? Then I have to do your forfeit'

Alfie said, 'Yeah. Looks that way. You want me to check the documentation.' He rolled away and picked up the contract Iris had typed which was lying on the bedside table. He snuggled back up behind Iris and held it up in front of her.

'Have you decided what the forfeit is?' Iris said.

'Actually, no. I think I'll just see how I feel at the time.' Iris bit her lip.

Alfie was still reading. 'Well it still seems pretty water tight. Absolutely no clauses here about anything resetting back to zero. And you've signed it. God, your signature is illegible.'

'You were fucking me at the time, remember. I'm pretty sure that makes a contract null and void, actually. Signed under duress.'

Alfie laughed. 'Does this scrawl actually say, Iris Instasi-Fox Tabernacle Friday?'

Iris laughed and reached out to grab the paper, but Alfie pulled it out of her reach and rolled onto his back behind her. Iris twisted after him. 'It so doesn't say, oh –' Iris stopped laughing. He was there again. Matthew. Standing right at the end of the bed. Iris pulled away from Alfie and sat up, drawing up the bedclothes to cover herself.

'What is it? What?' Alfie said, flipping into attack mode. Ready and guarded, sitting up himself to look where Iris was looking but clearly seeing nothing there.

'Matthew.' Iris's voice was barely a whisper.

'Matthew? I thought he'd gone when you killed the Beast.'

Matthew sat down on the end of the bed. Alfie looked at him then. Iris knew he was only following her gaze, but somehow she didn't believe Alfie couldn't see Matthew too. He was so real. Where Matthew had sat down the bed seemed to indent around him. 'I don't understand it,' said Iris. 'I thought he'd gone too, but I saw him at work yesterday, twice, and now he's, Alfie, he's right there.' Iris nodded in the direction of Matthew who smiled back at her.

'Is he normal? I mean, he's just the normal Matthew right? Not the bloody version you used to see right after he died?'

Iris shook her head. 'No, no, it's not the horror movie version with the face torn off. Just him. Normal him. He's not saying anything, though. Normally he doesn't shut up.'

You could talk to me, you know.

'You don't normally need any provocation to start going on and on.'

Alfie frowned. 'What? Oh. You're talking to him. Well, why don't you just ask him why he's still here?'

'Because he's just my imagination. I should know why he's still here.'

'Just ask him.'

Iris turned to Matthew. 'OK, Matt, what are you doing here? I avenged the thing that killed you. We shot the Beast. So now you stop haunting me, wasn't that the deal.'

There was a deal? You're not done, Iris; killing the Beast wasn't enough. The Silver Crown are coming. More Ancient Beasts. You need to kill them all.

Iris paused. 'Kill them all? All the Beasts or all the lycs? In Oxford? In the world? What about Alfie?'

Alfie looked at her, 'Me? What? What did he say about me?'

Iris was still staring at Matthew but he was melting away before her eyes. 'Matt! Don't go! I don't understand. I don't know what I'm meant to be doing.' But Matt was already nothing more than a translucent wisp before her tear-filled eyes. She looked at Alfie. 'I have to kill them all.'

'Well we knew that, that's what the prophecy said. Maybe Matt's just here to make sure you get on with it.'

Iris shrugged, sighing hard at the same time. 'I guess. But you know, I've been thinking. Do we even know what the prophecy really means? After all, everyone thought the first version meant you were going to kill the Beast.'

'There was no way...' Alfie started and Iris realised she had touched his sore spot.

'I know, I know, but what I mean is, no one seemed to really say what it meant until after it happened. "The kingdom is home to many Beasts and the Warrior Wolf will kill them all." It's not as clear cut as all that is it? Does Beasts mean Ancient Beasts? Werewolves? Something else? And is the Kingdom England? The United Kingdom? The World? Oxford? What? And am I even the Warrior Wolf? How can anyone be sure?' Iris shook her head and Alfie shrugged and didn't reply, but somewhere inside Iris couldn't shake the idea that Matt had really meant she had to completely wipe all werewolves off the face of the earth before she would be free of his ghostly presence.

'Iris, you know, I've been meaning to ask you, when

did you start seeing Matthew? I mean, I know that you started getting these hallucinations or whatever they are, after Matt died, but when after he died? I mean how long did you have to wait?'

'Alfie?' Iris narrowed her eyes. 'You really aren't good at nonchalant, are you?'

Alfie dropped her gaze and looked at the floor.

Iris sighed, sadly. 'I don't know if you're ever going to see Misty's ghost, Alfie. Or hallucinate her ghost. Or whatever it is I do with Matthew. I don't know why I see him all the time. I just do. But, God, Alfie, don't wish this on Misty. Or on yourself. She's better off resting in peace. If I could never see Matthew again, I would. Seeing him like this is far, far worse than never seeing him again. It's hard to explain why, but it is.'

Iris reached out and took Alfie's hand. Alfie's hand was so much bigger than hers; she could barely get her fingers around it. She rolled over into his arms. 'Was Misty your girlfriend? I know you were having sex with her when you flipped and bit her.' Iris said gently.

'Oh, no, not really. Not like that. We were just friends.'

'Sex friends?'

'Yeah, sex friends. My mouth was –' he paused and swallowed '– between her legs when it happened. The wolf went back to ... I bit her there.' Alfie turned his head. He was crying. He kissed Iris softly on the lips. It was a slow sad kind of kiss. A kiss that was about comfort not joy. It reminded Iris of the way they'd kissed right after the werewolf attack eleven years ago. Reminded her of Alfie pulling her down onto his hospital bed. About how they were kissing, knowing they shouldn't be, and both so shocked, still. Matthew was dead. It had only been half an hour since they'd been told. Iris had been the one crying then. She'd started crying again while Alfie was kissing her. Alfie had asked her if she wanted him to stop – said they ought to stop – but she'd said no.

She'd climbed on top of him. Had sex with him on his hospital bed. And that had been the first time she'd ever seen Matt's ghost. Standing there covered in blood and half ripped apart. Still there even when she closed her eyes.. But she'd kept going until Alfie had come inside her. Even now she didn't know why. And she'd never told Alfie what she'd seen that time.

With his lips still touching Iris's, Alfie said, 'There was no one else, Iris. I never stopped loving you. There was never anyone else.'

'I wish I could say the same,' Iris murmured.

Alfie laughed a little. 'I'll bet.'

'It was just a rebound thing. A weird reaction. Blake was a werewolf hunter so it made perfect sense at the time.'

'Yeah, I know. I do get it, Iris.'

Iris pulled back a little. 'OK, well, look, here's how it happened. I was in the Bodleian Library, doing research – research about you, about the Beast – and they were there: Blake and Jude and Dr Tobias. Lying in wait for me, of course. Waiting. Part of Tobias's recruitment pro-gramme. But back then it just seemed like a coincidence.' Iris started to kiss her way down Alfie's neck. He was flat on his back and she began to trace a path down his chest, dropping words between kisses. 'And as I got to know him, when I started working there, Blake just seemed like the only person who could . . .' Iris's voice drifted away as she started licking and nipping at the skin on Alfie's belly.

'Iris,' Alfie said darkly, 'you do know that's two, don't you?'

'What?'

'That's the second time you've mentioned Blake during sex. It's like a compulsion with you. It's a good job I'm secure in this relationship. You're really hopeless.'

Iris lifted her head and looked at Alfie, her lips pressed

into a tight little line. 'What? I was comforting you. You were sad.'

'Oh and you think that means I want to hear you talking about my love rival.' Alfie smiled and flashed his eye.

Iris screamed in frustration. 'God, Alfie! He is not your love rival.'

8

That morning, in Texas, Pearl dealt with Leon's leg on her own in the motel bathroom. There was no other way of fixing his injury that wouldn't have involved a mass of awkward questions and the niggling little fact that Leon had no kind of health insurance. Not to mention the fact that he also had no ID, no passport, not even any clothes – although that had been quickly remedied.

Leon was sitting on the closed lid of the toilet in the motel bathroom with his injured leg up on the side of the bath. He was still swigging from a bottle of Everclear even though the really painful stuff was over. Pearl had removed the bullet and sterilised and stitched the wound. Now she was applying a dressing.

Leon seemed different from the werewolf Pearl had met before. Or maybe it was she who had changed. She too was a werewolf now. But there was something new about Leon. Power? Charisma? No, he had those before. She didn't know what it was. But she knew she hated him.

Leon, who had, apart from his swigging, been stoic and silent throughout the painful procedure, said, 'It's normal, you know.'

'What is?'

'The way you feel. Your sire's sire. You hate him. You feel that heart-pounding love for Zac because he's your maker. But you know he feels that way about me. You know Zac'd choose me over you. And you're jealous. And confused. But it's normal. You should have heard how Misty talked about the Beast when Alfie wasn't around.'

Pearl sniffed. 'Well Zac doesn't hate Alfie.'

'Oh yes he does.' Leon watched Pearl work for a moment then said, 'You know he didn't come for me?'

'Alfie?'

'Yeah. The first time I changed. He didn't come.'

'I know. Zac told me. He'd Locked Down. Didn't know he'd bitten you. The wolf ripped his hands up trying to get out of the cage.'

'Yep. Then when he does find me the next day, nearly dead from changing in the middle of London and getting hit by a car, he brings me back to his pack. Carries me, hasn't brought me any clothes so I'm just wrapped up in that leather jacket of his. He had no idea what he was doing. And then what he calls his pack is just him and Misty anyway – plus me. And he thinks he's being a werewolf. He thinks that's it. Didn't even think he should explain to me about all the stuff the Beast must've explained to him about how this shit works. He says the Beast only told him the basics – but even that would have been nice. I bet Zac tells you I'm always giving him lectures, right? About werewolves. About how it is.'

'Yeah.'

'Ever wondered why I do that?'

'I don't really wonder about you all that much, Leon, to be honest.' Pearl had finished the dressing now and rolled Leon's new jeans back down over the bandage. She took a step away – the limit of the tiny room – and leaned up against the wall.

'Thanks, baby,' Leon said, adjusting himself a bit. He flicked his hair back over his shoulders and nodded to his crotch. 'You can suck my dick now.'

'What?'

'You heard me, love. What's that phrase?' Leon jerked his hips. 'It's not going to suck itself.'

'What? Leon, I'm not going to . . .' Pearl stopped talking and stood staring at Leon with her mouth open.

59

'I'm the pack Alpha round here, baby. That's how it works.'

Pearl swallowed hard, avoiding Leon's eyes. 'You're not my Alpha,' she said. 'Alfie is. And Zac's my sire. You're . . . you're just nothing.'

'You've got a lot to learn, baby,' Leon paused and made a noise like a snort and a laugh. 'Zac ever tell you about The Line?'

Pearl shook her head. 'No.'

'There's three kinds of power bonds. Pack and Alpha, sire and cub and The Line. We might be missing the first two, but I'm still above you in The Line. The Line is the thread of bonds and power that weaves through all werewolves. Sire to cub. It spreads out over every werewolf in the world and creates hierarchy, a chain of command that we all adhere too. You can't feel it now, with only two of us in here, and no direct connection, but the more related werewolves there are in a space, the more The Line will have a hold over you.'

Pearl shook her head. 'I don't understand.'

'OK, baby, I want you to suck my cock. You say no. But imagine if the whole pack were in here. Imagine if I got Zac in here. Now, if I asked Zac to suck me off, he'd do it. He wouldn't be able to refuse me. And if I asked Zac to make you do it – to tell you – he'd do that too. Wouldn't be able to refuse me.'

'You wouldn't ask him to do that.'

'Try me.' Leon grinned. It made his face look like a skull.

Pearl took a step forwards and got in Leon's face. 'No, honey, you try me. She reached out and put her hand on Leon's leg. Right on the place where his jeans covered his dressed wound. 'I just made you feel a whole lot better. And I can make you feel a whole lot worse if I want to. I know how the human body works, where its weaknesses are. And I've had to deal with way shittier patients than you, sunshine. Now, OK, you might be able to rule over Zac but I love Zac and I will do anything to protect him. And if that means making sure we get time alone together where I remind you, painfully, how important it is that you treat your cub nice, then that's what I'll do.' Pearl tightened her fingers around Leon's leg and started to squeeze slowly.

Leon held her gaze. But she could see the pain rising up behind his eyes. Arrogant bastard. Trying to keep it all tight inside. But he couldn't keep this up forever.

A little blood had already started to blossom through the denim before Leon cried out. 'Arrgh! OK, OK. I get your point.'

Pearl nodded and moved quickly, shoving his jeans back up and replacing the soiled dressing, without any of the tenderness she'd shown before. As she worked she said, 'And that's really nothing. I can make you hurt in ways you can't even imagine.'

'Ways I can't even imagine? Calm down, sweetheart. I'm a werewolf, my body rips itself open and puts itself back together once a month. I do have a pretty high pain threshold.'

'You been kicked in the balls, Leon?'

'That meant to be a scary threat?'

'No. I just wanted to know to illustrate a point about pain. The reason being kicked in the balls hurts the way it does is that the testicles are essentially internal organs, but a little bit of an administrative error has left them on the outside. But that pain you feel when your balls are damaged, that's the pain of having your internal organs damaged.'

'So you threatening my internal organs, are you?'

'If you're threatening Zac, then, yeah, pretty much.'

Leon said, 'What ever happened to "Do no harm". I thought you took a Hippocratic oath.'

'That's doctors. Nurses take a "Hit the arseholes where

it hurts" oath,' Pearl said as she brought her open hand down hard on the sticky dressing on Leon's leg and made him howl again. 'See.'

'You like werewolves, don't you sweetheart?'

Pearl paused. 'What?'

'You're a sniffer. Or, you would be if you were still human. It turns you on, doesn't it?'

'Maybe it does.'

'So, how come you don't want to suck my cock. Suck your Alpha's cock.'

'I guess you still don't quite understand me, Leon,' Pearl said, dropping to her knees and taking hold of his jeans. She started opening them up. 'I never said I didn't want to suck your cock. I do.' And she bent forwards and slipped her mouth over his cock, right over it, pushing down until her nose was up against the mound of his crotch. Leon sighed. Zac's woman. The head of his dick glided against the soft cushion of flesh at the back of her throat. He made a single soft noise. A purr of pleasure.

And Pearl pulled her head away and stood up. 'Oh yes,' said Pearl, 'I really, really want to. But I really, really dislike you, Leon. Just like you said.'

Job done, Pearl turned and walked out of the bathroom. In the tiny motel bedroom Zac and Pure were sprawled on separate beds.

'How is he?' said Zac, getting up and coming over. Twining his arms around Pearl's waist so she could see the concern in his eyes.

'He's fine. Healing up already.'

'Even with the silver.'

'Yeah. It's just like Alfie's eye. He had a bit of blistering but that got better. He'll have a scar, but you know...' Pearl shrugged.

'Did he say how he got shot?'

Pearl shook her head.

Zac let go of her and headed for the bathroom door. Pearl turned away. Pure was on the bed, lying on his stomach in his underpants and reading a comic book. She strode over and slapped his cotton-covered arse, hard.

9

'Misty's one thing,' said Alfie slowly.

Iris rolled over into his arms. It was afternoon, but Iris and Alfie often spent the whole day in bed now, fucking for lost time. The conversation about Misty had been hours ago. Iris was surprised this was still the agenda. 'Misty wasn't your fault.'

Alfie wrapped his arms around her and continued. 'But you know I'm messing up all over again, don't you?'

'You are?'

'Aurelia. I've barely spoken to her. I know she's been living here – she feels the pull, the need to be near me. Her sire. And I claimed her. But I haven't done anything to be there for her. To see how she's coping. She's gone all day at the Institute. It's Saturday. I should be spending more time with her.'

Iris's stomach flipped. Aurelia. His cub. Beautiful Aurelia. 'Yes,' she said quietly. 'I guess.'

'Hey,' Alfie said a few minutes later as he looked around the door of Aurelia's bedroom. The walls were honey beige. It had been Misty's room. It was slightly more feminine than the bigger, pale-blue painted bedroom at the front of the house, which Alfie still thought of as Leon's, and it was bigger than Zac's strange wood-panelled room, which was right at the back.

Alfie had told Aurelia she could take any room she wanted. She needed a room and deep down he simply couldn't bear the though of her taking the place of any of them. It hurt Alfie, bruised him deep inside to still be in this house, but, as he had told Iris over and over, he wanted them to be able to find him if they ever came back.

Iris had wanted to move back to her flat. Just the two of them. 'We can take the chains,' she had said. But this house was the only place where Alfie felt whole. Hurting and whole – he knew Iris thought it was penance. And Iris's flat didn't have room for Aurelia. Not that Iris understood the first thing about living as a pack. About how Aurelia was part of this now. About how Alfie needed to lead her and guide her.

Not that he had been doing that. But he would. He should. He shuddered inside when he thought about what Iris had told him about Blake stepping up to the plate.

In response to Alfie's voice, Aurelia looked up. Her face was red and slightly teary. Alfie had seen this before. Some people just couldn't come to terms with it. Never did. A lot of werewolves ended up killing themselves. The self-administered silver dagger through the heart was both a huge werewolf taboo and practically a cult. It was so common. It was sometimes claimed that more than half werewolves took that route. It was so understandable. Some werewolves even believed that to move fully into your wolfhood, a process that generally took a full year of transformations, you had to experience the silver night. A night alone with a silver dagger where the werewolf faced himself in the mirror and held the dagger to his breast. Truly looked inside himself and asked whether he didn't wish that bite had been fatal. Whether he didn't wish he had stood and fought rather than run away broken and bleeding to be reborn.

Alfie had done it. Silver nighted. It had only been thoughts of Iris that had pulled him through. He knew Misty had done it too. Aurelia was still a young wolf. She had only transformed twice, in Blake's lab and then in the cellar with Alfie on Christmas Eve. She still had a long way to go.

'Hey,' Aurelia said as she looked up at him. And Alfie saw it then. Thrall. Vicious strong. Thrall he didn't deserve. He was being no kind of sire to her.

'Iris says Blake's got you working for him.'

'I thought you knew that?'

'I knew you were working there. I didn't know you were working *for him*.'

Aurelia shrugged. 'Only way I could keep my job.'

'You know most werewolves cut their ties in the end. Sometimes it takes a while. There is usually a period, like the one you're going through, where they try to live both lives, the one you had and the one you've got, but you can't. You need to be part of the pack.'

'What pack?'

Alfie knew she was right. The two of them didn't make a pack. If only Misty were still here. Or if Zac and Pearl hadn't run. Or Leon . . .

Alfie knew Zac had come back to the house after he'd escaped. His passport was gone and a few other things belonging to him and Pearl. He wondered yet again if Zac had gone back to Texas. And if he had – whether he'd summoned Leon or not – Alfie didn't think he'd have any reason to come back to England. Zac had never liked the weather. And he'd always been the loudest voice in favour of not setting foot in Oxford in the first place. Home of the Vix.

Alfie crossed the room and sat on the bed next to Aurelia. She leaned into him, her slender body warm and relaxed against his big chest. It was a natural gesture for a werewolf and his cub. It felt right. Alfie felt a desire to protect Aurelia bubbling up inside him. Almost overwhelming him with its blend of guilt and poignancy. He could smell Blake on her. Faint. Not from today. Maybe from three or four days ago. But the scent was there. And Aurelia would know he'd be able to tell.

'I should be dead,' Aurelia said quietly. 'Vix have a policy about bites. Can't have a Vix switching sides. They should have shot me.' Then she turned her head and looked up at him. Alfie nodded. There was a certain look in her eyes. He knew what she wanted to do. He been though this with Misty and Leon. She wanted to show her sire what he'd done.

Aurelia lifted her fingers and flipped open the buttons of her white blouse. She worked from bottom to top, until she unfastened the last one and drew the edges apart, opening it to reveal her tight tanned belly and plain cotton bra.

The top part of her stomach was a mass of scar tissue. Still a little pink. Alfie knew Blake had stitched Aurelia up the night she'd been bitten. He and Iris both had basic field medical skills. Blake hadn't made a bad job of it. A little puckering here and there. Alfie could've done it better. He'd asked to, in fact. Probably too late, when he was human again and chained up in the Institute basement. But Blake had just laughed hard and then punched him harder.

So Blake had saved her life. She would have bled to death otherwise. Blake had saved her when policy said he should have killed her, or at least let her die. But hadn't Blake always wanted a WXX?

Aurelia made no move to remove her bra but Alfie could see that the livid marks extended past the edges of it. He'd only seen the full scar on her when she'd been in wolf form. When he looked at the marks vanishing under the edges of the cotton he inhaled sharply through his nose and looked away at the floor. Aurelia had always been beautiful. She still was. More beautiful in many ways. But Alfie knew that she would never really feel beautiful again after what he'd done to her. For some werewolves – for the Aurelias – the scar is the hardest thing to bear.

Lying on the floor by Aurelia's bed was a scrapbook. Alfie bent and picked it up, turning to look at Aurelia, wanting a kind of permission to intrude into her personal things. But Aurelia just shrugged.

Alfie opened the book. Stuck in a random sort of way across the pages, haphazard and overlapping with some pictures creased and upside down, was Aurelia's life.

A middle-aged couple – both beautiful and refined. Clearly her parents; Alfie didn't need to ask. Shots from her teenage modelling career. Pretty enough but not a world class beauty. Some lingerie ads. Her perfect stomach tanned and flat and unscarred.

Some blurry shots from her short time as a soldier. A family tradition she had mentioned once. Alfie's own parents had been in the military. He didn't think he'd ever told her about that.

Alfie turned a page and then the scrapbook was full of animals. Wolves and dogs. Pictures from magazines. Older, darker pictures. Pages torn from books. Probably Blake's books. She'd been through Blake's library.

That must be why she was spending so much time with him. Who else would she see as better placed to tell her all about her new life? Well, other than the one person who obviously should have been doing it?

From that page on the scrapbook was full of information about WXXs, about sex with them. Pictures of naked scarred women. Pictures of women posing with clearly doped wolves. The kind of fake WXX porn that Alfie had always known must exist and never seen. Trust Blake to have it. And to let Aurelia see it.

Alfie licked his dry lips and put the book down. 'It takes time,' he said. 'For different people, it's different ...' He thought of Pearl, laughing with Zac in the kitchen.

She'd wanted to be bitten. She hadn't said so, but she was drenched in it. And Zac, Zac had been stoic, known the score. *Happens, man.* Leon had been proud, bursting with it. Marked out as more than a man. And Misty ... Misty had been like Aurelia.

And so had Alfie. The Beast who bit him had abandoned him to his fate. Let him wander alone. Told him nothing more than the basics. Alfie knew he really had no idea how to be a sire or an Alpha or even how to be a wolf. Hadn't Leon always said that? Hadn't Leon always been right?

'Is there anything I can do?' Alfie said, his heart breaking.

Aurelia shrugged again. 'I doubt it,' she said quietly.

Her shirt was still open. Alfie looked again at the red marks that marred her perfect flesh. He bent his head and kissed them.

Under her sire's tongue, Aurelia melted.

When Alfie lifted his head Aurelia was crying. Alfie reached up and touched her cheek. Touched the dampness there. 'Did Blake hurt you?' he said as gently as he could.

'No,' said Aurelia, 'you did.'

In the attic Iris lay on Alfie's bed listening. Alfie and Aurelia's voices were just soft murmurs. She couldn't tell what was happening. She was blindingly jealous anyway.

She knew she shouldn't be. She was his cub. It was a pack thing. She twirled a silver gun around in her hand, practising quick draw and zippy trick moves Doctor Tobias and Blake had taught her. She thought about The Silver Crown. And about how, as soon as she saw Aurelia down and bloody, she should have put a silver bullet in her.

10

Before he closed the bathroom door, Zac looked back at Pearl and Pure now lying next to each other on Pure's bed reading the same comic book; both so similar looking so close together, same plump mouths, same body types, same classical face shapes. He couldn't quite understand how the sight of Pearl could make his heart sing and the sight of Pure could make his mouth dry.

He knew Leon had a lot he wanted to say. He wasn't sure if he hadn't said it in front of Pearl – perhaps because she was female or because she was another step down the hierarchy – or if he was not saying it in front of Pure.

'The queer that wants to screw your girl, he's a Vix,' was what Leon said as soon as Zac closed the door.

'Pure? Yeah, I know. We got captured by Vix. He let us go. He's Pearl's cousin.'

'He's one of the guys who broke in through Pearl's window that time, who hauled me off. I tried to kill him. Thought I had.'

'I know. I've spoken to him about it. He knew it was you I was summoning. I know about what happened. That scar right down his face is down to you. But he's changed his mind about werewolves now. And about Vix. He hates them.'

Leon was sitting on the closed seat of the lavatory, his bandaged leg stretched out in front of him. Zac couldn't stop staring at him. The tight jeans and the tight T-shirt Zac had run out and bought for him, the cloud of flyaway blond hair that was almost down to his waist now. He hadn't seen Leon for so long he felt like his eyes were starving for him. The way Leon looked. Like no one else on earth. The strange blend of ultra masculine and twisted feminine. His sire. His Leon.

'What about you?' said Leon, 'you hate Vix?'

Zac shrugged. 'Yeah. I guess. Broke into our house, hauled Pearl and me off to some lyc prison they've got. It was her they wanted. This nasty little guy they've got there made that quite clear. Some sniffer thing probably. Hot for female lycans.'

Leon tipped his head back in frustration. 'A nasty little guy? Damn it, you mean I didn't kill that one either.'

'I don't think you killed any of them, sire. Sorry.'

'Well that's going to change. Zac, cub, look, this isn't easy to say but Misty's dead. I don't know how . . .'

Zac nodded. He could see Leon was surprised by his lack of reaction. 'Yeah, I know about that too. It was Vix. They shot her while she was doing that transformation thing for Omega. I went back to the pack house after we ran and . . . well, I saw Alfie again before I came here.'

Leon's eyes flickered around the room as if he was checking for something. Then he said, 'Do you know where Alfie is now? I had a visitor. Told me the Vix had Alfie, that we needed to rescue him.'

'He was there when the Vix took us from the pack house. He flipped. Bit one of them.'

'He's still alive,' said Leon. 'I know that for sure.'

'You are? Well, then they must have kept him. They took me and Pearly alive. Pure said Iris went after him.'

'Iris?'

Zac nodded. He knew they both knew who Iris was. The woman who held Alfie responsible for her brother's death. 'So if he's still alive,' Zac said slowly, 'he is with the Vix.'

'Yeah. Him and his new cub I reckon. Aurelia. Yeah. He didn't kill her. He's sired another.'

'They told you all this? Your visitors? Who were they?'

Leon's face went tight and hard. He didn't answer.

'Were they the people who shot you?'

Leon's response to that was a nod so tiny Zac was pretty sure only a cub would see it. When Leon spoke he kept his teeth locked tight together. 'I don't know who they were – but they wanted me to summon Alfie for them. They want to find him. I don't know why. But I don't like it. Alfie's mine. Alfie's death is mine. No one touches him but me.'

'I thought you never wanted to see Alfie again?'

Leon sniffed. 'Changed my mind. Or had it changed for me. If those bastards want Alfie, then they'll have to get to him before I do. They know he's with the Vix. But they can't get past the Vix's cloaking. That place is hidden from werewolves, but did you say you were there and got away? That's what they wanted to know. Had I ever been there? There's some kind of loophole. And if we have a Vix on side too . . .' Leon's eyes drifted to the closed bathroom door.

'Pure,' said Zac.

'That's right. Even if you and Pearl can't be sure of the way back, he'll know.'

'Yeah,' said Zac, 'Pure knows everything there is to know about that place.'

Leon grinned. 'So having that creepy human on our team might be useful after all.'

'Might be,' said Zac, 'but if you want Alfie why go to the Vix to get him? Wouldn't it be safer to just summon him?'

'Safer, maybe, but no. I'm not giving Alfie the satisfaction of thinking I *want* him. That I need him. But we need to go there anyway, avenge Misty. And if daddy is locked up somewhere in their basement, well, it'll be nice to see the look on his face when I turn up as his knight in shining armour.'

11

Iris looked up as Alfie walked into the bedroom. He looked heartbreakingly sad. Beaten down. 'What is it?'

Alfie looked pointedly at the gun in Iris's hand. 'I'm a werewolf,' he said.

Iris nodded. 'Well, I actually know that.'

'You kill werewolves, don't you?'

'I – No. Yes. Not you. You're quite safe with me.'

Alfie didn't smile. He pointed down the stairs. 'Tell her that. Aurelia. Or tell Misty. You should have killed me. If you'd killed *me*, you would have saved them all.'

'It's not your fault you bit them, Alfie. You're not in control.'

Alfie crossed the room and climbed onto the bed. He knelt over Iris. Straddling her, looking down at her. 'If it were you. If you were bitten. What would you want?'

Iris swallowed. 'We have a policy. I signed something once. And there's the oath too. If I get bitten I die.'

Alfie nodded and Iris knew what he meant.

'You're safe,' she said again, 'the collar. Lock Down. It won't happen again.'

'It wasn't meant to happen at all.' Alfie said. He reached out, took Iris's hands and lifted them to his neck. 'Take it off me.'

'What?'

'Take it off me. Let me be what I really am. I don't deserve this. I don't deserve to be a man.'

Iris pulled one hand out of his grip. 'Why? Do you think I'm scared of that? Do you think I'd kill you if you didn't wear that? Do you think I only love you when

you're stable – you think I don't love what you truly are?'
She slapped his face and then grabbed the collar, pulling
it from around his neck. 'You think I don't love the
monster you are? Lie down,' she said. 'Lie down on the
bed.'

Iris moved so Alfie could lie down. Neither of them
spoke. The next moves were obvious. Iris pulled out the
chains and started to fix Alfie down.

'How do you feel?' Iris asked, her voice weird and flat,
as the last manacle magically drew itself tight.

'Fine. Well you know how these chains feel, not built
for comfort.'

'How does it feel to not have the collar on? And to
know what I'm about to do? You do know, right?' Iris
reached out and stroked the bulge at the crotch of Alfie's
light-blue jeans. His cock jumped under her hand. 'That
good, eh?'

Alfie swallowed. 'OK, Iris, I never really told you this
before because I thought it might seem a bit, I don't
know, a bit ungrateful, but it's better without the collar.
Sex. I can't really explain it. The collar numbs everything.
Only slightly. But it does.'

Iris pulled her dark-green T-shirt off over her head and
grinned at Alfie. She wasn't wearing a bra. Standing here
across the room, looking at the light in his eyes as he
stared at her, his twitching mouth and thinking of his
lips, his tongue, his teeth on her nipples, was enough to
make her hot and wet and hard. She pulled off her trousers
too, jogging bottoms, grey and old, and walked over to
the bed in just her black cotton knickers. Alfie was still
fully clothed, but chained down. It was a pretty little
dichotomy. Iris could feel Alfie's arousal uncoiling like a
snake. She felt so powerful as she climbed up on the bed
and straddled his jerking frustrated hips.

'See. Monster. You don't scare me,' she said as she
leaned down to kiss him. Alfie mouth was savage

beneath hers, desperate for her, his teeth snapping, his lips greedy.

'Oh God, Iris, you look so beautiful on top of me. I want to fuck you so much,' he panted. 'I want to rip free of these things and throw you down underneath me, I want to shove my cock inside you so hard. I want to see your face, full of surprise at how viciously I slam into you. But at the same time ... being like this in front of you makes me burn. Oh God, this is too good, oh, *oh*! Fuck. You better use the muzzle *now*.'

Iris ran her tongue over his lips again and then sat back and pushed one finger into his mouth, thinking about his jaws. Those jaws that had nearly savaged her more than once. It turned her on. The things about him that tore him apart just made her wet. 'Bite me, werewolf,' she whispered.

Alfie closed his teeth around her finger.

'Harder.'

Alfie bit harder. Iris closed her eyes and felt it. It felt so real. She thought of everything. She thought about the Beast the night everything changed, ripping into her brother, tearing Alfie's flesh. She thought about her old colleague Jude who the Beast had killed in front of her. She thought of Alfie attacking her in his wolf form. She thought of her wedding night with Blake when he'd handcuffed her to the bed and fucked her, saying, 'Sometimes I think you *want* the Beast to kill you. Go the same way as your brother. Maybe that's why it won't do it.' Iris hadn't replied, just looked away, rolling her face into her arm – her lean muscular arms pulled taut in the cuffs. 'Oh my God,' Blake had said, not breaking the rhythm of his fucking. 'Is that true? Do you want the Beast to kill you?'

Iris had looked up at him. He looked like the devil. 'Maybe, I guess that would be my second choice.'

In the attic, in Alfie's bed, Alfie kept on biting Iris's

finger hard enough to hurt. Iris wanted him to break the skin. Wanted him to taste her blood, but he didn't. Maybe he couldn't. Fingers weren't fleshy enough, probably. Iris opened her eyes and pulled her finger out of his mouth, letting his sharp teeth scrape her flesh.

She dipped her head and kissed him again, licking his teeth. *His fangs.*

But Alfie pulled his mouth free and said, 'Baby, you really need to put the muzzle on me right now.'

Iris picked up her silver gun from the bedside table. When Alfie saw it his hips jerked hard.

'I know,' Iris whispered as she scooted up his big body, placed herself firmly on his chest and, bracing herself against the wall behind the bed, she lowered her left breast towards his mouth. 'Soon.' Alfie's tongue slipped out and licked her nipples. 'Good boy,' Iris whispered. She reached down and grabbed his hair, twisting it and pulling him closer. Alfie gave a muffled gasp and sucked the nipple that was in his mouth harder, grazing it with his teeth and his fangs. Iris closed her eyes and leaned harder against the wall behind the bed. This was too dangerous. Alfie ought to muzzled by now and yet, somehow, all she wanted to do was play games with his mouth. With the darkest dangerous part of him. With his weapon.

She took a deep breath, slid off and back, right down his legs, far enough to undo his jeans and slide them down, to open up his underpants, to let his hard ready cock leap into her hands. Alfie said, 'Iris?'

'I know,' she said, still brandishing the gun almost idly. 'I'll put it on in a minute. I swear.'

She jerked his cock slowly with one hand, pushing up his white T-shirt with the other, flicking his nipples and pinching them with her fingernails. Then she let go of his cock and ran both hands around under his back. She felt his wolf back. The hard muscled plane, the ridge of his spine, the tautness around his neck. He gasped when her fingers grazed his bite scar, but she didn't linger there today. She had hitched forwards now. His erection was grazing her through the fabric that covered her pussy. She reached around, pulled the damp cotton aside and backed onto it.

'Iris!'

'In a minute.'

'Fuck. Iris, either put the collar on me or the muzzle. This isn't safe. Even with the gun this isn't safe.'

Iris slid up and down on his cock. 'It's OK, Alfie. I'm trained for this sort of thing.'

Alfie rolled his head against the pillows. 'Iris, please.'

Iris reached forward and shoved the gun in his mouth. 'Better?'

He shook his head violently and started pulling at the chains, but they were so tight there was barely anywhere to move.

Iris started to move up and down more violently. She watched Alfie's eyes. He moved his head roughly, ripping his mouth free of the gun. 'Iris! Now . . .'

'I know. It's too late.'

'Iris . . .' Alfie's voice was cracking. He was over his edge.

'Shush.' Iris reached out and pinched both his nipples and then dropped her body down flat onto his, moving fast, riding him hard, waiting, waiting.

There was a tiny moment of stillness before he came. She had always wondered how this worked. Did he get to orgasm? Did he feel it? Who came? The wolf or the man? The answer, as Iris felt her werewolf-hunter adrenaline spike, was both. As she leaped back, tumbling out of the reach of the huge snapping jaws she saw Alfie. And she saw the wolf. She rolled clear of them both and sat up on the floor, panting hard, the gun still in her hands.

So, we've established you're still the biggest fucking lunatic of all then, Iris.

Iris looked around. The ghost of her dead brother was standing at the top of the stairs. 'What are you doing here watching that, pervert.'

I'm a pervert! Matthew eyed the snarling wolf chained to the bed. *That's not what they mean by doggie style you know, Iris.*

'I'm your sister. Don't talk to me like that. You're freaking me out. And the question still stands. What are you doing here?'

Do you mean what am I doing here watching you banging werewolves? Matthew let his gaze flick over to the snarling animal chained to the bed. *Or what am I doing still in this reality when you thought I'd disappear once you killed the Beast?*

Iris bit her lip. 'Um both, actually, well, the latter.'

They're coming, Iris. The Silver Crown. You have eleven Ancient Beasts left to kill. This isn't over.

12

Sunday 20 January 2008

Alfie came up behind Iris while she was making tea. She jumped, not sure how he'd be with her after what she'd done the night before. But his breath was hot, close to her ear and seemed calm when he said. 'I've had an idea.'

Iris turned in his arms. 'You have?'

'I'm a wolf without a pack. Aurelia's rejected me as her sire. My other cubs have gone. I'm lost to the werewolf world. So lost I can hardly bear to think about what my wolf has done. There's only one place left for me.'

'There is?'

'Aurelia has it figured out. Vix. I want to be part of the solution. I want to help you.'

Iris reached up and touched Alfie's cheek. 'But you can't. You're a werewolf. This was the problem we had before remember?'

'Things are different now. And if Aurelia works for the Vix why can't I?'

'Because you . . .' Iris shook her head. 'I don't know.'

'So, what's the business of the day? I know it's Sunday, but what can I do to help?'

Iris turned around, taking Alfie's hand as she pulled away from him and led him to the table. She thought of Matthew appearing the day before. What he'd said. The Silver Crown. She hadn't really stopped thinking about them since Blake had told her on Friday. What Blake had told her just before she saw Matthew again. 'You know Alfie, there is something. Work stuff.'

Alfie sat down at the head of the kitchen table. 'What?'

Iris turned away and fetched the tea then set it in front of him. 'The Beast was part of something called The Silver Crown. Like werewolf police. Have you heard of them?'

Alfie slowly nodded. 'Yeah, mostly rumours, but I'm sure they're true. They keep the records. Hold The Line. Spend a lot of time covering up lycan attacks all over the UK.'

'They cover up attacks?'

'Course. You didn't know? You remember how with Matt and me, how the police dropped the investigation really quick and the coroner said those strange things at the inquest about our testimonies being inadmissible because of shock. Well, that was probably the work of The Silver Crown. They have really powerful seers and they keep track of everything that goes on with lycans in the country. Maybe even the world. And they keep attacks quiet. They have a lot of influence.'

'Blake thinks they'll be coming for me. Vengeance for me killing the Beast. He was one of the twelve. And the rest of the Crown coming for me means eleven more Ancient Beasts.'

'Fuck,' said Alfie. 'Are you OK? Is this what yesterday was about?'

'I don't know really. Maybe. I mean I am meant to be killing the Ancient Beasts.'

'But eleven at once.' Alfie stopped and shook his head. 'That's even more reason why I need to be there. At your side. As if it isn't enough that Blake is taking care of my cub, I'm not having him protecting you too.'

'Blake's hardly . . .'

'I want to come and work with you, Iris. This just confirms that I should. Protect you. You're the Warrior Wolf, Iris. That's your role. Well mine is to help you. Whatever's coming for you, well, it'll have to deal with both of us. Let me come and work with you. Join the Vix.'

Iris smiled – not in a happy way. 'Yeah. Well, you know who I'm going to have to ask about that, don't you?'

Alfie's mouth twitched. He didn't say anything. He didn't need to.

13

Monday, 21 January 2008

'Blake, I need to ask you something about Alfie.'

Blake was rummaging in a cupboard in the basement. He turned around holding a packet of tobacco. 'No, Iris, I do not know if his penis will get stuck inside you if you try and do it while he's hairy.'

Iris blinked.

Blake turned around, leaning against the cupboard as he closed the doors. 'Actually, I think it probably will.'

'Blake, do you seriously think that I –' Iris stopped and shook herself.

'Well, what then? What do you want to know about wolfman? Don't tell me, you had him bite you, did you? That didn't take long. You want me to put some silver in you? That is still the only cure.' Blake began to stroll across the basement towards where Iris was standing.

'Blake, I didn't. You know I didn't. I was here last full moon, with you, doing the sweep.' Suddenly Blake was standing far too close, but Iris's back was against the basement wall and there was nowhere to run.

'Yeah, except you don't need it to be full moon, do you? All you have to do is slip that collar off his neck, get on your knees and take his cock in your mouth. Suck him hard enough and he turns into a monster.' Blake somehow moved even closer. His words were hot heavy breaths. 'Does that excite you, Iris? That's he's so close to the Beast inside him? That he's so fucking dangerous? I know you like danger. Do you like showing the wolves that you're really not scared of them anymore. Is that what it means to you? Being with that monster. He's worse even than Tobias, the Beast, the thing you killed, because he can turn anytime. Are you trying to prove something, Iris? Prove you're not that scared little girl hiding up in that tree anymore?'

Iris almost couldn't speak. She knew Blake was just being Blake, but, God, he was so close to the truth this time. 'Blake . . .'

'Because, really if that's what does it for you these days, Iris, I mean, well, I'm not surprised you left me, because I could be all kinds of things for you, but I really couldn't ever be that.'

'You couldn't be anything I needed, Blake.'

'Now, Iris,' Blake said softly, his mouth moving closer and closer to hers. It was Blake that was dangerous; far more dangerous than Alfie. Alfie could kill her, but Blake could destroy her. 'You know that isn't true. I was lots of things. I was the thing that gave your nightmares nightmares.' Blake stopped with his lips a hair's breadth from Iris's. She was breathing him now. He smelled of cigarettes and wrongness.

Like a seduction, he whispered, 'Staff meeting, Iris, you coming?' The word 'coming' was long on his lips. Too heavy with meanings.

Iris jolted. 'What?'

Blake was already turning away.

Iris followed Blake up the stairs from the basement. In the foyer he looked through the open doorway into the auditorium, Blake stopped short. 'God, Iris,' he said, turning around, 'what is Fido doing here?'

Iris looked past Blake's narrow shoulder. This building had once been a cinema, then a bingo hall, then a derelict heap and now The Institute of Paraphysiology. The massive auditorium had lasted through all these incarnations with relatively few changes. Alfie was sitting on the edge of a low stage at the front of the vast shabby-chic space crowded with plastic tables and chairs. Next to him sat Aurelia.

There was something about the way he was sitting with her that rattled Iris slightly. The way their heads were tilted. There was an intimacy between them that made Iris jealous. She just couldn't help it.

Iris shifted. 'That's what I wanted to ask you about. Alfie wants to come and help us. Work here.'

'Tch, what a pity I've already hired Aurelia to make my coffee,' Blake said and started patting his pockets for his tobacco.

'He could do a lot for us, Blake. The amount he knows about lycs.'

'Yeah, yeah, Iris,' Blake was rolling a cigarette now; not looking at Iris, his head bent over it. 'Except *I* know a lot about lycs, remember. Also what with Aurelia and Cate we're in danger of having more paranormals on staff than humans...' He trailed off as he flipped the little tube into his mouth and then pulled a match from behind his ear, moving to strike it on the doorframe.

Iris jolted upright and looked quickly around the empty foyer. 'Shit, Blake, don't let Cate hear you saying that. Witches *are* human. Don't people who say different meet very nasty fates?'

Blake exhaled smoke. 'Oh, you know what I mean, Iris. Look we're down to you, me and Pepper as far as actual humans go. You made that point yourself, on Friday. We need more soldiers. People who can actually sweep on full moon. Werewolves – strangely – aren't much use for that. The Silver Crown, Iris. We need to be prepared.' And with that Blake turned and strode into the auditorium in a flurry of cigarette smoke and hair and the swish of his dirty white coat.

Iris watched Alfie look up and, noticing Blake

approaching him, he stood up. Alfie was much taller than Blake. But little-man Blake didn't seem at all fazed by this. Perhaps he was used to it. Blake was small but Blake was a lot tougher than most men. And he knew it.

'Hi, Blake,' said Alfie. 'Iris told me about The Silver Crown.'

Blake stopped. Iris was behind him but from the way he was standing she reckoned she could picture the exact expression on his tight little face.

'And I know a lot about the Ancient Beasts,' Alfie continued. 'I'm a Beast cub.'

Iris watched the back of Blake's head move, still picturing his expression, almost able to anticipate his drawling response. 'Oh so we're meant to go to lycs for our impartial advice on lycs, are we? Why ever didn't I think of that?'

Alfie didn't say anything. Iris watched the way he was looking at Blake. It almost looked like he was trying to stare Blake down, pull Alpha on him.

Then Blake said, 'OK, Fido, sit down for now. We'll see how much use you can be.'

Alfie sat back down on the edge of the little raised stage with Aurelia. Iris sat at one of the fixed tables right in front of it. Blake came and sat next to her. There was an awkward pause until Pepper strolled in.

Iris hadn't seen Pepper since she'd come back to work. In fact, other than the last full moon sweep she'd come in for, her most vivid recent encounter with Pepper had involved the two of them aiming guns at each other across Alfie's attic bedroom. But as she sat down at the next table across from Iris and Blake she didn't seem at all fazed and Iris decided that if Pepper wasn't bothered she wouldn't be either.

Ella Pepper was the only Red still standing from Iris's original team. Pure – or 'bloody Pure' as he always seemed to be called now – had gone AWOL with some werewolves he'd released from the basement two months ago. And, really, he'd been pretty absent before that too. And Aurelia, well, Aurelia was still here at least. Even if she had suffered the fate that werewolf hunters were supposed to ensure never happened to one of their number.

It was funny, Pepper had always looked a little dowdy next to Aurelia and Pure who had both been such tall, lean studies in human beauty, that Iris had sometimes wondered if Dr Tobias had, in fact, recruited them from a modelling agency rather than via his contacts in the military. But now Pepper seemed to have come into her own a little more. Her harshly cropped hair had grown out a little so it was more Audrey Hepburn urchin than brutal crew cut. Her eyes were a little sparklier too. And there was the new way she walked too – springy.

Then, Blake gave the exact same sort of little delicate cough that Doctor Tobias used to do when he held staff meetings and it commanded attention in just the same way. 'OK,' he said, 'full moon tomorrow night. It'll be just three of us again so we need to optimise everywhere we can. I want some lycs brought in to work on. It is vital we engineer some encounters. Iris, do you have a route planned?'

'Um, kind of,' Iris said. 'I thought we'd make a circuit of the city. See if anything caught our attention and, if not, drop in on a few of the usual haunts.'

Blake sighed. 'What? Seriously? That's just not good enough, Iris. We need to raise our game. I want you to be researching proper routes. Drawing up itineraries. You're our expert on the ground. As soon as one sweep is done I want you to be planning the next one. Scouting, researching. I want us to be anywhere that there is chance of stray lycs. This is your job, Iris. Have you forgotten?'

'No, Blake, I . . .' Iris shifted. Blake was trying to humiliate her. She looked down at the nasty plastic table top.

'But shouldn't she be training?' Alfie said. 'You don't need her to do the sweep. She needs to prepare for The Silver Crown.'

Blake stared at Alfie for a moment. 'What?'

'She needs to be on top form. She's the Warrior Wolf. She needs to be ready.'

Blake's eyes went narrow. 'She is ready. Ready as she'll ever be. How many werewolves have you fought with her? She can cope with anything that's coming.'

'With eleven Ancient Beasts? She needs to fight. She can fight me. What better training?' Alfie said, 'I need to be here. Let me stay here, Blake. Let me work with you. I could be very useful. She could fight me in wolf form even when it isn't full moon – because of the instability.'

Iris peered at Alfie's face. This was new. The idea that his flipping could be something useful. Something sexy, sure. But something *useful*. Useful to werewolf hunters.

Blake narrowed his deep-set eyes at Alfie. 'Maybe you could be useful to me somehow –' he said slowly '– with a few conditions.' He sucked his bottom lip for half a moment. 'She still comes on the sweep. But, OK, you can stick around. But for a trial period of one month. And you can take the Doc's old office next to mine on the second floor.'

Alfie smiled. 'Sure.'

'And you report to me. I'm your superior. Not Iris. You understand that, don't you?'

'Sure,' Alfie said again.

Blake looked oddly at Alfie for a second. Iris was about to say something too but at that moment the doors of the auditorium opened and Cate wafted in on a tide of green and purple hazy paisley. She glided over and perched herself on the edge of Pepper's table. 'Sorry, sorry,' she said, 'what did I miss?'

'Oh,' said Blake standing up, 'just everything. No matter, Iris can fill you in. Why don't you two meet before the sweep tomorrow and do a proper briefing?'

Later that afternoon, Blake knocked on the door of Dr Tobias's old office. He heard Iris shout, 'Come in, Blake.'

Doctor Tobias had always kept an office so Spartan and under furnished it bordered on the ridiculous. Of course Blake had always known why this was the case. Tobias was a werewolf. The powerful Oxford Ancient Beast. Why would he have anything much in his office? But no one else had ever asked – it had just been part of the Doc's eccentricity. The fact the room was empty apart from one desk and two hard chairs.

The more Blake thought about it the more he was pleased with himself for putting Alfie in here. No furniture. Good. Animals aren't allowed to use furniture.

Alfie and Iris were in the far corner of the room, with Iris standing just behind Alfie with her back pressed up against the wall. And Alfie half turned, looking over his shoulder towards the doorway. Iris looked so delicate and petite hidden behind Alfie's hulking bulk. They'd obviously been making out. He saw every heartbreakingly nostalgic tell-tale sign on Iris as she sucked her slightly swollen bottom lip: the pink highlights across her cheek bones, the nipples slightly raised under her shirt.

Fuck, this was so wrong. It was wrong that Iris was with Alfie. Iris was so different from him. The difference in their heights was just ridiculous. She looked like a doll next to him. A really kick-ass warrior doll, but a doll nonetheless. Alfie was just a lump of muscular meat. Iris was tight and wiry. In fact, Iris had a very similar body type to Blake's own; it had been remarked upon before. Iris had told him a few times that he reminded her of her dead twin brother – wondered aloud what that might mean. Plus Iris was a werewolf hunter, just like him. They were probably the best pair of werewolf hunters in the world. Alfie, damn it, Alfie was a sodding werewolf. Not even a human. This was so wrong. So fucked up. This needed sorting. Blake realised he had coiled both his hands into fists and was digging his nails into his palms.

'Do you want something, Blake?' Iris said, pouring cool condescension on his heated mood.

'Yeah,' said Blake, 'yeah I do. I need to talk to Alfie.'

'Well, I'm right here,' Alfie said as he turned around properly to face Blake square on.

Blake pressed his lips together. 'Yeah, right. On your own. Haven't you got any work to do, Iris?'

Iris shrugged. 'I'm on top of things.'

'Have you done that list for me for the sweep?'

'I'll do it tonight.'

'I want it by four o'clock, Iris. I want to study it and approve your proposals. Give me three possible routes and a risk assessment for each one.'

'What? That'll take me all afternoon. Doctor Tobias never . . .'

'Well, I'm sorry for expecting you to actually treat this as a place of work, Iris. You know, I'm sure the doc was thinking of getting rid of you. I suppose locking you in a cage with a werewolf on full moon is one kind of dismissal. Perhaps he had a point.'

Iris pushed past Alfie and stormed over to Blake. For a second he thought she might hit him. In some ways, he was rather disappointed when she didn't. She stopped right in front of him. 'Stop pushing me, Blake. I don't know what your game is, but this has to stop.'

Blake said, 'Iris, I really don't know what you're talking about.'

Iris made an exasperated noise and pushed past him out into the corridor.

Blake looked at Alfie. Alfie raised one hand and touched the corner of his mouth in a gesture that seemed unconscious but Blake knew that Alfie had just been marking his territory.

Blake clenched and unclenched his teeth a couple of times. Then he said, 'The job, it comes with another condition.'

'Really?'

'I need to be sure that you're safe. That you're on our side. I want you to Lock Down here. In our basement. I want you down there with the collar off two hours before moonrise.'

Alfie frowned. 'Two hours before? Why? I don't need to Lock Down two hours before moonrise. What kind of sick reasons do you have for doing that, Blake? If you think that'll give you a two-hour window to try and screw my girlfriend you're very wrong. It won't keep us apart. She'll sit with me, Blake. She'll wait. She likes to watch me change, you know. She likes it. The danger. The sense that I'm more than a man.'

'You're not a man at all and she's a freak if she gets off on it,' Blake said. 'I want you down there two hours before moonrise tomorrow night or you're fired. Gross misconduct. And one more thing, that collar locked around your neck – that collar that stops you killing my wife – belongs to me. Belongs to the Institute. It is extremely rare and valuable and if you don't want me to start taking steps to get it back you should really make sure you keep me happy.'

In a plane somewhere over the Atlantic, Zac sat between Leon and Pearl. Pure was across the aisle and Leon was leaning right across Zac and Pearl to talk to him.

'So you know where the Vix are based, right? You can get us there?'

Pure nodded. 'I worked there for over a year. Of course I can.' He looked over at Zac. 'Don't you know too. From when we broke out?'

'Maybe, I'm not sure.'

'I know, babe,' Pearl said gently. 'I've lived in Oxford all my life. I know just where we were. Let me show you.' Pearl took Zac's hand and turned it over. She picked up the felt-tipped pen she had been using to do a crossword puzzle and started to draw a little map.

14

Iris had, rather sulkily, put together Blake's lists and plans for the sweep and then he'd asked for so many changes she had to work late on Monday and come in early on Tuesday morning to get it done. This was fine with Alfie who claimed to be feeling guilty about neglecting Aurelia. 'She's all that's left of my pack, after all,' he'd said, and spent time with her. Which Iris didn't feel too weird about because she didn't let herself think about it.

On the afternoon of the full moon, Alfie told Iris that not only was he Locking Down at the Institute, but he wanted to be in his cage with his collar removed two hours before moonrise. But Iris didn't argue, just took him down to the basement and took off his collar, locked the door and made to leave.

'Iris, don't you want to stay here with me?'

Iris stopped and turned around. 'Um, well, I do have work to do. I've got that meeting with Cate before the sweep.'

'Oh.'

'Look, Alfie, it's two hours yet. This is weird. Do you want me to put the collar back on you and let you out until nearer the time?'

'No, no, I just thought you'd stay and talk to me, that's all. I thought you'd like to watch me change.'

Iris smiled at him. 'Well that's the great thing about you, my unstable wolfboy. I can watch you change any-time. Now, you sure you don't want out?'

'No, no, this is fine.'

'Pervert,' Iris said, laughing as she turned away and headed up the stairs.

Pure tried to keep up as Zac, Leon and Pearl whirled through Heathrow. Did werewolves have the ability to move extra fast when the full moon was near?

They suffered many delays on their journey; the worst of which was due to a serious misunderstanding involving the silver blade Leon turned out to have on his person.

He'd stolen it from Zac's weird magic shop. No doubt planning to stick it into Alfie. Probably didn't bother to ask if it was spelled for non-detection. Spelled like the one Pure always carried. (He might be a human trying to live in a werewolf pack, but he wasn't a fool.)

This whole thing was a mess. Everything was more impulsive and ramshackle now Leon was in charge. Back in the motel, Zac had made it quite clear he was stepping aside and that Leon was Alpha. And Leon did things differently. He'd scorned Pure's offer to arrange for a private flight back – explaining that for a fraction of the cost they could get Jin's coven to create magical documentation that would get them on a normal flight. This was, apparently, how things were done. Leon wasn't the first werewolf to find himself in a strange place with no ID after a summoning. Witchcraft was the usual way of dealing with it. Of course, Leon's affinity with witchcraft would have been way more convincing if Leon had remembered to ask the witches to cloak his silver blade, too.

So now they were late. It was full moon tonight and they were trapped in the middle of Heathrow Airport. Runways and security and people. Practically an urban jungle. Pure wasn't a werewolf. He was a human. He was a Vix. And he knew what three werewolves could do in the middle of a place like this if the moon caught up with them. They needed to get out of here. Not for their own safety – this place was full of security, but they wouldn't have silver blades or bullets – for the sake of everyone else's.

But Leon was in charge and Leon was still clinging to his plan of going back to Oxford, convinced there was time to get there before moonrise.

But there wasn't enough time, Pure was certain. It was already too late.

As usual, Cate was less interested in Institute business and more in Iris's state of mind. It wasn't long before Iris had told Cate everything she could think of about current operations and there was no way to avoid getting psychoanalysed witch style.

'So, are they coming for me? The Silver Crown? And is killing them part of my destiny. All eleven of them?'

Cate shrugged. 'You've read the prophecy too. What do you think?'

'Well, you know, if you could maybe explain that in more detail, I might be able to answer the question. I mean all this stuff about prophecies and destiny, well, it might make sense to you, but it's just so much mumbo-jumbo to me. Look at it this way, you have told me I have this special destiny to kill Ancient Beasts, but I also have this very dangerous job and, actually, this very dangerous love life. So, am I safe? I mean, I have to wonder. Does having a destiny mean I can't die?'

'It's complicated, Iris, it doesn't really work like that. Things that are meant to happen, will happen.'

'Well, can't you just tell me what things are meant to happen? Or, are they really coming. Just nod if they are.'

Cate didn't nod, but she was clearly about to say something.

Iris held up her hand. 'I know, I know,' she said, 'you can't "help" me. Unless it's part of your job and don't worry I'm not going to ask you to explain how that particular slice of witch morality works.'

'I can't get involved in your destiny, Iris.'

'You are involved, though. You've had your meddling witchy fingers in my destiny all along. And now, when I could actually use some of your meddling or, at the very least, some explaining, it's hands off.'

'I'm sorry, Iris. It's complicated. Witches aren't meant to get involved in human affairs. That's the vow we took. Human and witch don't mix. It's been proved time after time in every culture on earth.'

'Then why? Why are you here? You clearly are meddling to some extent. You help us fight the werewolves, for God's sake.'

'Iris, I'm not here to work for the Institute. I don't need to do this. I'm here for you, because we believe in what you're doing. We think you need protection. We think you're important. You're going to do important things. Or you should. You will.'

'Like kill all of The Silver Crown? Then help me. You think I'm important, help me. Tell me what's going on.'

'I'm not here to help you, Iris, or to explain things to you. You have to help yourself. I'm just here to watch you. To stop anyone else making things hard for you.'

'Anyone making things . . .? Anyone like who?'

Cate made an odd little gesture. Very unwitchlike. She seemed furtive for a moment. Looking around. Checking no one was listening. 'Some witches don't believe the same things we believe at the Clements and Castle coven, Iris. You remember stories you've heard about good and bad witches. Well, that is broadly true. Some witches, well let's just say that they aren't really very happy about the human attitude towards them. Some witches are still a bit sore about that whole setting us on fire thing. Some witches think it's payback time. Some witches think that any kind of creature that makes life miserable for humans – say werewolves, for example – is well worth their time and their assistance.'

'There are witches who help werewolves!'

'Yes. It's all about balance, Iris. Maintaining balance. There are also witches who help werewolf hunters.'

'Like you, you mean? Well then help me. Tell me what's going on. Tell me what's going to happen?'

Cate sat back. 'OK, I will. I'll help you and here's how. This is all you need to know. Don't have sex with Blake.'

Iris spluttered. 'I'm really not going to . . .' then she remembered who or rather what she was talking to. *Was she? Would she? Was this really in any way something she needed to be warned against?* Iris took a deep breath, shaking her head. 'I'm hardly going to have sex with Blake.'

'Maybe you won't have a choice.'

Iris raised her eyebrows, 'Blake's not . . . he can be a bit inappropriate, but he isn't like that. He knows when no means no.'

'I don't mean that. It won't be him that takes your choice away, it'll be you. Destiny is a tricky thing, Iris. Maybe you won't be able to avoid this one, I don't know. But if you can, well, some things are fixed and some aren't. Even those of us who know what will or should or may happen can't ever tell for sure what's negotiable and what isn't. There are some difficult decisions in your future, Iris.'

'Whether or not to sleep with Blake is hardly difficult.'

Cate silenced Iris with a look. 'The thing is Iris, killing the Beast has changed you. Forever. Do you know how many humans have killed Ancient Beasts?'

Iris shifted. 'I can guess? None? It's none, isn't it?'

Cate nodded. 'Yes. And more than that. None of them have ever died before. They're practically immortal. Killing the Beast wasn't an end, Iris. It was a beginning.'

15

'Hey.'

Alfie looked up. He wasn't at all surprised to see Blake looking at him through the bars of the cage, but this was, already, very awkward. Blake had an expression on his face that Alfie didn't want to think about. He had no idea where Blake was going with this. His best guess was, no place he wanted to be.

'Blake,' Alfie said, with a slight nod that he hoped hit the right note between respectful and dismissive. How were you meant to behave when you were a werewolf and leering at you through the bars of your cage was a werewolf hunter – a werewolf *torturer*, who was also the husband of your girlfriend? And your boss?

Blake smiled, his face becoming ever more creepy-sinister-predatory. He said, 'The job, the one Iris wants me to give you, there's one more condition I haven't mentioned.'

Alfie looked at Blake's hands. He was holding a small wooden box. Alfie felt his stomach roll over. 'If it involves you and a bottle of silver nitrate then there's no danger money in the world . . .'

Blake smiled slyly. Clearly he remembered the last time the two of them had been down here alone too. 'It's not that. Nothing like that. Well, maybe a little like that. But only a very little. I'm not going to hurt you. But it does involve certain aspects of my interests. You know I'm interested in your condition. I'd like to run a few experiments. The problem is I can only run them when you're not wearing that damn collar. I don't want Iris to know about this just yet, so I can't ask her to...' Blake paused and smiled like he was clever. 'But Iris lets you out of it before the change, so...' Blake opened the box he was carrying, set it down on the bench behind him and turned back around holding a syringe. 'Adrenaline. That was always her theory about how to flip you chemically. I think this would be interesting for a first trial, don't you think. I've already started the cameras running.'

'You're just like all the rest of them,' Alfie said, shaking his head as he started to take off his shirt.

'All the rest of who?'

'Oh, just everyone. Everyone wants a piece of me. A piece of the weird werewolf. Sometimes I feel like a fairground attraction. A freak show. You, Iris, Hera in Brazil, Lilith.'

Blake paused a moment and then spoke slowly, as if he'd only just processed what Alfie had been saying. 'Lilith? The witch, Lilith?'

'Yeah, you know her? From the C and C coven.'

'Um, there were a lot of covens...'

'More than seventeen?'

Blake smiled a knowing smile. '"More than seventeen covens"? Yes, actually she did say that.' Blake said. 'I only met her once.'

Alfie smiled back. The same smile. 'You "*met*" her, did you? She gets about, does she? She seemed the type that might.'

Blake blinked. 'What are you going to do to Iris if she doesn't stop talking about me in bed?'

'What?' Alfie took a step backwards.

Blake smiled and Alfie followed his gaze to the camera set high in one corner of the room. The camera Blake had told him was running. It was only small. A box with a blinking red light, but when he looked he realised he'd seen it before. 'There's a camera in Iris's office too.'

'One in every room. We need security. Imagine what

The Silver Crown would do to us if they could find this place.'

'Worried you might find yourself on the other end of some of your own more refined methods of torture?'

Blake paused a second and ran his teeth over his bottom lip. 'It's not me I'm worried about, and you know it. They'll come for her. She's the lyc killer. The Warrior Wolf. She killed the Beast.' Another pause. 'And your cub.' Alfie went to say something but Blake kept talking. 'So, I hear she talks about me all the time while you're fucking her?'

Alfie baulked then remembered the camera and realised Blake must have seen it all. 'She says your name. She doesn't scream it, you understand. She *says* it. She gets distracted, feels the urge to tell me what a terrible mistake she'd made ever getting involved with you. But I'm pretty sure I've put a stop to it. She's got one chance left. She isn't going to say it again.'

'Or what?' Alfie knew he had Blake now, Blake was so clearly intrigued.

Alfie walked forwards. Walked right to the bars of the cage so he was as close to Blake as it was possible to get. 'Anything I want.'

Blake smiled back. Tight and feral. 'Anything you want? Well, talking of which. Aurelia!'

Alfie looked over Blake's shoulder as Aurelia appeared through the archway at the bottom of the basement stairs. 'What is she doing here?'

Blake slipped the syringe back into the wooden box. 'Actually I thought we'd try another trigger today.'

Alfie shook his head. 'Blake. What? No! I can't. It's too dangerous. I could kill her.'

Blake cocked his head like Alfie was making an interesting point. 'She's a werewolf. Only silver can kill her.'

'An unstable wolf can kill a human-form werewolf. Don't ask me how I know. I just know.'

'Hmm,' Blake thought for a second, 'Well, I suppose that makes sense. But don't worry. I'll keep an eye on you. I'll tranq you right on the change over.' Blake shrugged. 'Not a problem. And Aurelia wants to do it, don't you?'

Aurelia nodded. She started to walk towards Alfie's cage.

'Blake,' Alfie said urgently, 'No. I'm with Iris, I can't just...'

'Iris, yes. Iris who is in mortal danger from The Silver Crown. Who you want to be with to protect. Who you can only protect by working here. And working here – werewolf – means answering to me.' Blake tipped a glance to Aurelia. 'So I guess it's your choice. Come on, it wouldn't be the first time for you two. And isn't it about time you did something for the only cub you haven't driven to death or banishment.'

Alfie growled low in his throat. The full moon was near. He could feel it. He could see it in Aurelia too. See it rising in her glossy pale skin. Sometimes it was hard to think straight when the moon was already in his blood. Blake's logic seemed to make perfect sense. This was the only way he could protect Iris. It was just coincidence that he also really wanted to do it.

Alfie nodded his head, all the time knowing very well that his dick had made so many bad decisions for him before.

The first thing he did when she approached him was sink to his knees in front of her and push up her blouse. He pressed his tongue to the scars that covered her and whispered, 'I'm sorry. I'm so sorry.'

Aurelia pulled his head back with a fist tangled in his hair. It hurt and he was glad of that. She looked at him for a long time. Her mouth was moving.

Alfie said, 'You want to spit on me, don't you? Animal. Filthy thing that ruined your life. You hate that you can't do it.'

Aurelia looked angry. 'I hate you,' she whispered.

Alfie said, 'I know. I know what I am. I know what I did. If you want to spit on me then do it. I give you permission to do it.'

But Aurelia didn't. She bent down and she kissed him. A kiss powered by anger and lust.

Alfie had fucked Aurelia in this cage before. Used Lure on her when she was a human. Spun her in his arms, forced her up against the wall. This time all he wanted to do was worship her.

Not Aurelia – Misty. This was more about Misty than anyone. Alfie's first cub. Misty who had never let Alfie back in her bed after he'd bitten her. Misty, who had died loving him.

All he wanted to do was give Aurelia pleasure. He wasn't sure what Aurelia wanted. Some part of it was revenge. Some part of it was about wanting to please her sire. He stripped off her clothes and pretended not to notice how bad the scars were that latticed her breasts. He put his tongue on them. One mark ran over her tight right nipple. When he touched his tongue to that point, Aurelia bucked and screamed as if in electric shock.

She reached down while he was still working his tongue on her scars, and guided his erection inside her. He fucked her without breaking contact. Using his hands with his cock to create an orgasm for her that he was sure was beyond anything she had experienced as a human.

And then he felt his own orgasm coming. Racing towards him with the wolf at its heels. He turned his head. Blake already had his hands on the cage door.

16

Iris went up to Blake's office to go over some last minute changes to the sweep routes he'd asked for. But there was no answer when she knocked on the door. Annoyed, she opened it. The office was empty but the door to the lab was standing open.

In Blake's lab, Iris stood very still, barely over the threshold. On the lab computer was an image from a security camera. It was the basement. Alfie's cage. Inside the cage Alfie was kneeling in front of Aurelia, kissing and licking the scars all over her naked torso.

As she stared Iris thought about a night a million years ago when she had turned up late to a student party and found Alfie pressing his ex-girlfriend Lara up against the fridge, kissing her and with his cock so clearly hard in his jeans.

Oh, Alfie, she thought. *Has so little really changed?*

Zac reached over and touched Pearl's hair. She was looking out of the window of the coach, but she turned when she felt his touch. 'What time is it?' she said, yawning.

Zac looked at his watch. 'I'm not sure. What's the time difference? Six hours?'

The bus pulled up at the St Clements stop and Pure stood up. Leon exchanged glances with Zac.

As he stood up, Zac said, 'It's too close, isn't it? We haven't made it.'

They started to file off the coach. Leon – still limping a little – close behind Zac. 'It'll be fine. But we need to get to open ground as soon as we're off.'

'We can go to the old pack house. Might still be empty.'

Leon's tone changed. Alpha. 'No way. It was only rented. It'll be let to someone else now. And the Vix know it. Just open ground. Quickly.'

Zac tripped down the steps of the coach and caught up with Pearl standing on the pavement. St Clements. Shabby and dirty. Strangely familiar. They cut through to Cowley Road where Pearl used to buy Alfie's steaks. The street the Vix's van was parked the night they found them. The park. Where was it? There was definitely a park around here somewhere. He slipped his hands around Pearl's waist from behind with a kind of sinuous urgency and put his lips to her ear. 'You feel it, don't you?' he whispered. Pearl nodded. 'Where's the nearest park?'

Pearl indicated with a flip of her pretty blonde head. 'South Park, just over there.' Zac looked. How could he have missed it? So obvious. A rising hill of green in the gathering dark. A minute away. Less if they ran hard. They needed to run hard.

Zac turned back to Leon, 'What about Vix? They'll be out tonight.'

But Leon had seen the park too and was already moving. He started to run, a weird disjointed movement favouring his uninjured leg. Zac could feel it then too. The moon. Suddenly so strong. He thought they had more time than this. He must have been mistaken. They were right on the edge of it. He grabbed Pearl's hand.

Pearl reached out as Zac pulled her away and touched Pure's cheek. 'See you tomorrow, Willy,' Zac heard her say as he dragged her along. 'Keep away from the park.'

In front of Zac, Leon had already taken off his denim jacket. Zac watched him vault the high fence around the park, yelping as he landed, his leg crumpling slightly. But he recovered in seconds, running again and slinging the jacket down in a clump of long grass. As Zac grabbed the fence to follow, Pearl looked up at the height of it, her eyes wide and said, 'Babe, I can't do that.' Zac looked at Leon, still running away from them. His heart was pounding. Sire or cub. The downward tide.

I can't lose him again.

He turned back to Pearl, not sure what he was going to tell her. That he had to follow? That last time he'd run out on Leon, left him behind when the Vix attacked, it had taken a summoning to get them back together. He couldn't go through that again.

That Leon was his sire and he was injured and Zac didn't feel ready to let him out of his sight again. If anything happened, Pearl could summon Zac easily if she went back to the pack house where he'd bitten her. Pearl was pointing, saying something about a gate, but her voice was going, fading. When he looked at her face he saw it was too late. The moon was rising. She was changing.

So was he.

Blake stood in the doorway of his lab and watched Iris for a moment. On the screen Alfie was fucking Aurelia on the floor of his cage. Blake coughed lightly.

Iris turned. 'Oh.'

Blake strode in and peered at the screen. 'Oh, Iris,' he said. 'I never wanted you to see this.'

'He'll kill her,' Iris whispered. 'He hasn't got his collar on.'

'Oh no,' said Blake, reaching forwards and switching off the monitor. 'I took care of it. This feed is on a fifteen minute delay.' As he finished talking, Blake threw the tranq rifle down on the desk. 'I stuck Aurelia in the other cage. Moon's too close for her to go home now. Oh, are these for me.' Blake grabbed the sheaf of papers that were still in Iris's hand then steered her away from the screen with a hand at her back. 'Come on, Iris,' he said. 'Let's talk and walk.'

* * *

Iris followed Blake, still slightly dazed and dumb with it. She wasn't sure what to say ... what to do. They both stopped in the yard, standing in front of the open back of the truck. Blake was still looking through the papers she had prepared. He twisted his mouth up in thought.

'Yeah, OK, Iris, I like the first one.'

'You made me do three and you like the first one?' she said stiffly.

'Three? I thought I wanted five. Next month, I want five. I'll drive.'

Blake turned and made to walk around to the front of the truck. Iris looked at Pepper, already sitting in the back; her face was pale with shock.

'Iris,' Pepper said jerkily, 'come listen to this.'

Iris climbed up into the back of the truck as Blake got into the front and started revving the engine. 'Stop it, Blake,' Iris snapped at him, crouching close to the short wave radio set and listening to what Pepper had found.

Blake turned around in his seat. 'Iris, you don't tell me to ... what? What is it?'

'... South Park ...' the radio muttered among blasts of static, '... three large dangerous dogs ... St Clements ...'

'OK,' Iris said, feeling her adrenaline spike as her shoulders locked back and her chin went up, 'we're on. Pepper, call Cate at home on the coms. Tell her to make sure the cops stay out of there. Just a mind wipe should do it. Blake, for God's sake, get going.'

'Iris, I really think ...'

'Just do it, Blake! Damn it. Go!' *Monsters. Something to kill. Oh Yes!*

17

Pure yelled at Pearl – not really words, just anything he thought might get her attention. 'Hey' and her name and 'please'. Zac had already gone, changed into a wolf and leaped clear over the fence. Pearl was on the ground. Still somewhere between blonde hair and white fur. Pure swallowed hard. He was trained to deal with difficult situations, to make tough calls, but he had never felt less prepared for anything.

During the long weeks of training in the Institute auditorium, Iris had built on Pure's army training, urging on him the importance of attacking fast, attacking first and attacking with silver. A silver weapon inflicting a fatal injury was what was needed. As always, Pure had his silver blade strapped to his calf.

He'd seen Pearl change before. On Christmas Eve in the cage at Omega's. As he ran towards her he tried to remember that process. But he'd been so overwhelmed. In a room full of shifty aroused men and with his own hard dick heavy at his crotch. Pearl had been naked, her pussy shaved bare. He'd never seen anything like it. He'd never even dreamed.

He wasn't even thinking about his dick now, only about scouring his brain to try and calculate how long he had before the woman he loved most in the world became a slavering uncontrolled monster. He wracked his brain trying to think of other wolf changes he'd seen. Alfie had flipped during that raid – but that had happened so fast. There had been some strange films that Blake had in his collection. Military experiments he'd said. They certainly *seemed* to show men changing into wolves in dirty white-walled rooms. Iris had said they were fakes. Blake had only shown them once. Cursed for hours trying to get the old abandoned projection equipment at The Institute working. When he'd succeeded and the flickering images had filled the screen, he hammered down the stairs, skidded into the auditorium and pushed Iris up against the back wall, kissing her and boasting about her having lost the bet that he wouldn't be able to get the projector working and now having to come and suck his dick in the basement. Iris had laughed. Liked it. God, it was bizarre to think of them together like that now.

Pure shook himself, trying to make his brain focus. This was so weird. It was like he couldn't make himself concentrate. Couldn't make himself concentrate on what he was going to have to do as soon as he reached.

Pearl was lying on the ground. A smallish white wolf. Pure kept running towards her. She looked so harmless as she lay on the ground. But then she sprang. Then harmless was the last thing she was.

Pure swallowed. He knew he wasn't going to be able to do this, but he didn't know what *else* to do. He thought of Iris, of her story of that first encounter with Alfie. How she's stabbed him in the eye. She'd been in love with him too, hadn't she? It was very strange to Pure to think about having something in common with Iris. But maybe he could do something like that, bring Pearl down with a debilitating wound but not kill her.

The white wolf turned. Snarling, mouth foaming. Pure moved, he raised his dagger and hurled himself through the air towards her, sticking the blade into her back. She howled and threw him off, batting him easily to the ground. The dagger was still lodged in her shoulder.

She was on him now, doing that hound thing where

they look at you before they begin. Iris had taught him about that too. Iris had had that done to her. Pearl was going to kill him. Pure reached up and found the dagger in her back. He twisted it, making her yelp – and his heart break – and then pulled it free. She hadn't been distracted enough to let him up, but now he was armed again.

He looked at her white throat. She was so beautiful. It was her or him. His eyes stung. He saw his move in front of him. Slit her throat.

Blake had once run a whole day-long workshop on blade care. Pure had a good memory. He kept his blade so sharp it could have cut the air. Pearl wouldn't even feel it.

Pure squeezed the handle of the blade tight. He still didn't know if he could do this. In a lot of ways he'd prefer it if she killed him. 'Pearl,' he whispered. 'Pearl, I love you. I've always loved you.' He told himself that if she killed him she would run and maybe hurt someone else. Destroy someone else. Worse, get caught by Iris. Worse still, get caught by Blake.

He raised the dagger and closed his eyes. Then closed them tighter. Then inhaled hard. The hound above him dropped onto his chest. But his hand – the hand holding the blade – still hadn't moved.

Pure opened his eyes to see a familiar figure standing over him and the heavy body of the wolf. 'So, Pure, you gone freelance?'

Pure looked at the rifle in Blake's hands. 'Is that . . . ? Was that . . . ?'

'Tranqs? Yeah, course. I seem to remember that this one belongs to me.'

'Pearl? No! I won't let you take her.' Pure reached up and clutched Pearl's wolf body to his.

'Oh for god's sake, Pure boy. Do you have make everything into such a drama?' Blake lifted his rifle and aimed.

There was nothing Pure could do. He watched the dart coming. Whirling through the air and sticking in the left shoulder, before everything went blurry, then muffled, then silent and dark.

18

South Park was a big hill with a fence around it. Deceptively big, in fact. And very central. Right in the middle of Oxford. Not a usual lyc hangout. Not much tree cover. Not much of anything really.

Running across the dark park, Iris felt her spirits roar and soar inside her. The image of Alfie and Aurelia – the image she thought she would never be able to get out of her mind – seemed to recede. This was where she belonged. All her questions, all life's complexity faded away. This was just ... running, hunting, killing. This was just it. Just her. Who she was. What the Beast had made.

It was like the very early days. With Blake and her and Pepper now instead of Jude. Silver guns. Silver blades. Chasing, tracing, hunting. Blake shouting directions, encouragement, obscure facts about lycs. Adrenaline whooshing, heart pumping, nerves zinging.

Oh!

This really wasn't the time to start remembering why she had fallen in love with Blake in the first place, but it was something about his capability, his confidence, his almost completely justifiable arrogance. The way he'd taken down Pearl and then Pure without blinking. The way he'd roped them both up and slung them in the back of the truck. Barking orders casually. Not agonising about right and wrong. Not worrying about shades of grey. Just doing. Being what he was. Blake destroyed werewolves. No questions asked. Anyone would think he was the Warrior Wolf. Iris didn't know why she found that capability, that simplicity, so damn attractive, but she did. She watched him running in front of her, calling out about the trail he had spotted and was following.

She watched his tight hard body under his red fatigues. It wasn't as if what he was wearing was particularly revealing, but Iris knew what was underneath it. Blake had a body that looked ordinary but could do extraordinary things. Built of tight, hard, wiry muscles. It had a strange tautness to it, like his body was permanently coiled and ready. Where Alfie was unimaginably beautiful – always had been – with muscles that moved like ripples on water, Blake was dark, nasty – scary even. Strange to think it, but really, Blake was far more of a monster.

Once, when Iris was in bed on top of Blake – who was sprawled beneath her, all dark hair and fizzing flashing dark eyes – he had whispered, 'You know, Iris, Nietzsche said, "He who fights with monsters might take care lest he thereby become a monster".' Iris remembered laughing and telling Blake that he must be the only man in the world who quoted Nietzsche in time with each viciously hard upwards thrust. And Blake had laughed too and reached up and pulled her down into a kiss, yanking her hair so hard it almost made her come, and said that he was pretty sure that he wasn't. But thinking of it now, running through the dark, she thought that Blake might have been telling her everything she ever need to know about what they did for a living.

'There,' Blake shouted. Iris followed his outstretched arm. They had run all the way up the hill from the St Clements end of the park. Over to Iris's left were some trees, grouped close to the perimeter fence. In among the trees, something was moving around.

Two wolves. Hounds. One oil-sleek black, one shaggy greyish brown and a lot like Alfie. 'The grey's injured,' Iris said softly, spotting the way it was keeping off one of its back legs.

'Well maybe we'll give him a bandage later. OK,' said Blake, 'take them. One hound for each of my killer chicks.'

Iris and Pepper both made the same annoyed grunt.

Blake laughed under his breath. 'What? I thought you'd like that. Tranq 'em, ladies.'

Iris bristled, even though she was already still bristling from Blake's last piece of smarm. 'I don't tranq hounds, Blake.'

'Yes you do, Iris. You do now. You've only got tranqs.'

In the dark, Iris met Blake's defiant eyes and there it was. The moment where everything came together. Her hot, hurt heart, her hard, hard clit. She felt strange. Itchy. Hot for Blake. *Blake!* Blake was over. She'd done Blake. No going back. Iris shook herself. Shooting things was probably the best medicine.

Pepper was ready, waiting. Iris gave her a nod and they began to creep into the trees. There was a good clear line to both animals and they really didn't need to get too close. Iris set her sights on the grey. 'You got the black one?' she hissed at Pepper.

'Affirmative, ma'am.'

'OK,' she whispered. 'On fire. Three, two, one, fire!'

There was a slice of time in which several things happened. Iris's dart hit the grey and he went down. Pepper shot too and missed and the sound the large grey had made going down startled the black hound and it streaked into the trees.

Blake came up behind them with a slender unlit roll-up cigarette clamped between his lips, 'Damn,' he said, not opening his mouth properly so the cigarette didn't fall.

'Sorry, sir,' said Pepper, 'it was me. My finger slipped for a sec.'

'Yeah. OK,' Blake took a lighter out of his pocket and

raised it to his mouth and lit up. He took a couple of draws and then took the cigarette out and said, 'Pepper, you rope that hound and put him in the back of the truck. Iris and I will go after the other one.'

'Don't be stupid, Blake. She can't move that thing on her own. You stay and help her. I can take the black one.'

'Rope him first then go to the van and get the gurney,' Blake said to Pepper, then he turned to Iris. 'Not having you out of my sight on full moon.'

'What? Why? What do you think I'm going to do?'

'It's for your own protection, Iris. I'm not leaving you alone right now.'

'What? That's ridiculous. I'll tell you what, I'll stay and help Pepper, you take the black one. One hound. It only needs one of us. I could have had it down by now if we weren't standing around here arguing.'

'I said, you are staying with me. And Pepper can't go after a hound on her own. She's not ready. So this is the only way, come on, Iris.'

'Blake?'

Blake's voice dropped down very low. 'OK. I was hoping it wouldn't come to this, but ... Iris, there are a million and one reasons why you need to start toeing the line around here. I'm in charge now. I need your respect. You know full well this operation is essentially paramilitary. Which means you obey the orders of your superiors, no questions asked.'

'Unless they're illegal,' Pepper said softly.

'Yes. Thank you, Pepper. Now listen, Iris, if you don't care about The Silver Crown coming for you, I want you to consider the werewolf I'm letting you keep, the Silver Collar I'm letting you use to fuck him, the many, many legitimate reasons I have to fire you. I have a file on you, Iris. Not that I have to answer to anyone if I do want to get rid of you. So let's just take a moment and imagine what would happen if I did let you go – see if we can think of anything else Iris is qualified to do after eleven years working for a secret werewolf hunting organisation.'

Iris swallowed. Being fired from The Institute was, at this moment, a truly terrifying prospect. Not because of her unemployability, just because she couldn't imagine life without The Institute. She'd already tried to turn away. She couldn't. Cate's voice in her head whispering about destiny was almost impossible to ignore. 'Fine,' said Iris, 'we're losing that lyc every moment we're stood here arguing. Let's go.'

Iris didn't look back at Blake as she started to run in the direction the lyc had headed.

They tracked it easily; paw prints in the soft ground. But Iris knew they had given it too much of a start. She ran over the crest of the hill and across some flatter ground to the children's play area. There was something eerie about swings and roundabouts deserted in the dark. As Iris neared the low fence around the play area, Blake overtook her, vaulted the fence and ran across the special bouncy surfacing of the playground. On the far side of the play area was the park's perimeter fence and then the road.

'Damn it,' Blake shouted; his voice a loud bark in the silent night.

Iris came pounding across the playground to stand next to him. 'What?'

'Look,' Blake pointed at the fence that divided the park from the road beyond. The fence was partially covered by a thick hedge and there, with a trail of paw prints leading up to it, was a huge dint, where something had cleared the fence but smashed though the hedge.

'Damn,' said Iris.

'We'll never track it if it's on the road.'

Iris paused a minute to catch her breath. 'OK, well let's get back to the van. Get on the radio for sightings.'

'Pepper can do that,' said Blake. Almost simultaneously

he flipped the microphone down from his coms earpiece. 'Pepper,' he snapped, 'Pepper? You reading this?'

There was a bit of crackle and fizz, then Iris heard Pepper's voice coming through on her own earpiece too, 'Sir.'

'Pepper. Are you back at the truck?'

'Just going back up the hill with the gurney to get the lyc, sir.'

'OK, look, we've lost the other hound. When you get back to the truck get the radio on and listen out for anything. Particularly any animal sightings. Cowley, Rose Hill, Headington.'

'Yes, sir.'

Blake flicked his mic back up. He turned his body a couple of degrees, lined himself up square on with Iris. He smiled. One of his nasty ones. 'Right then.'

Iris stared at him. She felt suddenly very, very alone in a dark park with a predatory, scary man. She shook herself – again. Not a scary man. Just Blake. Blake. Ex-husband, Beast-loving, werewolf-hunter Blake. 'Right then, what?' she said, horrified when her voice came out as a crackling whisper.

'No more bloody messing around. I'm going to fuck you now, Iris.'

The corners of Iris's mouth twitched into a smile. She almost laughed. 'What?'

'You heard me.'

'What? Blake. Don't. Stop it. We need to go back and help Pepper. She's got two lycs down there not to mention Pure – whatever he is.'

Blake cocked his head. His movements had suddenly gone all sinuous and seductive. Prowly. 'All tranqued, baby,' he purred. 'Pepper can handle it.' He took a couple of steps towards Iris.

'Blake? What about the other one? We need to get after it.'

'We can't track it without a sighting. We need to wait for Pepper to get back to us.' Blake was too close now. He reached out and touched Iris's hair, brushing a few stray strands out of her eyes and then reaching around and pulling out the band that held her pony-tail, letting his fingertips tickle the back of her neck. It was a familiar gesture. One he used to do all the time. It was his pre-sex thing. When they were dating and when they were married, he would do this at home, in the office, he did it once at Iris's cousin's wedding. His thin dry fingertips had the perfect texture for this move. They played – just for a spare moment – around the very start of her spine. That achingly vulnerable spot where her brain slunk into her body. His voice was silk, smoke. 'Come on, Iris. You always did used to like it out of doors. Out of breath. Out of – of control. You want to fight me a bit first? Wrestle? See who gets to be on top. I know you usually can best me, but I really want to win tonight and sometimes that can give me enough edge. Want to try me. I really want to win, Iris. Flip you over. Fuck you like an animal. I wonder why I should be thinking that way.'

Iris was shaking her head. Slowly, her disbelief winning out over her growing, conflicted arousal. 'Blake? Have you gone nuts? What on earth makes you think I'm going to have sex with you? I'm with Alfie. You know that. In fact, I know that you know that because you have been acting practically psychotic about it.' But Iris hadn't moved away from Blake and his hands were on her shoulders.

Blake moved his right hand and played with the collar of Iris's shirt. 'Yeah? Does he know that? You know you can't trust a lyc, Iris. He'll always betray you. They might look human, but they're not. They'll always put their own kind first. You saw that in the basement.'

Iris took a single step back. Away from Blake. Shaking her head. He watched her, almost as if he was just curious about what she might do. Like everything she did faintly amused him.

She moved fast. She kicked Blake hard in the shin and turned to run. She started pounding away across the playground and across the park. But Blake wasn't far behind her, shouting something about her wanting to play games.

Iris tried to sprint, but she was exhausted from pursuing the lyc. Her muscles were screaming too soon and she felt Blake almost at her shoulder. She swerved as she anticipated his tackle, but missed her footing in the pitted ground, going down hard on the grass.

Blake had her. He had dived half on top of her and he hauled himself up her body, rolling her onto her back. He had her arms pinned under his knees as he straddled her and he got his face very close to hers. He took hold of her chin, running the pad of his thumb across her lips. She jerked her head away. 'Blake. Get off me.'

'No.' Blake ducked his head, stuck out his tongue and licked her top lip.

'God, Blake.' Iris was panting now and it wasn't from the run. She was turned on. She was feeling very glad that Blake didn't have Alfie's sense of smell.

Blake stared at her for a moment. He was breathing just as hard as she was. He narrowed his eyes as if he was trying to work something out. Then he said, 'I know you know that I'm not a good man, Iris. But even I, your special nightmare, am not going any further with this game until you give me permission.'

'What?' Iris was horrified to find herself almost disappointed.

'Well, I don't want to get done for sexual harassment now, do I, Iris? Look, I'm going to give you a chance now. One chance. If you want to walk away, right now, I'll let you.'

Underneath him Iris almost spat. 'You'll *let* me!'

'Yeah. I'll be kind and let you get away.'

'You'll let me get away! I don't need you to. Fuck you, Blake.' Iris almost spat it.

'That's fuck you, sir. And actually I'm not the one about to get fucked. I'm going to fuck you. Just like you want me to. I'll even carry on playing the bad man for you, if you like, so you can tell yourself it was all my fault. You can fight me as hard as you want. You can hurt me – kick me in the balls, I know that's your favourite move – I don't care. Fight me. But I'll win, Iris. Because I want you more than you want me to stop. I know you, Iris. I know what you need.'

'Blake, have you lost your mind?'

Blake dived and kissed her. Hard. Slamming her head back down on the ground. Iris felt her hips bucking up underneath him, as, at the same time, she scrabbled for a weak point that she could use to get him off her. 'God, Iris,' Blake said as he broke away. He started to kiss and lick his way down her neck.

With a sudden cold feeling in the pit of her stomach Iris remembered Cate's warning about not having sex with Blake. Oh God. How did she forget that? Only this afternoon she had been telling Cate that this – that this very thing she was doing now – really wasn't going to happen. 'Actually, Blake, this might not be such a good idea.'

'Shut up now, Iris. That moment has passed.' Blake reached up and jammed a hand over Iris's mouth.

Iris pulled with all her might and got one arm out from under Blake's hard thigh. She brought it up and wrenched his hand off her face, making him cry out when she bent his fingers backwards. 'Blake.'

Blake pulled away from her grip, 'You can tell me to stop if you want. I'm not going to stop.' He took hold of her shirt and started ripping it open.

'Oh, fuck you.' Iris pulled back with her free arm and punched him very hard.

Blake was knocked right off her and onto the ground. The punch had hit his temple hard. Iris knew she had a very good right hook. She scrambled over him, reversing their positions as she set herself down astride his thighs. Iris was on top now, but she had no intention of stopping what Blake had started.

'Oh, fuck it, you fucking killer bitch,' Blake said.

'Cate said we shouldn't do this.'

'Fuck her, too.' Blake jerked his hips and his very obvious erection jumped, just in front of Iris's crotch.

Iris took hold of Blake's trousers and wrenched the fly open. Blake's hard cock sprung out. 'And Cate,' she said, breathlessly, 'is really only one of the reasons why this is a bad idea.' Iris reached out and curled her hand around Blake erection. Hot and smooth. 'But if this is going to happen, Blake – and, you know, I'm pretty sure it is, one way or another – it is going to be something that I do to you. And you need to know that I'm doing this because I want to. I don't need anyone to play the bad man for me. I'm not a werewolf. What I do at full moon – or any other time – I'm fully responsible for.' She tightened her hand around Blake's cock and pumped it a couple of times making him moan. Then she lowered herself down until she was stretched across his body, and she kissed him, long and slow and on her own terms. Blake. Never forever. *Blake*.

He rolled over, getting himself back on top. She let him. As she kept hold of his cock, his hands found their way inside her underwear. He kissed her hard. His kisses were always hard, spiked with teeth and determination. He tasted like all her memories.

When Blake got Iris's trousers and underwear down to her knees and got inside her, they were still kissing. They hadn't really broken the kiss at all. It was still wet and hot and Iris's lips were sore from all the times Blake had bitten them. The kiss – the endless kiss – was frantic and desperate and, at the same time, familiar and comfortable.

Blake broke away eventually and lifted himself up on his strong taut arms so he could fuck her harder. Physically Blake was so different from Alfie. Small and taut. Not as strong. Not as overwhelming in size. Blake's cock inside her still felt pretty overwhelming. He knew just how to move for her. He remembered the positions that reached her. Long strokes, almost pulling right out. Rolling his hips so the root of his cock danced on her clit, nudging it up against her pubic bone.

Fuck, the bastard was going to make her come with his cock.

She felt her breathing get quicker. Crackles of pleasure started to shoot over her body. Blake leaned down, still holding himself on his arms, and kissed her again, pressing his tongue into her mouth. She was so close then and he rotated his hips again. She grabbed him, both hands tight on his arse, and pulled him in. Pressed him deep inside her, opening her eyes to look at him. She looked right into his eyes and then over his shoulder at the big fat full moon.

And she cried out into his hot, damp, familiar mouth as she came.

19

Iris lay on the grass, still looking at the moon. Blake was sitting up next to her, smoking. He exhaled. 'You going to get punished by Fido for *this*, Iris?' As he spoke, he reached down and put the end of his roll up into Iris's mouth for her to take a post-sex drag.

And that was way to intimate. Iris spat it out and he pulled it away. 'What?'

'He told me. All about his little contract. Can't believe I never thought of that. But I heard that if you say my name one more time during sex . . .'

'He told you about that! I can't believe it. He shouldn't have told you.'

'Yeah, well, you're the one that seems to think she can trust a lyc.'

'It was just a dumb sex game. It's nothing to do with anything.' Iris got up huffily and started to get dressed. She pulled her trousers up and then found the only way to fix her shirt was to knot the two halves of the front together. Most of the buttons were missing. 'Damn it, Blake,' she muttered, 'you ruined my shirt.'

Blake didn't reply; he was on his feet too, adjusting his own clothes, his cigarette gone into the damp grass.

Iris started down the hill without looking back at Blake. He sprinted up behind her and fell into step. They both knew each other's pace, how to run together, how to say everything to each other without speaking.

Halfway down the hill, Iris saw something and stopped dead. 'Blake?'

Blake paused and saw it too. 'Shit.' He started to run

again, faster, leaving Iris behind. She raced after him but couldn't match his longer strides.

A little further down the hill, Pepper was lying on the ground. Blake reached her quickly and crouched over her, rolling her onto her back and patting her face. 'Pepper? Ella? Come on, darling, talk to me.'

Iris reached them and pulled her gun and her torch. Standing over Blake, she moved slowly around casting around with her torch into the darkness that seemed to be closing in around them.

'Sir? Blake?' Pepper had opened her eyes.

Blake turned around. 'God's sake, Iris. Torch. Here.'

Iris shone the beam of light onto Pepper's face. Pepper blinked. She looked pale and a large patch of red stickiness glistened across one side of her head. Iris winced.

Blake held up his hand in front of Pepper's woozy eyes. 'Can you see? Can you focus?' said Blake.

'No. Oh, Blake, it hurts.'

'What happened,' said Iris, still keeping her eyes on the perimeter.

'I don't know, ma'am. Something from behind when I was trying to get the lyc on the gurney.'

Blake looked around. 'Where's the lyc now?'

20

Wednesday, 23 January 2008

Leon opened his eyes. It didn't get any brighter. Something was covering them. He was lying on something comfortable, something soft. His hands were tied behind his back. The air was still and coolly damp and slightly sour. He was underground. He tried to rub his face against his shoulder to remove the blindfold.

'Really, that isn't going to work.'

He could scent her then. He'd probably been able to scent her all along. 'Sabrina!'

'Nice to see you again. How's the leg?'

'Fine. I've had much worse than anything you could do to me, bitch.'

Leon felt her hands on him, pulling the blindfold away. He blinked up into her painfully beautiful face. Her dark hair was like a black cloud floating around it. Storm was coming.

The room was dark − Sabrina's flashing eyes were lit by candles. It was also small. The walls not far beyond the canopy of the pink satin-draped bed he was lying on. They were rough stone. *Some kind of cave?*

Sabrina moved from sitting next to him on the edge of the bed to straddling his bound body in one easy movement. She caged him with her tight lithe form and then leaned down and kissed him. Or, at least, she dived down and smashed her mouth hard against his. Leon jerked and tried to pull away. It burned. The kiss burned. Silver in her mouth. That wasn't chromium alloy anymore. She pulled back from him smiling. 'You like it?' she said then opened her mouth and slid her tongue over the glinting metal. 'It was your idea.'

Leon shuddered just looking at it. Silver in her mouth. Silver somewhere so sensitive. It was obscene. He struggled, pulling at the ropes that held his wrists behind him. 'That's disgusting.'

Sabrina sat back. She looked amused. She was wearing a thin white dress. Stretchy and tight. Leon could see her hard nipples and it was while he was looking at them that he noticed that he was still naked from the change. He squirmed a little. Being naked had never made him feel vulnerable before.

Sabrina reached up and took a tangled silver circlet of wire from her head. Leon could tell by looking at it that it was real silver. It looked beautiful. Twinkling pain. Glinting stars catching the candle light. In her hands it looked like a piece of barbed wire. She turned it over and then toyed with it some more, untangling and pulling it out until it was one long piece of silver wire.

'Big scar,' she said. Her voice sounded breathy. She reached out and placed her palm flat on Leon's belly. Leon's scar was huge. Bigger even than Alfie's – and Alfie had basically had his shoulder ripped off. Leon's whole belly was covered in a spider's web of tooth and claw marks. He should have died – after what Alfie did to him that night – he should have died. No one should have lived through that. But the wolf inside him had wanted to live.

As Sabrina touched his scar, grazing it with her nails, he remembered it suddenly. A flashback so violent it whisked him out of the visceral realness of the dark cave and Sabrina and into a car park behind a seedy London pub with a huge wolf ripping out his entrails. He could feel it. The cold-hot ripping pain. So real. He screamed and opened his eyes and saw that Sabrina was pressing the silver wire against his belly. She scraped the metal across his skin and Leon gasped. With her other hand Sabrina took hold of Leon's cock.

She pumped it slowly, still toying with the silver wire over his bite scar then trailing it over his cock. Then she lowered her head and kissed him again, rubbing her silver tooth over his top lip.

Leon hissed. High on pain and pleasure. Delirious with sensation. He rolled his head against the bed beneath him. He barely knew where he was or what was happening when he felt Sabrina's lips by his ear. Silver sparks and then her voice saying, 'So, werewolf, I have a little proposition for you.'

'Huh?'

'Why have you come back to Oxford? Did our meeting make you remember how much you missed him?'

Leon's eyes flickered open. 'Missed who?'

Sabrina slid down his body and rubbed her silver tooth over his scar. Leon moaned. 'The one who did this to you,' Sabrina whispered. 'Him. Your maker. Your master.'

'Alfie?'

'That's who you came back here for, isn't it? Did you come to save him from us?'

'From you? Who cares about you? I came because you said he was with the Vix.'

'So you came to rescue him from the Vix. Daddy's in trouble.'

'Yeah. What if I did?'

'You going to summon him?'

'I wouldn't give him the satisfaction.'

'So how then? You can't find the Vix. They're cloaked. Has daddy kept in touch with you? Told you how to find him?'

Leon tugged again at the ropes binding him. They didn't budge, but he smiled. These clowns, whoever they were, wanted Alfie, knew he was with the Vix, but didn't know how to find him. Leon felt a little stronger, felt like he had some power here after all. 'Maybe I've got some-one on the inside.'

'Well that's rather interesting, Leon. So I suppose what I need to ask you now is what it would take to persuade you to hand your sire to us.'

'You know I can't do that. Not unless you can break my thrall.'

Sabrina laughed. She drew her sliver tooth in a bright line of pain all the way down Leon's belly and took his cock in her mouth. Leon yelled out, bucking up off the bed. Sabrina took him all the way into her mouth and then let it slide out again very slowly. It left her mouth with a pop. 'And do you want that, Leon? Do you want me to help you get out of thrall? Your sire's a Beast cub. That makes it very hard for you to ever betray him.' She licked Leon's cock again.

'Do you think I don't know that?' Leon gasped, his voice twisting as her tongue moved on his cock.

'What if I told you he was the traitor? What if I told you your daddy doesn't need saving from the Vix? What if he's there because he wants to be there?'

'What? What are you talking about?'

Sabrina sat back, but kept her hand on Leon's cock. 'What if your sire works for the Vix. Against werewolves like us? What if he's a traitor? What if he helped them kill the Beast. His sire. One of the greatest and most powerful werewolves in the world.'

'Aren't werewolves meant to kill their sires?'

'Not Beast cubs. Ancient Beasts are part of the most sacred werewolf governance organisations. Heard of The Silver Crown? You probably haven't, we're highly secre-tive even to other werewolves.'

'I've heard of you.'

'Oh. OK.'

126

'And Alfie isn't a traitor. He wouldn't be working with the Vix. And, hang on, *you're* a werewolf?'

Sabrina smiled. 'That's right.'

'But you can have that metal in your mouth.'

Sabrina laughed. 'It's just a spell on the tooth so you can feel it and I can't. I got it for you.'

'You . . . ? I . . . ?'

Sabrina laughed again. Her laughter sounded slightly different. Less pretty tinkly and a little nastier. 'I am sorry, Leon. I didn't mean to confuse you. I'm one of The Silver Crown. And we want your sire.'

Leon swallowed his confusion, trying to find the strength he'd had a moment ago, before he knew Alfie was a Vix and Sabrina was a werewolf. 'I . . . I can't betray him.'

'Not even now you know he's a traitor? *He's* the betrayer, Leon. He's working for the Vix. He killed an Ancient Beast. If you have a way into the Vix, Leon, you need to tell us. We've been trying to find our way into there for a long time.'

Leon twisted at the rope that held his wrists. His stomach was full of shards of ice. 'I can't . . .' but even as he said it he could feel it. Alfie was a traitor. A traitor to all werewolves. It wouldn't be a betrayal. His thrall was breaking.

'What if I offered you a place in our pack. A place in a proper werewolf pack. Not that traitor Friday's idea of one. The real thing. A place for you at last. A proper werewolf – part of a proper pack. Like a wolf of your standing ought to be. What, Leon, if I said I could take you home?' Sabrina let her mouth close over Leon's cock again.

Leon groaned as Sabrina sucked him. The spiky sensations of the tooth tumbled over the bliss of her hot wet mouth. He didn't know what he was feeling, experiencing. He felt his cock getting harder, that feeling low in his belly, his balls drawing up and tightening. And then her silver tooth, whisked the orgasm away. He moaned and thrashed. She did the same again, brought him close to his peak and then tormented him with silver.

It became a rhythm – pleasure then pain. Over and over.

Leon got so used to it that when, finally, she kept on sucking him, working him to a long strong screaming orgasm, he almost missed the cool hard feeling of her tooth.

21

Blake had dropped Iris at casualty with Pepper. In fact he had left them round the corner, leaving Iris to practically carry the concussed Pepper up the hill to the John Radcliffe Hospital.

He couldn't stay, of course. He had a truck full of doped werewolves and ex-employees to take care of.

He shifted the sleeping forms of Pure and Pearl into one of the empty basement cells. Aurelia was awake in her cage and Blake opened the door. He leaned up against the wall watching her casually as she dressed. She gave him a look that was practically an invitation, but he smiled and shook his head, enjoying her confused expression at the rejection.

She shrugged and slipped past him, heading up the stairs.

Alfie was still asleep.

Not for long.

Alfie could hear a horrible rhythmic clanging noise. He opened one eye. Blake was standing outside the cage, trailing the edge of his metal clipboard along the bars.

'Stop that,' Alfie growled.

'Oh come on, sleepy, I've been up all night chasing monsters with your girlfriend and you don't see me lounging around. Get up.'

'I need to sleep, Blake. I thought you were a werewolf scholar. The change is hard on the body.'

'I know. There was a study done in Madrid in 1983. In the twenty-four hours after the change you experience fatigue, thirst, increased appetite and increased sex drive.'

'Yeah.' Still lying on the bare floor, Alfie leered and rolled over so Blake could see his taut erection. And, God, Blake was right – he was so damn horny. The twenty-four hours after the wolf were renowned for leaving the man a little irresponsible – especially sexually. And Alfie knew he was more prone to bad behaviour in the twenty-four hour danger window than most. 'Iris knows about the sex drive thing,' he drawled. 'I expect she'll be down here any minute to take advantage of it.' He stretched out and closed his eyes as if going back to sleep, his hands folded behind his head.

'Well, maybe, except I think I kind of wore her out last night.'

'Hunting just makes her hornier.'

'Didn't say we were hunting.'

'What?' Alfie pulled himself up on his elbows.

'Oh nothing. Ask her yourself. You know, werewolf, there's an aboriginal saying, "Wolves make us human". You ever heard that?'

'It's dogs,' said Alfie. '"Dogs make us human."'

'Yeah. You're right, but I think it works better with wolves. You know what it means?'

'Yes. It means that what characteristics humans don't share with apes they share with dogs. Or, yes, wolves. The pack living. The interpersonal stuff. Some people think that humans copied canine behaviour to evolve their social structures.'

Blake smiled. 'Clever boy. And what do you think?'

'I think sociobiology is a bunch of crap. I think that we are what we are. We don't need to worry about why. It leads down paths where you start asking what's right and what's wrong.'

'And that's a bad thing?'

Alfie shrugged. 'Depends what you're trying to prove.'

'You don't think the way the evolution of humans and dogs is intertwined is relevant to you?'

'Not really.'

'You don't wonder about werewolves. Why they're here. Where they came from. How they began.'

'No.'

'The prophecies. The destiny. The Divine Wolf. The Line. The Silver Crown. You don't care about any of it?' Blake made a face like he found the idea that Alfie wasn't interested in these things slightly revolting.

Alfie just shrugged again. 'Can't say I do.'

Blake smiled. 'You don't even care about your girlfriend being the Warrior Wolf?'

Alfie shook his head. 'So long as she takes care; keeps herself safe.'

'Well, I say your *girlfriend*, but I don't know, do you have some kind of rule about her being able to play away when you're, well, too hairy to be boyfriend material?'

'Fuck off, Blake. Iris isn't like that.'

'I'm not like what?' Iris was just coming down the stairs to the basement. 'Who are you talking to? Oh. Blake. I thought you were ... um, well, I didn't expect you to be down here. Uh, what *are* you doing down here?'

'Talking to your boyfriend about last night,' Blake said.

Alfie saw Iris go a little pale. He frowned. She came down the steps and walked over. 'Blake, can I have a word with you a moment.'

'I'm actually quite busy right now, Iris. But perhaps you could help. I want to do some experiments on your boyfriend. I was going to keep you out of it, but I've decided that you might actually be quite useful. Go in there and kiss him.'

'She can't come in here when I'm not collared, Blake. It's too dangerous.'

'Oh come on, it's not all *that* dangerous. She can get out long before you come. It wasn't right with Aurelia. I need to see you with a human.'

'What? Iris, I . . .' Alfie turned to Iris, who was looking at him calm and even.

'It's OK, Alfie. I know. I saw.'

Alfie didn't know what to say to that. He looked back at Blake, who was grinning nastily. 'Come along. This is crucial to my study. And really, Alfie, this is in your interests as much as anybody's. The more I know about unstable wolves the more likely it is that we'll be able to cure you.'

'I don't want you to cure me, Blake. When did we ever say that was what we were doing here?'

'What *are* you two doing here?' said Iris, looking at Alfie and then turning to Blake.

'I'm training your doggie for you,' Blake said, Alfie watched him practically leer at Iris.

'Oh cut that crap out for once, Blake. What is wrong with you?' Iris walked over to the cage and put one hand on the bars. She was staring at Alfie. Right at his cock. 'You want to see him fuck me?' she said. She was still looking at Alfie, but she was talking to Blake. Or, at least, he assumed she was.

'Yeah,' said Blake behind her.

'Well that really isn't going to . . .' Alfie began.

But then Iris said, 'I think you should just do what he says, Alfie.'

'What?'

'Just do it. He knows what he's talking about. He might be able to help you.' Iris walked over the door of the cage and started unfastening it. Alfie stood up. She walked in and over to him.

'Iris? You're not seriously going to . . .'

'Oh, yes, I am.' Iris draped her arms around Alfie's neck and kissed him. He felt his blood surge. It was always better without the collar. It felt freer. More real. Iris broke the kiss and found his ear. 'You could kill me like this,' she whispered.

'Iris,' Alfie hissed, he pulled out of Iris's arms a little and looked through the bars, 'Blake.'

Iris put her hand on Alfie's chin and turned his face back to look at her. 'Screw him. I don't care about him. Just you. Vicious and raw. There's an animal under your skin and it could escape at any moment.' Iris slid her hand down his body and circled his cock with her fingers. It was still hard from the change. 'Show him,' she whispered. 'Show him what I let you do to me.'

Alfie snarled, low and soft. He knew what Iris meant. He knew this was about more than just Iris having seen him and Aurelia. There was more. Some fucked up shit between Iris and Blake. He actually knew that if he thought hard enough about what was going on here he could probably work out what had happened between them. But the blood that he would be using for that, the blood that ought to be in his brain had all rushed to his cock. It was the day after the change, and Iris was telling him she wanted it rough and right now. Being rational about things was a long way down his to-do list. He snarled again. Louder.

Alfie took Iris by the shoulders and shoved her up against the stone wall at the back of the cage. He was naked, she was clothed, that needed to be sorted out. He tore her shirt away, noticing – and not caring – that it was already ripped at the front and that most of the buttons were missing.

Iris got her elbow up in between their bodies. And jabbed him hard in the belly. He stumbled back. She tried to come at him. She wanted to fight. Always fighting. When would she ever learn? He could best her. She *knew* that. She *liked* that. He twisted her around and got her arm up behind her back as he pushed her against the wall, grazing her face against the stone. As he held her, he set about subduing her by running his teeth over that one special point on her jaw that made her melt. She went softer in his arms. Submitted to him.

But Alfie was a werewolf and he knew what her moves really meant. Iris wasn't submitting to him for his benefit. This was for Blake. This was all about Blake.

Fine. He turned her around and started to kiss her, then ran his tongue over the white-pink abrasion the wall had made on her cheek. She hissed at the sensation and he saw that her eyes were over his shoulder. She was looking at Blake. Challenging him.

Iris screamed and squirmed in his arms for a moment and then tipped her head back, showing her neck like an animal submitting. Alfie pushed his head into the hollow she had made for him, running his tongue over the pale flesh of her neck. Dragging his teeth. Leaving marks there. Feeling the blood pulsing under her skin. Iris was writhing, fighting and moaning. She wasn't looking at Blake anymore. But she still didn't belong to Alfie.

Outside the cage Blake snarled, 'Now shag her. Do it. From behind. On the floor. Like an animal. Fuck her like an animal, werewolf.'

Alfie looked over his shoulder. He knew Blake was hard. Alfie could smell his arousal. Alfie started to say, 'It's not safe . . .'

But Iris interrupted. 'Just do it, Alfie. Just bloody show him and do it.' She pulled out of Alfie's grasp. Alfie stared at her. She looked incredible. Her shirt was off and her bra was torn and her throat and shoulders were covered in bite marks and scratches. His bite marks and scratches. Her cheek was bleeding a little. She got down on the floor on her hands and knees. She was looking right at Blake now. 'This what you want, Blake? This what *you* want?'

And Alfie knew then. He knew what had happened. Either Iris and Blake had had sex last night or they'd come damn close. He kept his eyes on Blake's too as he moved over and covered Iris, reaching around to cup her neat little tits. Blake was staring at them and actually writing something on his clipboard with the tranq rifle tucked into his belt. Alfie whispered, 'Iris, I don't think I can do this?'

'Why not? Is it because he's watching? Forget him. I'm not ashamed. I'm more ashamed that I ever got married to him than of what I feel about you. Let him watch, then he can go upstairs and get Aurelia to suck him off.' Iris said all this in a voice that was easily loud enough for Blake to hear, but he – playing the part of impartial observer to the hilt – didn't react.

Perhaps it was all the other stuff going on. Perhaps. As Alfie reached down and pushed his way inside Iris, he tried not to notice Blake watching them. He concentrated on taking his weight on his arms and trying to keep most of it off Iris's back – Iris was strong for her size, but he was a big man. As he moved and let his body overtake, he started to lose most of his rational thought anyway. The wolf was coming. He was coming. *The wolf was coming. So soon.*

When Blake shouted, 'Fuck, Iris! Fuck.' Alfie, in his wolf-addled state thought Blake was urging him on, but then the door clanged as Blake slammed it open. Alfie felt Blake's metal clipboard hit him in the face, but he was on the edge of the change then and it was just one sensation in the midst of many.

22

Pulled clear of Alfie, Iris rolled and sprang to her feet. Blake was screaming, standing over Alfie who was convulsing on the floor. Blake was hitting Alfie in the face with his metal clipboard, over and over. 'Jesus, fuck! You disgusting piece of lycan crap. You fucking leave my wife alone. You hear me? Leave her alone!'

Underneath Blake, Alfie was more wolf than man. Blake was a werewolf hunter, but even Iris wouldn't expect him to win a fight like this. Close quarters. Armed with just a rectangular piece of aluminium. 'Damn it, Blake!' She threw herself across the cage, tackling Blake around the waist. Bowling him away from Alfie and scrambling to her feet in order to drag Blake out through the cage door by his collar.

Once they were out, Iris pushed Blake away from her and fastened the cage door. Her ripped shirt was still in the cage with the wolf. She pulled her torn bra over her breasts as best she could as she turned to look Blake in the eye. 'Give me your lab coat.'

'Why?'

'So I can go home and clean up,' Iris replied. Blake could be deliberately obtuse.

'You can't go home, it's post sweep. You need to do a debrief.'

Iris let her eyes slide over to the cage. Inside it the wolf was going crazy, angry and snarling. 'Well Pepper's not here, so there's only you and me to debrief. So I'll keep it sharp. We fucked up. OK? What more is there to say? Now give me your coat.'

* * *

Zac woke up under an apple tree in an overgrown back garden. He was alone. No Pearl. No Leon. No cub. No sire. No pack. He'd chosen to follow Leon. He'd lost them all.

But he did have his memories. All of them. Neat and ordered the way they were sometimes after the change. He remembered everything about his night as a wolf. He remembered the Vix. Looking back and seeing the Vix truck through his wolf-eyes. Seeing them shoot Pearl and Pure. Then later, the Vix had shot Leon. Zac swallowed hard.

Just then he noticed some movement in the house that backed onto the garden. He sprang to his feet. He was naked. He vaulted the fence and cut and leaped through several more patches of lawn and flower bed, before instinct told him he had reached an empty house. He broke in deftly and located some not-too-hideous clothes. He was crying. He wasn't even sure who for.

But as he looked at himself in the dingy mirror in this dereliction site of a teenage boy's bedroom – now wearing a pair of reasonable jeans and a T-shirt bearing a video game logo – he remembered something Pure had said about Blake not liking to shoot to kill. Wasn't Blake the guy in charge now? And hadn't Leon been certain Alfie was still alive – even though the Vix had found him?

So then.

He screwed up his mind, trying to remember. What had come out of that rifle and hit Leon, a bullet or a dart?

What was the loophole in the cloaking spell? A wolf who had been to the Vix HQ before would be able to find it again. Zac's memory of escaping from the Vix's HQ with Pearl and Pure was hazy, but he didn't need to rely on that. He turned over his left hand and peered at the map Pearl had drawn there on the plane.

According to that, the Vix HQ wasn't even that far away.

23

Blake was sitting in his lab sulking. Thinking about Iris. Replaying the image of her in her ripped bra holding out her hand for his lab coat and then stalking out without a backwards glance. Usually the day after the sweep Iris did a debrief in the morning, then some of them would grab some lunch and call it early doors. Blake had been looking forward to Iris's debrief – he had some choice remarks all planned out.

He was so lost in his thoughts of Iris, that when he saw on the camera in the basement that Alfie was in his human form and sitting up, he couldn't be sure how long he'd been awake. But he did have a gratifyingly nasty bruise across his chin and half his left cheek.

They didn't talk to each other so much as grunt.

Alfie said, 'I'm not doing anything else for you now.'

Blake said, 'Yeah. I know. Done enough anyway. How's your face?'

'Sore. I bet you enjoyed that, didn't you? You vicious fucking cunt.'

'Oh nice. And you kiss my wife with that mouth?'

'Don't call her that. She's not your wife. Where is Iris, anyway?'

'Gone home.'

'Gone home? But I need her. I need her to put the collar back on me.'

'Well, she seemed in a bit of a strange mood. You want me to lock you back in the cage and call her?'

Alfie looked at Blake. 'Uh, yes ... actually, no. I need to talk to her. Can you take me home? Mark me?'

'Do what to you?'

Alfie rolled his eyes. 'Mark me. Get one of your tranq guns and come with me in case anything happens.'

'Oh, right.'

Zac rounded the corner and stopped dead, his mouth hanging open. He couldn't believe it. 'Leon! Sire, dude. How did you escape? I was coming for you.'

Leon and two other werewolves were standing on the pavement a few doors down from the huge grey concrete building Zac recognised as the Vix HQ despite the long vertical sign advertising BINGO.

Leon looked a little confused. 'Coming for me? What?'

'Yeah, man, I was going to rescue you from the Vix.'

'Oh, oh right. Look Zac. The Vix didn't get me. I came here to try and find them, though. I tried to follow what Pure had told me, but I can't seem to find the building. I mean, I know that's what's meant to happen, but I can't really believe . . . it still feels damn weird.'

'You can't find it? Man, it's right there. Woah, sure, the cloaking spell. You can't find it unless you've been there before.' Zac grinned at his sire standing mystified right in front of the building he was trying to find. 'That's why I can find it, sire.'

Out in the yard, walking towards the truck, Blake dug the nose of his gun into Alfie's back. 'You don't actually have to do that you know,' Alfie said. 'If I feel it coming I'll give you enough warning to . . .'

'Yeah, like earlier when you nearly bit Iris's head off.'

'It's different during. Oh. Oh, god . . . oh!'

'What?' Blake's finger went taut on the trigger – but he realised quickly that Alfie didn't mean he was changing. It was something else.

Three men had just walked in through the side gate. One tall and blond, one tall and dark and one other. Blake recognised the other very well. Some faces you just don't forget. And Blake had certainly never forgotten the face of anyone who had ever tried to kill him.

'Oh, am I pleased to see you again.' Blake pulled the gun out from behind Alfie's back and pointed it at Leon.

'Yeah, hi,' said Leon. 'Sorry I didn't kill you properly before. I'll do it right this time.'

'Oh will you really?' Blake said.

'Oh yeah. And put that stupid tranq gun down, would you? I know you've only got two darts in there and there are three of us. And, what's more, I know you need to keep one by in case daddy switches sides on you. You just can't trust traitors, can you?' He smiled. 'So take one of us down if you like, but really, that'll only make it worse for you later, Mr Vix.' Leon grinned a sharp-toothed grin.

Blake shuddered. He always knew it would happen one day. Lycs. Lycs had found a way in through the magic. This had to be something to do with The Silver Crown.

Leon had turned his attention to Alfie. 'I'm here to rescue you, sire. Are you pleased to see me?'

Alfie growled. 'Leon, don't make me bring you back into line . . .'

'Yeah. Didn't think you'd be pleased. Because you don't need rescuing do you? Not now you've gone over to the other side. Traitor. Working with the Vix. Helping them kill werewolves. And after what these bastards did to Misty. You make me sick.'

Blake felt Alfie bristle behind him, pulling his body more erect. 'This has nothing to do with Misty. She died. She was killed. But it was an accident.'

'Killed by your friends. The Vix.'

'You don't know anything about it, Leon. You weren't here. You left. Split the pack. People die when packs split.'

'Me leaving had nothing to do with Misty. I know all

about it, sire. We were closer than you ever knew, Misty and I. Pack siblings. She told me everything. Misty always loved to talk. I know what you did to her. Made her fall in love with you then told her you didn't want a relationship but you'd be interested in her as a friend. As a friend who you could sleep with. She was so crazy in love you. And you exploited her for easy sex. Right up until you bit her. Then you kept her around as a damn servant. The night she died you weren't even there to protect her. She died while she was out earning money for you. Helping you.'

'You don't know what you're talking about, Leon. I didn't ask her to fall in love with me and you know I would have given anything not to have bitten her. You know that. You've got it all wrong.'

'So you don't work for the Vix now, sire?'

'Leon. I . . .'

'Oh fuck this,' said Leon, 'let's kill them.' Weapons appeared. The two men flanking Leon each pulled out a dagger and a cricket bat and brandished them.

Blake pulled himself up, trying to coax every last inch of height from his five foot nine inch frame. All his life Blake had sought out ways to look more fearsome and intimidating than he really was. He pushed back his strong shoulders. Alfie had at least six inches of height on him. Blake had never let himself delve too deep into how he felt about his love rival being such a big, obvious, hulk of a man. But right now, with Alfie the only thing between him and an armed snarling mob, Alfie could be as big and hulking as he pleased.

'Take Leon out,' Alfie hissed. 'Tranq him. Don't let him get hurt.'

Under any other circumstances Blake would baulk at taking orders from Alfie, but right now, he did just as he was told. He aimed at Leon and fired. Leon crumpled as soon as the tranq stuck him and the two men flanking him snarled when they saw it and charged across the dusty concrete.

Blake looked from one man to the other. His mind raced. A simple plan – the only possible plan – was to take one of them down then he and Alfie could take the other. Easy. 'Which one? Which one?'

'Get in the truck,' Alfie said.

The truck was behind them on the concrete – about fifty feet away. Blake looked at it then at the two men then back at Alfie. 'What? I can't leave you to fight them alone. I can take one down.'

'No you can't. You'll need that tranq for me. Just get in the truck and make sure I don't touch Leon's bod –'

Alfie's last words were snarls and Blake – suddenly understanding what was happening – was running, running and diving into the open back of the truck.

Blake didn't look back. He knew Alfie wasn't in control of what the wolf did. He knew that if the wolf spotted him it might decide to come after him instead of doing whatever it was doing to the two men outside, which already sounded horrifying. Blake had never heard a werewolf kill before. He'd shot werewolves that were attacking, sure, but he'd always taken them down in time. And he hadn't been there for Jude's death like Iris had. He tried to shut out the sounds of screaming and tearing and snapping. Tried to find something useful he could do.

They always kept a gun in the back of the truck. Blake took a moment to search around in the back of the truck, but it didn't seem to be in the equipment box.

A few moments later, Blake drew the canvas at the back of the truck aside and peered out. The two men lay on the floor. The dark-haired man was decapitated. His head two feet away from his body. The wolf was standing on the blond's chest, ripping at his face. Leon looked undisturbed. Blake wasn't surprised by that. Wolves liked the chase. The capture. Playing dead was said to be a reasonably successful way of staving off a lyc attack.

Blake raised the tranq gun and calmly shot Alfie in the shoulder.

After Alfie went down, Blake slipped out of the back of the van. He felt in his pocket for his coms. He realised he didn't have it – at the same time remembering it was in the pocket of his lab coat that Iris had gone home wearing. He walked round to the front of the van. There was usually a spare coms set in the glove compartment.

Sitting in the driver's seat of the van was a tall good-looking young black man. He was holding the gun that was usually in the box in the back of the truck.

'Oh shit. Not another one.'

The black guy grinned. 'Indeed,' his accent was a lazy American drawl. He looked rather familiar. 'We thought a second front might be a good idea. You guys can be so slippery. So now, as it turns out you've got most of my family either knocked out or locked up around here, so I think we need to come to some kind of arrangement. Blake.'

Iris was in her own flat. She hadn't been back for a few days. She'd needed to pick up her post, take a shower with her own familiar toiletry brands, spend some time alone.

She was so wound up. As she made a jam sandwich and ate it she found herself wishing she'd never killed the Beast. Life was so simple when she had a clear goal like that. She could have chased the Beast forever.

Well there are other Beasts.

'Yes, yes, I know. But it isn't the same.'

And they're coming. You know they are. So you going to kill them, or are you too busy destroying your life?

Matt was sitting on the kitchen counter right next to where Iris had made her sandwich. She didn't look at him. 'They can't get here soon enough as far as I'm concerned.'

Iris ate the rest of her sandwich in silence as Matthew faded slowly out of existence. She thought about The Silver Crown. Eleven Ancient Beasts. Coming for her. And she could kill them all. Killing Beasts. That felt so right. But why wait? She should find them before they found her. She should sit down with Alfie and Blake and figure something out.

A plan. When she'd finished her sandwich, she walked through into the bedroom. She threw Blake's lab coat down on her bed along with the rest of her uniform and her coms set. Her shredded bra went in the bin.

In the shower, she lost herself to the roar of the hot water, so it wasn't until she turned it off that she heard it.

They had an emergency signal. Flip a certain switch on a coms headset and every other set in range would light up and emit a distinctive beeping. That was what Iris was hearing right now. And her response to that signal was trained into her so hard, she didn't have to think.

Iris jumped out of the shower. Naked and wet she dashed and skidded across her polished wood floor to the bed and picked up her own coms set. She peered at the screen, flipping her dripping hair back over her ears. The code said the signal was coming from the set they kept in the glove compartment of the van. She frowned as she noticed an echoing set of beeps coming from the pocket of Blake's lab coat, also lying on the bed. She fumbled in the pocket. Blake's coms. So if she had Blake's set, who else but Blake would currently be using the spare set in the van?

Was Blake in danger?

Her heart turned over. *Or Alfie.*

She jabbed the buttons on her coms to get a trace on the set emitting the signal, but the co-ords wouldn't settle. Perhaps whoever had the set of coms from the truck was still in the truck. And the truck was moving. Iris didn't bother getting dressed, or even getting dry. She pulled out a map and started to plot the truck's movements.

24

In the back of the truck, Blake was sitting on the floor with his hands cuffed behind him. The stupid fucking lycs hadn't even put the safety on the cuffs that stopped them getting tighter and tighter. Stupid uneducated, unprofessional animals. His wrists were in agony. In front of him lay the huge unconscious wolf that had stolen his wife and the sleeping piece of detritus that had once tried to kill him. Leon. Sitting across from him on the benches were Aurelia and Pure. Both his ex-bloody-employees. Both of them now on the dark side. Didn't things used to be simpler than this? The hunters and the hunted?

The black guy was sitting in the front, next to Pearl – Blake's other WXX – who was driving. He tried not to wince as the too tight cuffs bit into him while, behind his back, he fiddled some more with the coms set he'd managed to palm from the glove compartment.

Come on, Iris.

'Where are we going, babe?' said Pearl. She was related to Pure, wasn't she? Figured. She looked like him and she had the same slight burr to her voice. Local. Didn't Pure's family live in Oxford? He was a local boy like Blake.

'Not sure, honey,' said the black guy, Zac. 'I guess we need to wait for Leon to wake up and tell us the next step.' Zac turned around. He looked nastily at Blake. 'How long before that crap you shot him with wears off?'

Blake shrugged, then winced as the move pulled at his wrists. 'Depends. Not much longer on a lump like him.'

Aurelia tossed her hair back. 'How about we go back

to the pack house for now. It isn't far and I need to get my stuff if we're going away.'

'The pack house?' said Zac. 'Is that still there? Leon was sure someone else would have taken it.'

'Nah. Alfie kept it on.' Aurelia gave a little laugh. 'Hoping you'd all come back. I think he wanted to play happy families again someday.'

'Well,' said Zac, 'looks like he's going to get his wish.'

Iris had figured out from her map that they were heading for the pack house at St Clements. She took her bike and cut through the fields. She was just chaining it up in the empty street, when a truck she would recognise anywhere rounded the corner.

Iris dived back and then watched from a shady doorway. Aurelia and, yes, Pure got out of the back of the van and went into the house. They looked relaxed, laughing together.

Then Zac and Pearl got out of the front. She recognised them straight away. Both of them so strikingly distinctive. Iris had two silver guns tucked into her waistband and a blade in a shoulder holster. She pulled one gun and crept closer, keeping tight to the walls, silent in her soft shoes.

Pearl and Zac opened the back of the truck. Iris couldn't really see inside, but then Zac hopped up and emerged back through the canvas doors with Blake handcuffed and at gun point.

Iris squinted at the gun Zac had on Blake. That was Institute issue. The one from the box in the truck. Then perhaps it was the only weapon they had.

Well if that were the case then at least Iris had one advantage. She drew her second gun and snuck around the side of the truck, pressing the muzzle of one gun to the back of Zac's neck and pointing the other at Pearl, who was still standing on the pavement.

'Oh,' said Zac as the metal pressed against the back of his beautifully shaped head, 'it's Missy Vix. We were wondering when you'd turn up.'

'Take off his handcuffs,' Iris said, looking at Pearl.

'Zac, I . . .' Pearl looked confused.

'Do what she says, darling,' said Zac. 'The keys are in the back of the truck, remember.'

Leon opened his eyes. He was lying on the floor of the truck and Pearl was crouching over him, slapping his cheek gently. 'Leon,' she hissed. 'We've got trouble.'

Leon sat up, quickly. Too quickly. 'That so, darling? You've decided to be nice to me now, have you?' he said, steadying himself against the dizziness.

'Don't start Leon. This is important. Iris. Vix bitch. Out there. Got a gun on Zac.'

Leon nodded, trying to process what must have happened after he was tranqued. His eyes pulled into focus and he saw Alfie's wolf, fast asleep in front of him. *Ah, perfect.* 'Good cub he is too. My Zacky. OK. What about that nasty creature, the little man? Blake? Where's he?'

'He's cuffed. Zac's got a gun out him just outside the van. But Iris has a gun on him and a spare. She wants to take Blake back.'

'Well,' said Leon, 'I'm not quite sure how things worked out with daddy and his long-lost woman, but I reckon we might have something right here that the Vix bitch wants even more than rat face.'

Iris almost jumped when the canvas back of the truck was flung open. Standing in the opening was a lyc she had seen once before with Zac. 'Leon,' she said softly to herself.

But she didn't look at him for long. She was more interested in what was lying on the floor of the truck. Alfie. Sleeping wolf-form Alfie. Leon was holding a silver blade. He dropped into a crouch holding it to wolf-Alfie's neck. 'Well then,' said Leon.

Iris held her body perfectly rigid, perfectly still, but inside she was shaking. 'Alfie's your . . . that's your sire.'

'Yeah,' said Leon, nodding over at Zac, 'and that's my cub. Drop the guns, sweetheart.'

Iris swallowed hard.

'Fuck's sake, Iris,' Blake muttered almost to himself. 'That's just a fucking lyc he's got there. Part of his pack. He's even in his wolf form. An animal. Leave him. Iris, we need to get out of here. These bastards could be connected to The Silver Crown.'

Iris just stared at Alfie.

'Damn it, Iris,' said Blake, 'if this creature wants to kill a lyc, well, he's just saving us a job. It's his bloody sire, anyway. That's what they do.'

But Iris was already dropping her guns on the ground, raising her arms above her head. 'I can't,' she said softly, shaking her head. 'I can't.'

25

Alfie wasn't sure where he was, he tried to roll over but couldn't.

'Three changes in twenty-four hours, Alfie. No wonder you're feeling bad.'

He was in his bed. He was wearing his collar and he was chained down. Iris was sitting on his bed stroking his chest. He was naked, but the quilt covered him from the waist down. 'Leon? Did I . . . did I hurt him?'

'He's fine. He's downstairs.'

Alfie lifted his head a little and saw that she was wearing handcuffs. The familiar rigid style that they used at the Institute. Just one piece of solid metal with two holes. Alfie knew how uncomfortable they were. 'What going on, Iris? Why am I chained? Why are you cuffed?'

Iris twitched. 'I don't know exactly. I think you'd better talk to Leon about that.'

'Leon?'

'Everyone's here, Alfie. Zac and Pearl and Pure and Aurelia. Blake's locked in the cellar. I don't know what they want. What they're going to do . . .' Iris wasn't crying but she seemed pretty close to desperation. 'I thought The Silver Crown were going to come for me. Find me somewhere. Try and take me. Have me fight. I thought . . . not this. Not you and Blake, too. I don't know what this is.'

'Iris. This isn't The Silver Crown. This is just my pack. I'm sure we can straighten this out.' But even as he said that, Alfie knew he had no idea if that was even slightly true. He remembered what Leon had said about Misty and about treachery. 'I think you'd better tell one of them to come up here.'

Alfie was half-amazed and half-reassured by the sight of Zac. There had always been something calming about Zac but it seemed more pronounced now. Alfie thought it might be Pearl. Ever since Zac had bitten her and got himself a cub and girlfriend all rolled into one he'd been so much more assured.

'Leon wants to kill you, dude,' Zac said, pacing around.

'Right.'

''Cause of Misty. I thought we were s'posed to be rescuing you, but the plans changed. Apparently you're a traitor. Leon's ready, he says. Out of thrall.'

'Well, I don't know if we can really stop him. It's his birthright to kill me. If he thinks he can do it now, then he won't rest until he's stuck some silver into me.'

'Yeah,' said Zac, 'except he doesn't want to kill you himself. He says you've been working with Vix. Says you're a traitor. Killed an Ancient Beast. The Silver Crown want you, dude.'

Alfie started. 'The Silver Crown want *me*?'

'Yeah, man. You killed the Beast? According to Leon, you shouldn't have done that. A werewolf killing an Ancient Beast is really bad shit.'

Alfie swallowed. Holding it together. *They thought it was him!* Concentrating on not giving anything away, he said, 'And you're going to hand *me* over?'

'Yeah. They're coming to get you tonight.'

'What about Iris? What's going to happen to her?'

Zac shook his head. 'Dunno. She told us she killed Misty and that she was romantically involved with you now.' Zac stopped talking.

Alfie had a lot on his mind but he couldn't help spending a split second thinking how odd the phrase 'romantically involved' sounded coming from Zac.

Zac sniffed. 'She's your mate, right?'

'My *mate?*'

'Iris. She's your life mate. You were in love with her when you were bitten, right?'

Alfie shook his head as far as he could. 'That's just werewolf fantasy. I don't believe in life mates. How is she? Is Iris OK? Leon didn't touch her, did he? Didn't hurt her?'

'Didn't hurt who? Iris?'

'Yes. If he hurt her to make her talk, Zac . . .'

Zac shrugged. 'He didn't hurt her. She just told him. She seemed quite matter of fact about it. I mean, she doesn't think there's anything wrong with it, does she? Killing us? Even shooting Misty. She just said she had no choice.' Zac was still pacing. 'Perhaps she's right. People were going to die. Misty shouldn't have been there in the first place.'

'Did he ask her about the Beast? About, uh, me killing the Beast, I mean?'

Zac shrugged. 'Nah. He seems to know all about that already.'

Alfie felt his stomach flip. They'd got it wrong. They'd come for him, not Iris. Used his pack to get to him. But they'd made a mistake. They'd assumed it was him. Maybe they'd even read the same mistranslated prophecy that had made the Beast himself so sure it would be Alfie that took his life. Alfie looked up. Zac was looking at him as if expecting a response. Alfie didn't know what to say. Zac came closer and sat down on the edge of the bed. 'How much do you remember? You were hairy almost as soon as we got there and Blake tranqued you not long after, so I guess nothing. I went to Texas and got Leon back. I guess you figured that. He told me everything. About Misty. About you. And you working for the Vix. About you killing the Beast.'

'Leon doesn't know shit,' Alfie said tightly.

'Don't, man. I know. Leon's telling the truth, isn't he?'

Alfie looked at Zac. There was something simple about Zac's face. Something straightforward. Somehow, lying to Zac wasn't really an option. Alfie said, 'OK. Zac, it is true. All of it. But it's not how Leon makes it sound.'

Zac's face turned colder. 'Sure, man, OK. I think you'd better get dressed and come downstairs.'

26

Pure and Leon had met Iris as she came down the stairs from Alfie's room in the attic. They escorted her down the next flight and opened the door to the cellar.

Pure took hold of her wrists and started to unlock her handcuffs. The firm gentle way he held her as he did it – it was the way she had taught him to take off cuffs.

And then she realised where they were standing. Just when things looked like they couldn't get any worse. 'Oh God, Pure, don't lock me down there in the cellar with Blake.'

'Why not? I thought you liked Blake. Isn't he on your side? And last I heard you were still fucking him, anyway,' said Pure. Iris looked at the scar which ran right down Pure's pretty face. Pure – fixed by witchcraft. He ought to be dead. What Leon did to him should have killed him.

'It's complicated . . .' Iris said, before realising there was no point in explaining her domestic crisis to Pure.

Leon sniffed. 'It really isn't, baby. You and your boyfriend – your *other* boyfriend – kill lycs. You killed Misty. And you'd be dead right now if I had my way.'

Iris looked back at Pure. 'And isn't he the one that did that to you?' Iris's arms were both pinned, one by each of the men, so Iris had to indicate Leon with a jerk of her head.

Behind her a familiar cut-glass voice said, 'Just get her down there. She's just trying to squirm her way out of this.' And Aurelia's kitten-heeled court shoe hit Iris in her lower back as Aurelia kicked her down the stairs saying, 'Really, darlings, you don't know what she can be like.'

Iris hit the stone floor of the cellar. She didn't lose consciousness but there was a small moment where she didn't know where she was. When she realised, she almost wished she had lost consciousness.

Being locked in a cellar with Blake in adrenalised fear of their lives was not what she needed right now. Lying on her back, she could only see the ceiling but the cellar was familiar. Alfie used it to change at full moon – although she'd never been with him when he did it. She knew the four cages that had once belonged to Alfie's pack, were stacked in a pile in one corner.

Blake was crouching over her. He had a bloody nose but looked fine otherwise. He touched her face. 'Iris, are you OK? Did those damn lycs just throw you down the stairs?'

'Um, yeah, well, it was Aurelia. She kicked me.'

'Oh, really. Aurelia? Well she's never liked you.'

Iris sat up. 'What do you mean she's never liked me? Aurelia always liked me fine.'

'Nah. She always thought you were weak, she blamed you for her getting bitten and ever since then she's been seething about the fact that you took her sire away from her. "Hate" might be a better word for it. She hates you.'

'Well thanks, Blake. If things weren't bad enough, why don't you give me a run down on all my colleagues who secretly hate me . . .' Iris's voice trailed off into a gasp of pain as she attempted to sit up.

'What is it? What?' Blake touched her shoulder.

'Actually, Blake, where Aurelia's heel hit me in the back hurts quite a bit.'

Blake sniffed. He didn't say anything more. He used both hands to roll Iris casually onto her stomach and then lifted her backside up into the air so she was on all fours. He swiftly pulled her jeans and her underwear down to her knees.

Iris shivered a little, but only because it was chilly in the cellar. Even after the twisted sexual power games that had gone on in the last twenty-four hours this half naked position didn't feel uncomfortable or awkward. In fact, it felt familiar. Blake was – almost over and above everything else – a professional. He ran his thumb over the place where Iris was hurt and she winced.

'Hmm,' he said pressing a little harder.

'Ah! What? What do you think?'

'Well. It's nasty. You'll have a very sexy bruise here but . . .' Blake paused.

Then Iris screamed as she felt something else. The heel of Blake's hand pressed her wound hard. She collapsed onto her elbows, feeling like she might throw up. 'Blake!'

'Yeah. I mean, if you had a ruptured kidney I think you would have passed out when I did that,' Blake said casually. 'Then again with a crazy hard-ass bitch like you, who knows?'

'And if I *have* got a ruptured kidney?'

'You'll die in a lot of pain.'

'Well thanks, doc, nice bedside manner.' Iris froze, realising what she had said, but it was too late.

'Don't call me doc, Iris. I'm not *him*.'

Iris felt herself tighten inside. She looked at Blake with her face hard. 'If I thought you were him, Blake, you'd be dead.'

'OK, OK, hang on. Hold still a minute.'

Iris sensed Blake rummaging in his pockets, then felt some cool on her injury. She sighed with relief. Anaesthetic gel.

As Iris turned around and started to scramble into her clothes and up, onto her feet, she said, 'You've got your med kit.'

'Yeah. They never searched me. I guess they thought if I had a weapon I'd have used it.'

'And have you? Got a weapon, I mean?'

'Got a scalpel. But it isn't silver. I don't think it'd be much use for digging my way out either.'

Iris reached around under her T-shirt and poked at the numb spot on her back. 'You think that gel will sort it?'

Blake said, 'Maybe. But don't worry, even if it is terminal we aren't getting out of here alive anyway. Not now we've finally got ourselves captured by a group of disgruntled lycs. And that's if they don't decide to subject us to a bit of our own medicine first.'

'Our own medicine?'

Blake raised one eyebrow. 'Torture, Iris. I torture lycs. They wouldn't have shut me down here if they were planning a nice neat execution, would they?'

'Fuck? You think? Well I sincerely hope they understand our division of labour then.'

'Well that rather depends how much your darling boyfriend told them about us, doesn't it?'

'My? Alfie! You think Alfie betrayed our location?'

'They are Alfie's pack. You did get that, didn't you? He probably planned this all along. The Institute is cloaked. You can only find your way there if you've been there before. Well, except for that weird thing where Fido managed to scent you across several counties. But someone sold us out and, well, Fido would seem the obvious candidate.'

Iris swallowed. 'No. It wasn't him. Blake he didn't. They have him chained to his bed upstairs. They had me go in there and put his collar on him. He's a prisoner too. On our side.'

'Really,' Blake said looking at her sceptically.

Iris exhaled. 'If you want to know who sold us out, well, you don't think that maybe letting one of our Reds run off with a pack of lycs was a bit foolish? We should have gone after Pure. They knew where the Institute was. They could get past the cloaking. Why didn't you ever try to find them?'

Blake went pale. 'Pure. Oh God Iris, you're right. We never went after them because Tobias said not to bother. Except that was because, by that time, he knew it was Alfie who was going to kill him. Or thought it was. Oh God. You're right Iris. We let a major security breach happen. We should have had special measures in place until we recaptured those lycs.' Blake face went even paler. 'This is all *my* fault Iris. I fucked up.'

In her wildest dreams, Iris had never thought she'd hear Blake say that.

27

Zac fumbled in his pockets and found the keys to Alfie's chains. He unlocked them and Alfie sat up stiffly – like a hundred-year-old man.

'Come on then,' said Zac, turning away.

Alfie sighed and started to pull on a pair of jeans that were bunched on the floor.

In the kitchen Leon was sitting at the head of the table. The Alpha spot. Alfie positioned himself facing him – standing broad and tall. Pearl was making tea and refused to catch his eye.

Alfie fixed Leon with a look and then made a small dark noise at the back of his throat.

Leon didn't even flinch. 'Don't bother, sire. I'm out.'

'Out of . . .'

'Yes. Out of your thrall. Not now. Not after what you've done. Traitor.'

'Traitor?'

'We've already talked about Misty, sire. And she was slain by them. Vix. That's bad enough. But you're actually working for those Vix bastards now, helping them kill the most Ancient werewolves. You killed the Ancient Beast who sired you. It's disgusting. And you're a traitor.'

Alfie closed his eyes. 'Werewolves are meant to kill their sires.'

'Not Beast cubs,' Leon snarled. 'So you admit it then? You killed him?'

'Yes,' said Alfie. 'Yes I did.'

Leon got up from the table and started to walk around it, towards Alfie. He was limping.

Alfie said,' What's wrong with your leg?'

Leon stopped. 'Nothing.'

'Yes there is. What's is it?'

'Got shot. Pearl fixed it.'

Alfie took a quick step towards Leon and dropped into a crouch. 'Let me take a look.'

'No fucking way,' said Leon, bending to put his face close to Alfie's. 'You're not touching me. You're disgusting. I can't believe I was ever thralled to you.' He made to spit in Alfie's face, but Alfie was too fast. He brought his hand up and clapped it around Leon's mouth, then stood, twisting and using his grip on Leon to barrel him back against the kitchen counter. Making Pearl, who was standing right there, jump backwards.

Alfie bent Leon backwards until his head was pressed against the cabinets above the counter. 'OK,' said Alfie, 'you're out of thrall. I get that. So stop messing around and do what you're meant to do and fucking well kill me.'

'I don't think so.' That was another voice. Alfie looked round. Pure stood in the doorway. 'We have Iris shut down in the cellar, you know. I suggest you start treating us with a little more respect.'

Alfie took his hands off Leon and turned around. 'If you touch her . . .'

Behind him Leon laughed. 'What, the woman who killed Misty. You know she's as good as dead already. But there are a lot of different ways to kill that Vix bitch. And how clean her death is depends on how nicely you behave, sire.'

Alfie glanced over his shoulder at Leon, then back at Pure. 'And me?' he said softly. 'You're handing me over to The Silver Crown.'

'They're on their way right now,' said Leon. 'When it

comes to you, I don't think there's any question of your behaviour buying you anything less than a very painful slow execution. A werewolf killing an Ancient Beast is unprecedented. What they're going to do to you really doesn't bear thinking about.'

28

Iris was sat in one corner, her back against the wall, her knees drawn up tight.

Blake was against the opposite wall.

Neither of them had said anything for a long while, then Blake said, 'One of us should cry.'

'What?'

'One of us should cry then the other could comfort them. It would make this so much easier.'

'Neither of us is going to cry, Blake. This is *us*. I have never seen you cry.'

'I cried at Jude's funeral.'

'No you didn't. You were mostly shouting – or at least whispering far too loudly – something about since when was Jude a "bloody Christian", and if you'd died would we all now be sitting in a synagogue, and then you persuaded me to come outside with you so you could smoke and you...'

Blake semi-grinned. 'Oh yeah. Over a gravestone, wasn't it? God, you used to be so filthy, Iris. Some poor old bird trying to rest in peace could probably have done without your orgasmic screams, you terrible woman. Anyway, more to the point I've never seen you cry. Now that's weird. I was a terrible husband to you so many times and you never cried once. You threw things, you destroyed my stuff, you knocked me unconscious several times, but no tears. And you're a girl. You're meant to cry. Especially when you're married to a horrible bastard like me.'

'You weren't a...' Iris stopped. 'I do cry. Just not in front of you.'

'How much did you cry for your dead brother?'

'Blake, I . . . oh.' And Iris stopped talking because suddenly, Matthew was there. Almost like he'd been there all along, slumped against the wall to Blake's right. 'Matthew?'

'Yeah,' said Blake, 'Matthew. You must've cried over him. Therefore it is possible. So how come you're not crying now?'

Iris looked away from Matthew's still shadowy figure. 'Because, we are going to get out of here.'

'We are? There are five lycs up there, plus Pure for some reason. God, that's weird. I never took him for a traitor.'

'Maybe he's a sniffer.'

'Well, you'd know about that. Anyway I did him once, so if he's a sniffer he doesn't mind taking on the hunters as well as the hunted. Oh God, who does that remind me of?'

'Hang on, what? Wind back, Blake. You and *Pure*?'

'Oh yeah. Oh I don't know, Iris, you kept on at me about whether or not I thought he was gay – it just seemed like an easy way to find out. It was after we'd split though, Iris, don't worry. I've told you before *I* never cheated. Anyway, Pure was just one of those things. You know about those *things*, surely?'

'I guess,' Iris said giving Blake a heavy look. Then she glanced back over at Matthew who was still sitting next to Blake. 'Are you going to say anything?'

'Who me?' said Blake, looking confused.

'No, Matthew.'

Matthew lifted his head and looked at Iris. *Me? I thought you'd forgotten about me.*

'I haven't forgotten about you, Matthew. I mean, I avenged your death, didn't I?'

What and then, that's it? You're done with me? I might as well have never existed?

'Never existed? Matthew, where am I right now? Why am I here? Why am I locked in this cellar? Because I gave up my life to hunt werewolves. For you. I'm here right now, about to be killed by lycs because of you.'

You're not going to die, Iris. You have a destiny, remember?

'Yeah, I kind of thought that too. But how do I get out of here, Matthew? Do you know? Can you tell me?'

The same way you got in, Iris. Right through that door.

There was a slight haziness in the air and Matthew blinked out of existence. Blake seemed to sense he had gone somehow, because he said, 'So what did your mental illness have to say for himself?'

Iris looked past Blake and up the cellar steps. 'He said we should just leave through the door. I think . . .'

Blake opened his mouth, but before he could reply, the cellar door opened. Iris gasped out loud. Thinking for a split second it was Matthew's doing somehow, but then Alfie – his big muscular body obviously couldn't be any-one else – came half-tumbling, half-stumbling down the stairs. The door was slammed shut behind him.

Alfie reached the bottom of the stairs and landed on his hands and knees.

He lifted his head. 'Hey,' he said to Iris as he got up, pretty much ignoring Blake who had clambered to his feet too so he could meet Alfie eye to eye. Or, at least, eye to eye give or take six inches.

The two men stood for a moment, sizing each other up. As she looked at them Iris wondered if they were going to stand there forever, neither of them seemed willing to be the first one to sit down.

Eventually, though, Alfie moved over to where Iris was sitting and slumped down next to her. Once Alfie was down Blake went back to his spot on the opposite wall. Iris had a glib remark dancing on the tip of her tongue. Something about how the two of them ought to get a room or hug it out. But she knew better than to say that now. Instead she said, 'So what's happening up there?'

'Well, Leon seems to be out of thrall. Not quite sure how that happened. He thinks I'm a traitor for helping you. And they're working for The Silver Crown. Or, it seems, the Crown used my pack to find, uh...' Alfie looked up and caught Iris's eye. 'To find you, Iris. Their coming here for you now, it seems.'

'What about me?' said Blake. 'What about you and me?'

'Well they didn't exactly show me a timetable of executions. I don't know what they're doing with us. I don't know what they know or what their plan is. If they have a plan. The Silver Crown are coming for Iris. I guess you and me are expendable. Here to make sure Iris doesn't try anything, perhaps.'

None of them spoke for heavy seconds. Iris looked at Alfie. There was something wrong. Some false note in what he'd just told them that she couldn't quite place. Then Blake said, 'Well, you know, as we're all going to die quite soon, perhaps we should do something nice to while away the rest of our time here.'

Iris felt herself bristle. She could hardly bear to think what Blake might mean by that. She said, 'This isn't how it ends, Blake. We're not going to die. We get out of here. Matthew said so.'

Blake rolled his eyes. 'Iris, you killed the Beast and now you're locked in a cellar – a cellar that has been secured for lyc Lock Down –' Blake paused a second and exchanged a glance with Alfie who nodded '– and The Silver Crown are coming for you. There's no way out of this, Iris. So forgive me if your delusion told you everything would be OK.'

Alfie sniffed. 'Delusion? Matthew? Same delusion that helped her kill the Beast. Same delusion that told her Leon and Zac were werewolves?'

'God, werewolf, will you shut up. When I want fantastical creatures to give me advice on logic . . . and, anyway, weren't you meant to be the logical one, Iris? What about all this "We're going to get out of here"? Doesn't your logic say different?'

Iris nodded. 'Yeah, maybe . . .'

29

Pure was standing in the dark front room, looking out at the road outside. Across the street was a petrol station lit up in multicoloured neon. Pearl had gone out to buy provisions. The smears of colour through the dirty window were the only light in the room until the door opened, throwing a yellow oblong onto the carpet.

A familiar refined voice behind him said, 'Hey.'

He turned. The perfectly back-lit figure was clearly Aurelia. She stepped into the room and into her own square spotlight. 'Hey,' said Pure. 'I wondered where you'd gone.'

Aurelia looked a little shy. 'I've been in my room. I have to keep out of Alfie's way, don't I? I'm still thralled. I need to be really careful.'

'God, are you OK? Aren't you having a bad time with the whole betraying your sire thing then?'

'I'm OK. It's not me doing it. That seems to work out all right. It's really good to see you. Properly, I mean.' There was an awkward little dance for a few moments as Aurelia made to hug Pure, but Pure moved back, unsure, then realised that he really, really did want to feel Aurelia's arms around him and opened his. But by the time he was responsive, she'd pulled back. They ended up shaking hands.

'So,' said Aurelia, as she dropped his hand, 'how have you been?'

'Weird,' said Pure. 'Hanging out with lycs when you aren't one. Just bizarre. Um, no offence.'

Aurelia smiled. 'Don't worry. I kind of know what you

mean, actually. Hanging out with Vix when you're a werewolf, pretty damn weird too.'

'How's it working out for you? The werewolf thing?'

'Um, well, not great, really. Alfie's been, well, kind of distracted. So I never really got to be in a pack. I think that might have helped. Blake has actually been the person who's taken the best care of me.'

'Blake!'

'Yeah, I know, but give him his due, darling, that man knows an awful lot about werewolves.'

'They're going to kill Blake.'

'Yeah. I know.'

'Well, how do you feel about that? I mean, if he's been taking such good care of you?'

'I don't know. Numb, really. I mean, Leon has said he's getting the pack back together. Him as Alpha. Zac, Pearl and me. And you, I guess. Not sure how that part works.'

Pure dropped his eyes and looked at the carpet, embarrassed. 'Nor am I.'

Aurelia moved a little closed, a frown furrowing her peach-cream brow, 'So, er, Pure, what *are* you doing? You're a human hanging out with werewolves. You helped them escape from The Institute.'

'Pearl's my cousin. What could I do?'

'But this. Coming back with them. Helping them. Helping them kill Blake and Iris. I know they kill werewolves, but werewolves kill people: Iris's brother, Jude, Leon tried to kill you. Even I can see that. God, Pure, this is so fucked. I can see why they say that a Red ought to get silvered if they are bit. My head is so screwed. I don't know what I am. How can you do this?'

Pure's felt his face twisting as a variety of emotions were fighting for control of his features. 'I don't know. I just wanted to be with her.'

'With Pearl?'

'Yeah.' Pure wasn't crying but he felt on the edge of it.

But balanced safely on the edge. Not about to tip over. 'I just can't believe I let that happen to her.'

'You know, darling, I've seen Pearl and she seems OK. I mean, this is all a bit intense but she's with Zac and that's all pretty sunny. She's happy. If anything's causing her problems it's probably worrying about you.'

'But she's infected. She's a lyc.'

'I know, darling,' Aurelia said, shaking her head slowly. 'And so am I.'

It was that that tipped Pure over. Not into tears. Something else. He looked at Aurelia for a moment. Really stared at her. She was standing square in front of him, almost regal with that excellent posture she had always had, and the look on her face, the smile painted on her lips, clear as a signpost.

Pure knew Aurelia had always wanted him. There had been one time they'd almost had sex. Out on a full moon sweep – not long after the two of them had joined The Institute. Usually when they had split into pairs it had always been one of them with Blake and the other with Iris, but that night Iris had said she wanted to experiment with the two of them patrolling together. Pure remembered joking with Aurelia that Blake and Iris probably wanted to go and fuck each other in a dark corner of the industrial estate they were searching. But now, knowing the two of them better, Pure was sure that neither Iris nor Blake would do anything so dumb as have sex during a sweep. They had probably wanted to go somewhere and have a row.

Aurelia and Pure, however, weren't so committed.

They found a large deserted warehouse with a low concrete wall that crossed the vast, otherwise empty, space. Pure leaned against it. In front of him Aurelia was oddly lit, smattered with shapes of moonlight from the broken ceiling. He dropped his trousers, which made a spooky dark-red pool around his ankles. His red shirt was hanging open showing the pale flesh of his chest. And as she dropped to her knees, Aurelia's cheek bones were grazed with a shade of murky crimson that perfectly complemented her own dark-red uniform.

At first she sucked him lazily, not with any particular rhythm, she seemed to be speeding up and slowing down at random. Pure squirmed with frustration.

As things began to escalate Pure's memory of what had happened was more blurred. Aurelia had started working on his cock more forcefully and his orgasm had begun to build, he had been gliding on it, shooting off into the atmosphere, and then there had been a massive crashing noise. Aurelia had slid her mouth off his cock and looked around. The wolf was in mid air, leaping for them. A big one, not one of the usual strays. And Iris was right behind it, her boots throwing up puffs of dust as she thundered across the warehouse. When Pure realised she was shooting as she ran, he yelled out, diving back over the wall and taking Aurelia with him.

By the time Pure was together enough to think about giving Iris some back up, it was too late. The wolf was down and Iris was bending over the wall grinning at the pair of them clearly pumped up high on adrenaline. As Pure had stood up, Blake had appeared with a little roll up cigarette clamped in his mouth, giving Iris a lazy round of applause.

Iris had saved his life. Saved both of them.

But they were going to kill her.

And Aurelia had never finished what she'd started in that filthy warehouse.

Pure moved forward. Surged.

Aurelia did look a little like Pearl – tall and blonde – but her face was put together differently. Aurelia had a kind of tight formal slender beauty, where Pearl had a loose warm sexiness, but they were both lycs, both lost, both betrayed. Pure fell into Aurelia's arms and kissed her.

Aurelia answered his need. Within a few moments she was driving into his mouth harder than he was kissing back, and twisting him around, steering him back onto the sofa, pushing her hands up under his white T-shirt.

'I always wanted...' Aurelia gasped in the spaces between kisses, '... Always wondered ... Even after that one time when we nearly ... I thought maybe you were gay, even ... Never though it was something like ... Do you love her?'

'Who?'

'Pearl.'

Pure buried his face in Aurelia's hair as she pressed her face to his chest. His T-shirt was up around his neck now. Aurelia's mouth was hot and delicious on his left nipple making it hard for him to resist her; impossible for him to lie. He whispered it. He had never ever admitted it to anyone before. 'Yes. I love her. I'm in love with her. I always have been.'

Aurelia teased one of Pure's nipples into a taut peak and then moved her mouth over to the other one. Pure squirmed, lying back on the sofa, seeing nothing but a blonde head and feeling nothing but a long female body. His mind softened, convincing itself that it was fine to let himself think that this was Pearl. Pearl. Not Aurelia. Not another blonde lyc he didn't save.

When Aurelia slid her tongue down the mid-line of his chest, popped open his jeans with her warm fingers and swallowed his dick, it was even better. Looking down, through his heavy-lidded eyes, everything half-hazy with lust, he saw nothing, no one but Pearl. The top of her head. Her wide soft mouth hot round his dick. He reached out and placed a hand on her head. 'Pearl.' He said it so softly. Nothing more than merely forming the shape with his mouth, but it made his hips buck and his blood pulse. He said it again and a voice from the doorway said, 'Pure?'

Pure opened his eyes. He was convinced he had imagined it even when he saw her face. Her eyes sparkling in the almost-dark.

He stared at her watching him from the doorway as Aurelia sucked him. Not breaking eye contact. Mouthing her name.

She smiled and took two steps into the room. She got close enough to reach out and touch him. Touch her fingertips to his mouth.

Pure squeezed his eyes tight shut, grabbing Aurelia's head and holding her to him, reaching for Pearl's fingertips with his other hand. But her touch had gone. And he was coming already; thrusting hard into Aurelia's mouth.

A moment later Aurelia was sitting back on her heels in front of him. Wiping the corner of her mouth with a fingertip and sniffing the air. 'Was someone here?' she said.

Pure shook his head.

'I heard you, you know.'

'What?'

'You said "Pearl". I heard you. You sat next to me in Iris's lectures. You know about the lycan sense of hearing, sense of smell. Even in human form we have an acuteness.'

Pure felt strangely dirty suddenly. Exposed. He'd confessed. Aurelia knew. She knew everything. She knew too much. He felt himself curl up tight. Defences armed. He wanted to attack. Hurt her for the way he was hurting. He said, 'If you were paying so much attention in the lectures then you'll know we should have killed you.'

Aurelia frowned. 'What?'

'Like you said. Reds who get bit ought to be silvered. You agreed it. We all did. We all swore. Remember how

Iris said that her and Blake and Jude had done it. Silver gun in each hand, one pressed against each of the other's chests. Swearing to silver anyone who got bitten. I know she didn't make us swear like that but I'm pretty sure she meant that should apply to us too.'

Aurelia stared for a moment. 'Right, so you, you who have just sold out Iris and Blake to a lyc pack, are now preaching Vix codes.'

'Why do you keep going on about how we've sold them out? You're upset about it, aren't you? Just pretending you're not.' Pure looked at her for a moment. He ran his tongue over his top teeth and all he could think of was how unlike Pearl she was. What had he been thinking? 'In fact, you're just as much of a traitor as Alfie, aren't you? I mean, you've been working for the Vix as well. What's the difference? Perhaps you should answer to The Silver Crown too.'

'Perhaps she should.'

The voice from the doorway was Leon's. Pure stared at him as Aurelia turned.

Leon's smile was only just visible in the light leaking around his body from the doorway. 'And so should you, Pure.'

Aurelia made a harrumphing noise and made to stalk out of the room, pushing past Leon, but he caught her arm. 'The two of you are bloody Vix, no matter what else you might be. Things need cleaning up around here.' Leon spun Aurelia around in his arms so she was pressed close with her back to him, his weathered muscular forearm against her throat. Aurelia looked terrified. There was a long moment and then a bang as the front door was flung open. Pure couldn't see, but he saw Leon turn pale and a strong female voice said, 'Let go of her, Leon.'

As Leon crumpled a little, Aurelia shot out of his grip, running straight for the front door. Pure ran past Leon into the hall just in time to see her pushing past the figure on the doorstep. An incredibly beautiful woman with a cloud of dark hair and a silver tooth flashing in her mouth as she smiled.

Zac looked up as Pearl walked into the tiny bedroom.

'Hey. You OK?'

Pearl shrugged. 'Oh, kind of. I'm worried about Pure. Do you think Leon might hurt him?' As she spoke she crossed the room and climbed onto the single bed, covering Zac's body with her own.

'I really don't know,' said Zac as Pearl shifted and started licking his jawline in little kitten flicks. 'The whole thing with Pure is fucked up. Maybe you should bite him. That might be for the best.'

Pearl sighed a little when Zac said that. Her hips moved against his thigh. Pearl muttered, 'Yeah. Bite him. I should . . .'

Zac moved his body, shifted so Pearl could roll around underneath him and he could get on top of her. He slipped a hand down her body, flipped up the hem of her uniform and touched her soft cunt. She was wet. Slick and hot. She gasped at the feel of him there, repositioning herself a little so his fingers could slide into her. Anything about werewolves got Pearl excited. Talking about what they were, what they might do. Changing, running, killing and now, biting. Turning someone. Zac'd never used this particular line to arouse her before. He couldn't think why it had taken him so long.

He had two fingers working inside her before he'd even said anything more. 'You'd like that, wouldn't you. Feeling your wolf jaws breaking someone's skin. Changing them forever. Human blood in your mouth.' Pearl writhed on his hand, desperate as he teased her with the prospect of a third long finger. Zac felt his own cock growing heavier. The way Pearl got off to this stuff – it was so disturbed, so wrong. It made Zac feel like he was going to die of horniness.

He was almost lost to her when the door opened. He started, adrenaline spiking through his body as he turned. Pure's eyes met his. 'Oh god, mate, sorry...' Pure stammered. 'I was looking for Pearl. Fuck. Sorry.'

'No, no, Pure man,' said Zac, softly, 'C'mere a minute. Maybe it's time you got some of what you've been craving.'

30

There are ways to have a bad time, there are ways to have a truly awful time, and then there's being locked in a cellar with your werewolf hunter almost-ex-husband and your werewolf boyfriend. Iris had never read a book on etiquette in her life. But if she had, she seriously doubted there would have been a chapter that handled this situation. The fact that the disgruntled werewolf pack that had locked them down here were going to hand her over to some kind of jumped-up werewolf justice organisation to be killed felt like the least of her troubles compared to this overwhelming social awkwardness.

In the heavy silence, Iris leaned her head on Alfie's shoulder. Blake said, 'You know what I think would be a shame?'

'What,' said Iris, hoping her gritted teeth were audible.

'If Fido dies without giving you a good hard spanking.'

'God, Blake,' Iris said, 'you are so inappropriate.'

'What? You're not going to let him? You let me.'

Under her cheek Iris felt Alfie twitch. 'I didn't, Blake.'

'Yes you did.'

Iris sat up and looked at Alfie. 'I didn't.'

'Twice,' said Blake. He turned to Alfie. 'She let me twice. Birthday presents. Both times.'

'Stop it, Blake,' said Alfie, his voice dark with unspoken threats.

'All I'm saying is you told her if she mentioned my name one more time during sex then you'd make her pay a forfeit. Well I'm here to tell you that she did. And I think you should spank her.'

'What?' said Alfie. 'She did what?'

'She said my name during sex. I had her last night, full moon. Did I not make that clear? Was your head all wolf-brained before? She said my name more than once. That counts as during sex, right? It doesn't have to be sex with you.'

'Damn it, Blake,' Iris muttered.

Alfie said, 'What the fuck, Blake? Are you so bored you are trying to get me to fight you? Is that what this is?'

Blake shrugged. 'Nah. But I am bored. Thought we could do a bit of truth or dare.'

'Oh get lost, Blake,' said Iris.

But over her shoulder, even as she was saying it, Alfie said, 'I think that would be a good idea.'

Iris turned to him, 'What?'

'Oh you know, Iris.' Alfie smiled. 'Just pass the time.'

Iris looked at Alfie. She knew her eyes were pleading. She knew that after what Blake had just said, everyone in the cellar knew what the first question was going to be. It was just a matter of who was going to ask it.

Iris said, 'OK, I'll save you both some time. I'll answer the first question – the one you both so obviously want to ask – yes, I do have some sort of feelings for Blake.'

Blake made a predictable sort of 'ha' noise.

'But it's complicated,' Iris went on. 'When I look at Blake there's some history there. A familiarity. It's weird. And most people don't have to work with their ex-husbands everyday. Last night was ... I never would have, but ... I mean, I'm with Alfie.' Iris turned around and looked at Alfie who looked blankly back. 'I'm with you. I know that. I would never have done anything like that otherwise.'

'Anything like what?' said Alfie, 'what did you do?'

'It was sex. Just sex. During the sweep. It was stupid.' Iris looked away from Alfie and put her head down. 'You know I saw you with Aurelia. On the CCTV.'

Alfie narrowed his eyes at Blake. 'You . . .'

Blake shuffled. 'I never meant for her to see it . . .'

'Oh, of course you did. That was your plan. Make me screw Aurelia. Make sure Iris sees. Fuck her while she's confused. You really are a prize piece of shit, Blake.'

Iris could barely speak. 'Blake. Did you?'

'No, I . . . I don't even know. I wanted to see him change from sex. I thought it might be different from moon changes. It does seem to be faster. And I knew Aurelia wanted him. I didn't mean for you to . . .' Blake caught Iris's eye. 'OK. I did think you might. I didn't make you go into the lab.'

'God, Blake. I can't believe I . . .' Iris twisted around. Alfie still had one big arm across her shoulders. She turned so she was nestled in his chest. 'Can you forgive me?'

Alfie shrugged. 'For screwing Blake? For being unfaithful? How can I not? I did it.'

'OK. But Aurelia . . . well, that wasn't really your fault.'

'I didn't mean Aurelia.'

'Then who? What did you . . .? You never . . .?'

'You know I did, Iris. We split up. It was because of that – the split – that I agreed to the damn photo shoot in the parks with your brother and that led pretty directly to us all being locked in this cellar eleven years later.'

'Oh God. I didn't think you meant right back then. Anyway that was a kiss, you didn't *sleep* with her.' For some reason as she said this Iris looked away from Alfie and at Blake, meaning that she didn't so much see Alfie's facial expression as see it reflected in Blake's.

As Iris turned back to Alfie she heard Blake say, 'Ha! Bad dog. Oh yes he did.'

Alfie said, 'You saw us kissing at the party and left. I thought I'd totally blown it. So I went ahead and slept with her.'

'Oh,' said Blake, 'well if it was after Iris stormed out then technically you were split up when it happened.'

But Iris wasn't listening. She was pulling out of Alfie's arms and standing up. She would have stormed out but there was nowhere to go. 'I ... I thought, you might have meant that thing with the witches.'

'Witches don't count,' Blake snapped. 'Witches don't count as cheating,' he went on, talking too fast. 'Because if they did then when a witch came on to you you'd have to choose between cheating and being a corpse.'

Iris scrutinised Blake for a second. 'You cheated on me with witches too?'

'With *a* witch, singular. Yes. But it was a *witch*. It's OK if it's a witch.'

Iris stood in the middle of the cellar. Blake was slumped against one wall, Alfie against the other. How long had she even been down here with both of them? It felt like days. She was going crazy.

'So, Blake,' said Alfie, 'Iris has told a truth and so have I. How about you?'

'I've told one. About the witch.'

'Do you still love her?' Alfie said.

'The witch?'

'Iris.'

Blake looked Iris right in the eye. 'No,' he said, with a kind of slow carefulness which gave him away so clearly that Iris thought it must be deliberate. 'No, I don't.'

Up in Alfie's attic bedroom Leon was watching Sabrina turning Alfie's chains over in her hands with a contemptuous expression on her face. 'It's disgusting. He's an aberration. He shouldn't still be alive. Eleven years. That's not our way. And for a Beast cub to kill his sire. Beast cubs are, oh, I don't know. We need them for the line to continue, but they just cause us many problems.'

Leon sniffed. 'You don't have to tell me.' He looked at Sabrina. She looked so strong. So capable. So relaxed with her wolf. He said, 'So you're an Ancient Beast too? You must be if you're part of The Silver Crown, right? Do you have a scar?'

She laughed. 'No, wolfie, I don't have a scar. It's different with us.'

'I thought Ancient Beasts were loners?'

'Nah, that's just some dusty old bit of nonsense. Tobias liked it that way – he used to nag Pious about it, but really, we need each other. We needed protection from the Warrior Wolf. The one who we knew would be coming for us. Tobias always said he'd find him for us. And he did. Poor soul paid with his life to save the rest of us. We can't let him down.'

'Alfie's the Warrior Wolf.'

'Yes.'

'Alfie should be dead,' Leon said, really mostly to himself.

'That's right, honey,' said Sabrina, 'that's how you have to think about it. He's lived too long anyway. You're doing him a favour.' She held out her arms to him. 'Make love to me Leon. We can deal with your sire in the morning.'

Leon came limping over. Sabrina looked at his wobbly leg and bit her lip. Leon closed the gap between them and kissed her.

As he kept on kissing, Sabrina seemed to be laughing a little into his mouth, but he didn't stop to find out why. He used his strength to push her down until she was sitting on the bed and then sank to his knees in front of her. He shifted a moment, finding a way to be comfortable on his damaged leg, then pressed his face to her crotch. Sabrina was wearing jeans. He moved close and positioned his face so the seams rubbed against his cheeks. Even through the denim the scent of her was overwhelming – almost destructive in its power. Leon felt lost, hypnotised. In his mind he pictured Sabrina forcing his face between her legs, demanding his tongue on her, strapping him to her thighs. Almost without realising he put his hands behind his back. Then he lifted his head and pulled the zip of her jeans open with his teeth.

Sabrina petted the top of his head. 'Good boy,' she said as she lifted herself up and helped him get her jeans and knickers off with his eager mouth.

As he buried his face back between her legs Leon felt almost overwhelmed with joy – that what he was doing was a kind of worship. He kept his hands behind his back and let his wolf tongue glide over Sabrina. Taking it slow. Making her burn. Grazing her clit but paying most attention to other hidden places. Finding her secrets and whispering to them.

When Sabrina was twisting his hair in her hands and gripping him tightly with her legs, he slipped his tongue right down and pushed. In. Out. Then he finally brought his hands back around and pushed two fingers up inside her, letting his tongue slide up and create an answering pressure and rhythm, making circles. Her clit was so eager for his touch – big, aching, sticking right out to meet him. He kissed it, drawing it into his mouth, and she came.

Pure squirmed. He was naked and Zac was behind him, half underneath him, holding him. In front of him on the bed, Pearl's eyes were dizzy with lust. Pure couldn't speak. This was more than a dream.

Zac whispered, 'Show him how you'd do it, baby.'

Pearl swallowed and moved closer.

Pure twisted. His cock was so hard and his hips wouldn't stop moving. 'This won't ... in human form her bite won't ...'

'Nah, man, nah,' Zac cooed, stroking Pure's face as Pearl bent down and let her mouth cover his left nipple.

Pure bucked and jerked in Zac's arms as Pearl bit him there, then on the other nipple, then everywhere. Her head bobbing up and down, making huge red marks on his chest.

After a few moments Zac slipped out from underneath him and climbed up behind Pearl on the bed. Pure watched as Zac slid himself inside her, fucking her slowly as she kept on biting at him. She barely reacted. Pure knew her mind was full of her wolfen self. Of how she might do this next full moon. Take Pure as her cub and continue the line.

Both of Pure's hands were on his cock. Stroking himself as he looked at Pearl. Her naked body. He remembered those few nights in Texas, watching Zac fuck her. Close enough to smell the intoxicating scent of her arousal. But this was so much more. Her mouth on his skin. His only wish in the whole world was that she would kiss him. Just that. Just show him that she wanted him even as Zac was fucking her.

But she didn't. She lifted her head and turned, to kiss Zac instead.

To kiss the werewolf.

Zac's eyes were open, tight on Pure's. Watching him. This wasn't a moment of compassion. Zac hadn't decided to share Pearl. He had decided to show Pure just how much power a sire had over a cub. Pure was nothing to Pearl. Family, blood ties, were nothing to a werewolf.

As Pearl started to come around Zac's cock, twisting against his fingers on her clit, Pure knew he was the last thing on her twisted mind.

31

The cellar was like a box. Four walls, a floor and a ceiling. One wall was mostly taken up with the door and the steps. Against the wall to the left of the steps sat Alfie, against the wall to the right sat Blake. And against the back wall sat Iris.

Blake was saying, 'See I get the whole thing with you two. You had the big passion thing. You were young and in love. Then he gets bitten and turns into a were-wolf and, yeah, Iris maybe you'd have been able to go with that if it wasn't for the whole dead brother thing. But, oh, and oh, and oh, and oh, because you never stopped loving each other, when he comes back into your life it's just simmering brimming passion ready to explode. And it does. I saw it explode. But nothing's changed. And really, if it wasn't for the whole werewolf thing, would you two still be together now? It doesn't sound like it was even such a great relationship back then.'

'Well, thanks for that summary of the situation, Blake,' Iris said.

But Blake practically talked right over her. 'And then there's me. Let's face it if you two had stayed together you'd have split at some point. Just a kind of puppy love. Heh. But I'm your husband, Iris. You met me at the office and married me. That's what real happy ever afters are made of. In the real world.'

'I met you at the office! What office would this be? The one where we train to kill paranormal monsters? Since when did we live in the real world, Blake?'

Alfie shifted himself against the wall. 'Anyway, she'd left you before I came back.'

'What?' said Blake.

'It was already over before I came back. She'd already split with you. Don't blame me. Or the paranormal reasons for why me and Iris are, well, me and Iris. You fucked it up all by yourself. She'd already left you. You're her ex. Her first husband.'

'You were just a rebound thing, Blake,' said Iris.

'A ten-year rebound!' Blake shouted back.

Alfie looked at Iris, frowning. 'I thought you two were only married for a year. Less than a year you said, Iris. I thought you split up during the blood moon. That was, what, March last year?'

'Well actually we are still technically married . . .' Blake began.

But Alfie wasn't listening to him. 'When did you start seeing him, Iris?'

'I don't remember exactly. It was a slow burn thing. Organic.'

Alfie sniffed. 'When did you sleep with him then? The first time.'

Iris swallowed. 'The day I met him. That was about six months after you left.' It was true. The day she'd met Blake with Jude and Dr Tobias in the Bodleian Library she'd gone back to Tobias's house in Summertown with them and talked – really talked – about Matt and everything that had happened. They had been the first people she'd ever told about the fact she saw Matt's ghost. And Blake – god, young baby-faced Blake who wasn't even thirty then – had put a hand on her shoulder and said, 'It's OK, baby, it's OK. Whatever hurt your friends, we'll find it and we'll kill it. That's what we do.' Blake had been the first person who had ever stepped up and offered to help Iris get revenge on the Beast. The authorities had lost interest, ruled Matt's death an accident;

Alfie, the only other witness, had decided he was on the side of the animals. It was Blake, only Blake, who had offered to understand. Of course she'd slept with him that day. It had been quick. Nothing really. The first man since Alfie. They'd been upstairs in Dr Tobias's rambling old Summertown terrace. Blake had been lounging up against the wall when Iris had come out of the bathroom and he'd invited her into the bedroom to 'show her something'.

The bedroom was full of nothing but dusty junk. There was barely room to move. Furniture was in piles. Paperwork on ever surface in huge teetering stacks. And in the middle, a musty-looking double bed.

And what Blake had shown her had been the last thing she'd expected. Something she didn't know how much she wanted. He whirled her around, overwhelming her then before she had learned much about combat. He pushed her against the wall and kissed her. His height and his build were just like hers – and therefore just like Matthew's.

And then Matthew. The ghost of Matthew. Her imaginary Matthew. Whatever he was, standing right behind Blake. His blood-smeared face glittering wetness in the sun coming through the dusty window.

Iris gasped.

Blake took hold of her face and turned it a fraction so she was looking at him, 'It's OK,' he said.

'Monsters,' Iris whispered. 'I keep seeing monsters.'

Blake pushed his thumb into her mouth, 'I kill monsters, baby.'

He turned her away from the wall, guided her backwards onto the bed. Matthew was still standing there, staring at them. Blake saw her looking.

Blake was wearing a suit. This was way back before they ever had their uniforms. Blake used to wear a suit a lot. He knelt up over Iris's body and pulled off his tie. 'Let me see if I can help you to not see those awful things,' he said softly; like he believed her. And he leaned forwards and tied his tie around her eyes.

Matthew was gone. The room was gone. Everything. It was all just dark and soft. All except Blake's body, which didn't seem to have a square inch of softness anywhere as he stripped them both and made Iris gasp as their skin connected.

He teased her with kisses. Using the fact she couldn't see to torment her with his mouth. Slipping his tongue between her lips for bare seconds before pulling away and leaving her gasping after it. He pushed that tongue into her belly button. He bit her ears. His cock was hard against her thigh.

When he pressed inside her she was wetter than she knew. He went in deep. One long movement. Steady.

He fucked her slowly. Iris bucked her hips to try and increase the pace. He put his lips to her ear and said, 'I promise I'll kill everything that has ever scared you.'

He was pinning her hands above her head, but not with a grip that expected her to try and pull free, so it was easy enough to yank her right hand out of his grip and pull off the blindfold. She looked him in the eye. 'Don't.'

'Don't what?'

'Don't kill the things that scare me. I don't want you to.'

'Sorry. I didn't mean that. I know he's your brother.'

'I don't mean that. I mean I don't want you to kill them. I want you to show me how to kill them myself.'

Blake grinned down at her. His smile was sharp and feral. 'Oh yes, baby,' he said, right before he resumed fucking her, harder than before, driving her into an orgasm – a shuddering jolt of a climax, quickly becoming mutual – that shook the teetering furniture all around them.

* * *

Back in the cellar under the pack house, Alfie was still reeling from the news that Iris had fucked Blake the day they met. 'Really? I never . . .' Alfie looked over at Blake. 'I never knew that. I never knew he'd been there the whole time I was gone.'

'You know we were married, werewolf,' said Blake. 'You must have thought that we would have had some kind of relationship before that. You think that was the only time we'd split up? We used to split up all the time. We were still fucking. We would have got back together.'

'You think so, Blake?' said Iris, her voice dark and low. 'You think that I would have ever got back with you after I found out you knew Dr Tobias was the Beast. That you knew all along. All the time we were together. I married you, Blake. You knew.'

'We. Are. Still. Married,' Blake shouted. He turned to Alfie, almost as if he couldn't face Iris. 'We were together a long time, werewolf, and it's complicated. But it wasn't some kind of fling.'

Alfie said, 'I guess. I just never really let myself think about it. The fact you must have lived together. Done all kinds of things.'

'Really, Alfie,' said Iris, 'it was just a stupid mistake. I didn't know who he was then.'

Blake shuffled against the wall. 'You knew who I was last night.'

But Alfie's mind was clearly elsewhere. 'What did you do with him in bed, Iris? What other kinds of kinky stuff did you do with him? Did you play rough with him? Let him tie you up? All the things we do – those things you want – did you do them with him first?'

Iris looked down at the floor between her hunched up knees. 'Pretty much.' She stopped and swallowed slowly. 'There was a time when, with Matthew, with my hallucinations, when it got really bad. He was there all night. On the bed. Screaming. His face covered in blood. I don't think I've ever really told you how bad it was sometimes. Hunting werewolves seemed to help. Rough sex helped. I let Blake help. Blake has certain skills . . .'

'He tied you up?'

'Yes.'

'He hurt you?'

'Yes. Sometimes. Well, we did different things. We used to fight a lot, wrestle, like we do now, Blake didn't always win.'

'Did he used to hurt you?' Alfie said again, his voice tighter and more angry.

'Yes. Sometimes. If I wanted him to. More at the start, when things were really bad.'

Alfie got up, making straight for Blake. Blake tried to scramble to his feet and as he did so Alfie reached him and lifted him by his red shirt collar, shoving him hard up against the wall. 'How could you?'

'What? It's the same stuff you and she like now. Except with us sometimes *she* got to be the one on top. I've seen the two of you going at it, remember. You just overwhelm her. And so what? She likes it rough, sometimes. She likes it rough with you – she liked it rough with me.'

'She was damaged then. Her brother had just died. You exploited her.'

Blake dropped his voice but Iris could still hear him. 'She's damaged now. He's still *dead*. But it's got nothing to do with the way she likes to fuck, werewolf. The Silver Crown are coming to take her away any minute. How about you cut her some fucking slack?'

Alfie let go of Blake and turned around. He looked at Iris. His eyes were burning. 'This is so messed up,' he said.

Iris rolled her eyes. 'You reckon?'

Alfie crossed the cellar to Iris in two giant strides. He bent down and lifted Iris to her feet, trapping her against the rough wall with his big body. It was just like what he had done to Blake, but full of gentle tenderness. 'I never wanted to hurt you, Iris,' he whispered.

'I know. It's complicated. But it's OK.'

'I can't believe I'm going to lose you.' Alfie moved in and kissed her. It was so soft at first, so teasing and gentle. He used his tongue to tease and pluck at her lips. He played with her. It was like a dance. Each moved perfectly judged to take her higher. Iris melted. Alfie's big arms were perfect for melting into. Big and strong and safe. As Alfie's mouth got harder and tighter, as his grip on her got rougher, as his teeth replaced his lips as the main instruments of his kiss, Iris sighed and lost herself in the sharpness of his fangs. Alfie. Alfie was a werewolf. Alfie was on the other side.

Alfie's mouth moved, until he found her ear. 'I want my forfeit Iris. And I want to see you with him.'

Iris pulled back. With the wall behind her she had to fight to get free of Alfie's mouth and look at him. 'What?'

'I just want to know, Iris. I need to know if I'm the same as him. That's what he wanted this morning in the cage. It's what I need too. I need to see it. And you promised. You signed. He's right. You fucked him, well, surely that counts as saying his name a third time.'

Iris frowned. 'What? Is this just some kind of over-elaborate pissing competition between you two? No. The contract was ... that was just a game. This is different. You can't ask this.'

'You did it for him, Iris. You wanted him to see. And it's not like you have some kind of problem having sex with him when I'm not around.'

'God, Alfie, I ... no. No, I can't.'

'We had a deal, Iris. If you mention Blake's name three times during sex I get the forfeit of my choice. You said that it was a game. Well, fine. Isn't it all just a game when you think about everything else that is going on right now? It's my choice. And this is what I chose. The forfeit is this, Iris. Let him fuck you. Let me watch.'

Alfie let go of Iris completely and moved away from her. He went back to his wall and sat down, leaving Iris standing, still panting and dishevelled from Alfie's kisses, looking at the two men.

And then Blake stood up. Posturing like he was about to address some kind of formal gathering.

'OK, Iris, this is how I see it. Fido's got a point. Why shouldn't he get to see? We did it last night after all, and you might have the excuse of being all overwrought from seeing him and my WXX going for it, but I don't. So, come on, Iris. I mean, really, what the hell? We're going to fucking well die.'

Iris looked at Blake. Was he right? She thought about Matthew telling her she was going to get out of this. She thought about Matthew being a figment of her imagination.

She stood up fast and ran — insofar as it was possible to run in such a small space — at Blake. She really didn't know if she was fuelled by lust or anger. Passion, perhaps. At this moment she was willing to give Alfie anything he wanted. Alfie's forfeit. Even if what Alfie wanted was something as down and dirty as an accurate demonstration of how it was between her and Blake.

She twisted before impact and hit Blake with her shoulder, sending him back against the wall. She still didn't know, even then, whether she was doing this out of anger or as an agreeable overture, but the next thing she knew, Blake was on the floor and she was on sitting on top of him, straddling his pelvis.

Iris looked down at him. She cocked her head. 'Sometimes,' she said, 'I really don't know what I ever saw in you.'

Blake shrugged. 'Nor do I, really.'

Iris slipped down, let her body run along Blake's until

she was almost lying flat on top of him, then she brought her face close to his and kissed him quite gently. It only felt weird for a second. 'I'm actually sorry you're going to die, Blake. I always thought you'd be the one that got away. Once Jude went I thought I'd be next. I thought you'd be the boy who lived.'

Blake laughed. He reached up and grabbed a handful of Iris's hair, twisting his fingers tight. Then he flexed his hips and practically flipped his whole body up off the floor in a move Iris had no idea he could do. He turned the two of them over – almost in mid-air – and had Iris on her back on the floor.

He grinned down at her. 'Don't lose your edge now, Iris. Don't let your guard down. Don't go mistaking me for one of the good guys.'

Iris fought back. But Blake was so damn strong. He pinned her wrists in one hand; a move that always seemed natural with Alfie, but with the smaller more compact Blake it seemed wrong that she couldn't break his iron grip on both wrists at once.

Iris didn't have the same physical power Blake had. She had enough moves and balance tricks that his superior strength was hardly ever much of an advantage. But in a situation like this – when it was all about his grip and whether or not Iris could break it – Iris was looking like she didn't have an escape route. Almost.

As she struggled Blake moved closer and licked her face. 'Come on, baby,' he whispered, 'have you run out of moves already.'

Iris never ran out of moves. But in this situation she only had one. And she knew Blake would probably be anticipating it – but, really, that might not matter at all. She knew she couldn't get her knee up hard enough or fast enough to be really debilitating, but a tap might be enough. She let her eyes flick to Alfie, slumped against the far wall watching them like he was watching TV. She looked at his crotch, wondering if he was hard. Then, when Blake let his gaze follow hers, she struck. She brought her knee up between their bodies and twisted it in Blake's crotch. It was enough. Blake's hand on her wrists loosened enough for her to pull free. She pushed down on Blake's shoulders and scrambled wildly against the cellar floor, sliding her whole body out from under him. Then she sprang to her feet and got one foot on his chest as he rolled over. Iris wasn't heavy, but she knew where to put her weight to crush the air out of him.

Iris was still smiling down into Blake's face when she heard Alfie coming up behind her.

'You want me to help you out there?' he asked Blake, practically laughing.

'I'm fine,' Blake gasped and then Iris slid her boot up his chest and squeezed Blake's neck. 'Oh God, Iris,' he gasped.

'I'll say it again,' said Alfie, 'you want some help there? You want me to tame her for you? You see that's the difference between you and me, Blake. You can only best her – what? – about half the time. It's not enough. A woman like Iris needs to be with someone she knows can take her down every single time.'

Alfie took hold of Iris as he spoke, pulling her off Blake and twisting her around, rushing her across the room with her feet off the floor and slamming her up against the far wall. He drove his hot mouth onto hers. This was show-time. This was about demonstrating to Blake how he could take Iris apart. Iris was helpless in his arms, knowing she wasn't going to have any choice in the matter.

He ripped her shirt open, covered her breasts with his hot damp breath. Licked her and bit her. Made her roll her head against the cellar wall. He used his fingers on her nipples while he used his teeth to tease her jawline, working her three most desperate points at once. Turning her inside out. Turning into his property. When she started to collapse, to slide down the wall, his big thigh was between her legs to support her. He took her onto it, grinding once or twice into her hot twitching cunt and then helped her float to the floor.

He got between her legs, got her trousers off, got close. He slipped his wolf tongue inside her and Iris wasn't even in the room anymore.

But then she felt and heard something that brought her back. Alfie lifted his head and then said, 'Come on then. Come on, Blake.'

Then Alfie's mouth was back covering her pussy. Hot and wet and too, too much. Her clit was so sensitive. She squirmed and cried out. But he held her thighs tight and said, 'Come on, baby. I want you to come for me, right now.'

Iris shook her head no. 'Too, uh, too soon.'

Alfie drew his tongue lightly across her ultra-sensitive clit again, pitching it just right. Just the tiniest fraction over the edge of too-much that made her feel helpless and out of control. Alfie was choosing whether she came or not. She didn't have a say. Alfie whispered, 'This is just the first one, baby.' And he touched her clit again. Twisted his tongue. And her world exploded into pleasure.

Hands were on her. Mostly Alfie's but Blake's too. She was on all fours. Alfie was behind her. His cock sliding inside her and making her ache and burn while she was still super sensitised. Blake was in front of her, one hand in her hair and the other jerking himself in front of her face. He brought her mouth to his cock and when she opened up and took it inside she thought this might be enough to make her come again. Just this. Just the fact she had Blake and Alfie inside her at once. Not the fact that it was a deep dark fantasy fulfilled, so much as it was so twisted and never-ever and forbidden.

She felt Alfie's thumb glide over her oiled clit in a move so familiar it made her ache and want to cry out.

Again. And then she was coming for the second time. Bigger than before – like the second ones often are. Arching over everything. Her arms gave way and her mouth lost contact with Blake's cock as she collapsed onto the floor.

Alfie's thumb was still on her clit as he withdrew. He moved it once and she screamed out. Too much. Alfie rolled her onto her back and replaced his thumb with his mouth again. Light hot breaths. Super-soft nothing-touch. Iris writhed. Blake moved in and kissed her.

Alfie's tongue wasn't on her clit anymore. Which was beyond sensitive – now just a throbbing sparkling piece of flesh so taut and hot if felt like a shard of glass. Alfie's tongue was lower down, feeling almost as thick and satisfying as his cock as it plunged into her. Having Blake and Alfie's tongues both inside her at once was possibly more overwhelming than having both their cocks. She wasn't really kissing Blake back. Not really capable. More just writhing and moving underneath him as he thrust into her mouth.

Not long after that, she started to lose track. Alfie made her come at least once more with his tongue before he entered her again. Blake was lying next to her, kissing her and rolling her nipples with his fingers. He licked her ear. They swapped around. Blake licked her and fucked her. Alfie filled her mouth with his fingers, then his tongue, then his cock.

There had been many times in their relationship when Alfie had delighted in torturing Iris by making her wait. Teasing her to the very edge of her orgasm over and over, holding her there forever, on the edge of space – but this was different. This was like sensory overload. Too, too much. She didn't feel like she was capable of coming again. But as Alfie moved inside her and used his fingers between their bodies to tantalise her, and again, she didn't feel like she had a choice.

She whispered, 'This is like torture.'

Blake laughed. A typically dark laugh that seemed to mean that she was right. She came again with Alfie's fingers on her clit and Alfie's cock inside her and Blake pinching both her nipples hard.

When she opened her eyes again, Alfie was over her. Still inside her. Close to his own orgasm. He leaned down and kissed her. He tasted of her, wet and dry all over his face. Blake was kneeling up behind Iris's head, holding her by her hair. As Alfie thrust again, Blake leaned forward, caught the back of Alfie's head and found Alfie's mouth with his own, kissing him as he came inside Iris. Iris caught her breath as the image swam before her exhausted eyes.

32

Thursday, 24 January 2008

A long time before morning, in the sleeping pack house, Sabrina threw open the cellar door and stalked down the steps. She thought it was best to do this quick and clean. She had a gun. That should be enough, but she knew that as she was going up against one hard-built werewolf and two trained werewolf hunters, being armed wasn't a guarantee of anything.

She hadn't expected them all to be naked. Or so clearly post-coital and comatose. She placed the gun to Iris's forehead and twisted Blake's earlobe.

Blake opened his eyes. She watched him take in the scene. Her gun on Iris. 'You wouldn't do it,' Blake whispered.

'Why not? She's going to be killed anyway.'

Blake frowned. 'What do you want? In fact, who are you? You're not one of Fido's pack? Are you one of them? From The Silver Crown?'

Sabrina nodded. 'Just come with me, Blake.'

'What about them?' Blake nodded at Iris and Alfie.

'Aw, that's sweet. Well Blake, the best thing you can do to help them is exactly what I say.'

Blake paused for a moment and then slid himself out from under Alfie's arm.

'Good boy,' said Sabrina. 'Now, if you come quietly, I'll let you get dressed.'

'I'll come quietly,' said Blake, 'I don't want Iris waking up.'

'Not one for heartfelt goodbyes?'

'Something like that.'

Sabrina watched Blake while he pulled on his dark-red fatigues. He wasn't pretty like Alfie, sleeping naked only feet away, who, even for a werewolf, was exceptional. The muscles under his skin rippling and undulating as he breathed. But Sabrina still found she was looking at Blake's tight hard body and biting her bottom lip. Strange. Something about him. She'd heard about him of course. Blake had a certain reputation among the circles she moved in. Although he probably didn't know it.

Over in the corner Iris sighed and moved closer to Alfie, closing the gap Blake had left. Blake looked at them. 'They have to die?'

'I think so.'

'And I take it there's nothing I can do to save them.'

'I really doubt it. She killed Misty. He killed the Beast. It's hard to make a case for letting them go.'

'He killed the . . .' Blake stopped and blinked.

Sabrina looked at him. 'What?'

'Oh, nothing.'

As Blake walked up the cellar stairs in front of the woman and her gun, his analytical mind clicked through the only logical path. The Silver Crown had it wrong. They thought Fido had killed the Beast. Well, of course they did, their information came from Tobias, didn't it? And that was exactly what Tobias had thought would happen when Blake mistranslated that prophecy.

OK, in reality, Fido had rolled over full of thrall and Iris had been the one who shot Tobias. But Tobias had been in no fit state to let The Silver Crown know that things had worked out differently after that. And with their circle of twelve broken The Silver Crown must simply have not had enough power to realise their mistake. They'd assumed what Tobias feared had come true.

And the one thing Tobias had always thought was certain, was that it would be a werewolf, not a human, that took his life.

Blake wondered if Alfie knew about the mistake. And then, replaying the events of the last night in his head he realised that of course he did. Fido knew The Silver Crown had got it wrong and he was letting that mistake lie to try and save Iris.

Typical bloody self-sacrificing werewolf hero.

Blake was still thinking about this, trying to see if there was anyway he could use this information to his advantage when the woman ushered him into the empty living room. 'On your knees, please, facing away from me, hands on top of your head.'

Blake assumed the execution position as instructed, realising it was probably too late for any new information to help him. He felt the gun against the crown of his head. 'Further down,' he said harshly, 'make sure you take out the brain stem.'

The woman repositioned the gun a little lower on Blake's skull.

'You know, you're a very interesting man,' she said.

'Really. Does that make the execution more fun for you?'

'I hear you torture werewolves.'

Blake swallowed. *Oh God, no.* 'No, ma'am. Pure's got that wrong. We hunt werewolves. I know you know that. But really, we only hunt them a little bit. And I've already told you we were working for a lyc up until recently.'

'Yes, yes, right up until you helped Alfred Friday kill him.'

'I didn't help anyone do anything.'

'That's really not important right now. What is important,' the woman said, walking around Blake and crouching down right in front of him, 'is that you know a great deal about werewolves. Oh, I know just who you are. You have quite a reputation. You could be very useful to us. But I don't really believe in werewolf–human partnerships. That Pure creature, for example. I don't know why they don't hurry up and bite him. It all feels a bit snifferish otherwise. So, if I took you, you'd have to agree to be bitten. Would you do that?' And she leaned in close and kissed him.

Blake was a man who lived his life by as few rules as possible. But, really, if a woman who seconds ago had a gun to your head about to blow you away execution style started kissing you, Blake made it a rule to kiss her back. Hard. As if his life depended on it, even.

They moved in to each other's arms. Kissing deep. She was a beautiful woman. Dark colouring – body a wonderment of curves. She tangled her hands in his hair as she climbed on top of him, twisting it tight in her fists as she mounted herself on his twitching cock.

She had shed her jeans but was still wearing her pink sweater, which was pushed up over her tits. Blake had one hand on each, his fingers pinching her nipples. Every time he twisted them, it made her head roll. 'So,' she said, looking down at him and panting hard. 'Will you take the bite?'

Blake narrowed his eyes while he kept on thrusting up with his hips. He said, 'You want me to, what? Come and work for you?'

The woman nodded. 'Yes. We could use someone like you. Information retrieval is your speciality, I believe.'

'You want me to torture lycs for you?' That thought made Blake's cock rush and pulse. He was near now. He moved one hand between the woman's legs and found her swollen clit.

'Yes, in a manner of speaking.'

He thrust again. So close. 'And by "lycs" I take it you mean Alfie in particular. You're going to torture him, right? As he killed the Beast.' Blake felt his heart beating harder and harder in rhythm with his desperate upwards thrusting. The woman was barely moving on his cock at all.

The woman nodded.

'And that just so happens to be someone you know I'd be rather keen to torture.' Blake paused then too. Still inside her. 'Except, you don't want me human. So in order to do that, I'd have to be bitten. Turned. And you actually want me to be willing?'

The woman smiled. 'That would be my preference, yes.'

Blake made two huge thrusts and paused right on the brink of his orgasm. He lifted his head from the floor. 'Well, listen, sister, I've been in this game fifteen years. No lyc's broken my skin yet and I'm pretty proud of that. You think, after all that, that I'd *ask* you to do it? You really think I'd ever *help* you?'

Blake spat in her face and it made him come.

Without missing a beat the woman slapped Blake hard on the cheek. He was gasping on the floor. She climbed off him. Still wearing only her sweater. 'Oh, I should have known you'd be a waste of my time. Now where were we.' She picked up her gun from the floor and pointed it in Blake's face.

'Hang on, hang on,' Blake stammered, sitting up. 'What if I did say yes?'

The woman smiled. 'Yes to being turned? To willingly receiving a bite? I thought you just said . . .'

'Never mind *that*.' Blake was fastening up his trousers. 'What I want to know is, are you actually offering to bite me yourself, sweetheart?'

'Why? You want to make sure you get to be a Beast cub?'

Blake stood up, raising his arms above his head as the woman gestured with the gun. 'Oh no, fuck that lyc shit. And more to the point, you're not an Ancient Beast, are you? You're not even a werewolf. So I just wondered how you were planning to turn me.'

The woman paled. 'What?'

'How did you find this place, sweetheart? You weren't with us in the truck.'

'Leon told me how to . . .'

'Yeah. Great. Except that wouldn't have been enough. I had a cloaking spell put on this house. Iris needed the protection. A lyc can't find his way here – even with instructions – unless he's been here before or he's with someone who has. And you hadn't ever been here before. So you're not one of The Silver Crown. You're not even a lyc. In fact, thinking about it, there's only one thing you can be. I can spot your kind, you know. And they are always trying to bloody fuck me. But those wolves upstairs think you're a lyc, don't they? They'd never give you their Alpha if they thought you weren't one of them.'

The woman looked at Blake, her face like stone. 'I'm going to kill you. It doesn't matter what you know.'

Suddenly Blake found it very hard to think about anything but the gun that was right in his face. He screwed up every bit of courage he had into a tight hard ball and spoke right into the barrel. 'Just take him. Alfie. He's all you want, after all. Let me have Iris. There must be some sedatives around here that they use for Fido. Give her a dose and I'll take her away from here.'

The woman shook her head. 'Why should I?'

'Or you shoot me, and you take a chance on how loud I can shout your secret before the life runs out of my body.'

33

'Hi.'

Alfie opened his eyes. He was still in the cellar. No Iris or Blake. In front of him stood someone new. A beautiful woman with a light musical tone to her voice that made Alfie's spine thrum slightly. She was tall and elegant with her dark wavy hair dancing around her head like a black cloud.

'Hello Alfred. My name is Sabrina. I work for The Silver Crown. I've come to take you to them.'

'Right.' Alfie let his eyes scan the tiny box of a room again, wondering if maybe he'd been mistaken. But, no, she wasn't anywhere around. Iris was gone.

'Do you know what we're going to do with you, Alfred?'

Alfie didn't look at her. Couldn't. He felt queasy and his eyes were suddenly prickling and sore.

'There's going to be a trial, Alfred. We take treason very seriously.'

'Yes,' Alfie said, gently, 'I understand.'

He didn't care. *Iris was gone. They'd killed her already.* Killed her while he slept.

Sabrina handcuffed Alfie and took him out to her car. The house was silent. Was everyone else still sleeping? The daylight was greyish and damp. Still early.

'Where are they?' he said quietly. He didn't want to ask. He knew what the answer would be, could hardly bear to hear the confirmation.

'Dead,' said Sabrina. 'They're both dead. Werewolf

hunters, kind of hard to make the case for keeping them alive. Look on the bright side though,' she said starting the engine, 'at least neither of them were werewolf *traitors*. It'll be much harder for you.'

As she drove away, Alfie twisted in his seat to watch the pack house recede into the distance.

Going, going, gone.

Sabrina drove Alfie into the centre of Oxford and parked in the big multi-storey. Alfie's insides felt like lead. She was dead. Iris was dead.

There had been many times, during the years they'd been apart, when Alfie had wondered if Iris was still alive. He'd known she was part of the Vix – known how dangerous werewolves were. Occasionally he'd received a copy of the magazine from his college alumni society. God knows how they'd found him; these people have their ways. He scoured the pages for any mention of her, for any clue. Never a word. He'd typed 'Iris Instasi-Fox' into Google time and again and never got anything except a mention of her degree being awarded to her *in absentia*. But he'd never really believed she'd go first. Never. Even locked in the cage at the Institute with her and the moon rushing towards him.

She'd been the one up a tree when the Beast attacked. She'd been the one left untouched. Iris was a survivor.

Not anymore.

'OK,' Sabrina said levelly. I think we'll just wait here a few moments.

'Wait for what?'

'For some people who will help you understand your place in the world.'

It was, in fact, less than moments. Sabrina and Alfie had only sat in the car for a couple of seconds before they appeared. Nine of them. Werewolves. Ancient Beasts. Each of them wearing a twisted silver wire circlet on his head. They were walking across the concrete, their faces twisted and solemn in the light from the harsh fluorescent strips overhead.

And the power. So much power. It was making Alfie's head swim.

Sabrina smiled like she could read his mind. She reached over and fumbled behind him, unlocking the cuffs. 'You can get out the car now, Alfred,' she said in her gentle musical voice.

Alfie did so. Turned and opened the door, unfolded his body from the car and stood up. It made him slightly light-headed to be able to feel the air moving around him. And as the other wolves came closer the strong overwhelming feelings of submissiveness escalated. His sense of his place in the world – of a kind of order and meaning to all things – pacified and delighted him. The Line.

On Sabrina's delicate command, they walked out of the car park and along the High Street until they reached a large pub called The Bishop. It was open and busy with customers, but Alfie, Sabrina and the Beasts walked straight through, out through the back and down a flight of steps which led to a long tunnel.

Alfie felt like he was gliding; free of his responsibilities he followed wherever he was led.

They went underground. The air got darker and damper. They followed the cambered tunnels down and down until they arrived in a rough-walled room, an underground cavern. The room contained a table surrounded by twelve chairs – thrones – and at its head sat a young rangy man with sandy-coloured hair and long misshapen nose that looked like it might have once been broken. He too wore a silver crown. The man stood up as Alfie entered the room.

The other Beasts hadn't followed them into the hall. It was just Sabrina, Alfie and the tall man, but the tall man had a power that was coming off him in waves. Another Ancient Beast. Even more powerful. Alfie swallowed hard.

The tall man offered a hand. 'Alfie. I'm Pious. We've gone to some real trouble finding you, my boy. I believe you killed my brother.'

34

'Ow!'

Iris opened her eyes. In front of her swam an image of Blake. Blake holding a syringe. Iris rubbed at the sore spot on her arm. 'Blake?' She looked at the syringe again. 'Blake, what did you just give me?'

Blake shook his head disparagingly. 'Oh, this? Nothing. Just a stim. I knew you'd go mad if I let you sleep the day away.'

Iris sat up. Quickly. 'Oh God. What's in that, Blake?'

'It's nothing. A stimulant. Cold war Russian military thing. It's fine. I use it on myself all the time.'

Iris looked around the room. She was in Blake's office. 'Blake? How did I get here? Oh, God. Where's Alfie?'

'He's not here. I could only take you, Iris. Although that was hardly Sophie's Choice.'

Iris shivered. 'But how come they let you take me?' She paused a moment, crinkling her brow. 'What happened?'

'They didn't really want us, Iris. They wanted Fido. They fucked up. The Silver Crown got it wrong just like Tobias. They thought Fido killed the Beast. They've taken him for, whatever, something gross and lycan. He's the traitor. I don't think a lyc has ever killed one of the Ancient Beasts before. I'm not even sure an Ancient Beast has ever been killed before. But you're off the hook, Iris. They took him instead.'

Iris shook her head. 'No . . . no. They can't have.'

'Look, Iris, I'm pretty sure Fido knew about the mix-up. They way he was in that cellar. He knew they thought it was him. Maybe they even told him so, I don't know. We were just leverage. There to make sure he behaved until The Silver Crown arrived. He knew, Iris.'

'Then why didn't he tell me?' Iris sniffed, suddenly and strangely, remembering what Blake had said about never having seen her cry.

'Because he bloody well knows what you're like, Iris. If you'd found out you would have been banging on that door demanding to explain that you had killed the Beast yourself. Fido's no fool.'

'Oh God,' Iris said, feeling the first tear slide down her cheek. 'The stupid bastard.'

'Yeah, but don't be like that Iris. He's not dead yet. They'll torture him first.'

Blake smiled and turned away, walking towards his lab.

Iris got up, wiping her face with her sleeve. Feeling her head start to clear. 'What? Blake, where are you . . .? Oh. Oh!'

Blake carried on walking, Iris followed him into his lab. He was already sat at his computer, pulling up a map.

'Have you got him?' Iris said, leaning over his shoulder.

'Oh yeah,' said Blake, 'nice strong trace on him coming through loud and clear.'

All three of them were traceable.

Very late, very post-sex, the night before in the cellar, Iris had been slumped against the wall with Blake next to her, lazily rolling a cigarette. Alfie was lying on the floor, his big head in her lap. His eyes looked a little glazed. 'You OK?'

'I'm kind of hungry. That might not have been such a good idea. It's been a long time for a werewolf to go without food.'

Blake leaned over. 'You want a cig, puppy? Nicotine buzz might help.'

'Not really,' said Alfie.

'Lucky they didn't search you, Blake. Never mind the med kit – you'd be going nuts if you didn't have your tobacco.'

Blake grinned, 'Did they search you?'

'Nah. They took my guns and my blade. That blond one said he could smell silver. He knew just where all my weapons were.' Iris reached over and picked up her jeans, lying on the floor. 'I've still got both of these, for example.' Out of the back pocket she pulled two coms sets.

'Heh, well yeah.' Blake picked up his own dark-red trousers and pulled out the coms set from the truck. 'Lot of use they are with Pepper hospitalised. There's no one to hear if we try and use them.'

Iris was holding hers in her hand. Turning it over. 'There might be something. Inside. What can I use to get the back off?'

'The wire from your bra?' said Blake.

Iris tutted. 'I'm not wearing a bra, Blake. Didn't you notice? But there must be something.'

'Blake picked up his own shirt and pulled the med kit out of the top pocket. He opened it. 'Here,' he said, skimming a scalpel across the stone floor.

Iris stroked Alfie's hair as she leaned over and took it. 'Are you sure you're OK?'

Alfie opened his eyes. 'Oh yeah,' he said. 'Takes more than this to kill me anyway.'

Iris leaned back against the wall to use her new tool to prise the back off her coms set.

'Iris,' Blake said idly, he was lying on his back on the floor now, blowing smoke rings up into the air, 'that is Institute property.'

'They're going to split us up,' Iris said, half to herself. 'They'll take me off somewhere. Who knows what they'll do with you, but as soon as The Silver Crown get here the first thing they'll want to do is split us up. It's a strategic nightmare, locking us all up together. Ah!' she grunted as the back of the coms snapped off. Inside was a mess of electronics. 'The coms sets all have a little chip that emits a constant signal. For tracking. That's how I tracked you. We have three of those chips here. We ought to use them.'

'Use them for what?' said Alfie.

Blake blew out another smoke ring. 'Oh clever girl.' He pulled himself up on his elbows. 'Cheer up, Fido. Iris has got something for you to eat.'

'No,' said Iris, 'we can't eat them. Our stomach acid would destroy them.'

'Then how?' said Blake.

We've got a scalpel and there's a field suture set in the med kit.' Iris was already wiping down a patch of skin on her upper arm with a sterile wipe. 'I think we ought to get ourselves chipped.'

35

The first full moon after Alfie was bitten by the Beast he was sitting at his computer in the house he shared with four other medical students in Marston.

His shoulder was patched up, awaiting reconstructive surgery, and he was trying to catch up with the work he had missed while he was in hospital. After the animal attack the university had offered to defer his place for a year, but he wanted to get on. It already took long enough to qualify as a doctor.

But it was heavy going getting back into his studies. He felt different. Nothing he could name or place, but a strong sense of dislocation and an even stronger one of anticipation. Something was coming. Something bad and good. Awesome and terrifying. He was sure of it. But what? And the fact he was so damn horny didn't help much. He'd pretty much had a permanent hard on since he'd left the hospital. And Iris – strangely – had welcomed it. She was barely able to talk to him, but she was happy to fuck. To turn up at this house, go straight to his bedroom, strip, lie on his bed and welcome him to her body with a stone face and an obvious ache inside that Alfie knew he could never reach.

Iris's grief was strange, unearthly, savage. Alfie knew she was using him. He wanted to be used. If Iris wanted a fuck machine, a hard body over her, a hard dick inside her, a conversation wrought of moans, that was fine. He would do it. He couldn't save her brother. Perhaps he could save her. Fuck her back to life. She was desperate for it. Crazy. His cock in her cunt or her mouth or her arse. His big fingers too. Every part of her that could be filled, stuffed tight with him. Yet, he was nowhere near reaching the void inside her. She was distracted when they fucked. Not present. Often she seemed to be looking at something over his shoulder. When she came she usually cried.

That night as he worked, on the bed behind him, the covers were mussed and the indent made by Iris's small body – as he driven her down hard into the mattress that afternoon – was still visible.

When the moonlight had hit him – filtered through closed curtains – it felt, at first, like a simple urge to stretch his body. Similar to the way he often felt when he woke in the morning. But as he began to respond, stretching out his limbs the urge grew stronger, stronger. He stood up and stretched harder, further. He stretched until his limbs began to cramp.

He heard footsteps running down the hall; then banging on his door. His housemate George's urgent voice saying, 'Alfie, Alfie! Are you OK in there?' It was then that Alfie realised he was screaming.

Then he knew. Or he knew something. He knew he needed to get out of the house, and fast.

He shoved the door open so hard that George was slammed into the plasterboard wall. But Alfie didn't look back.

He thundered down the stairs. Suddenly unable to see properly. Running on instinct. Getting out and as far away as possible as his world changed into one of intolerable sounds, oppressive odours and a million shades of grey.

Then he was out in the open. Parks, marshes, river, countryside. His memories of that first change were always strong and often sharply nostalgic. He ran, he howled, he ran again. He tasted blood.

The other wolf appeared after the first kill. He knew

the Beast at once. His sire. His Alpha. He'd followed that wolf out of Oxford and into the countryside, running forever.

Later, when Alfie woke up a man, the Beast was still there. To become the thing Alfie hated and loved like nothing else.

And in the underground chamber of The Silver Crown, when Alfie looked at Pious, standing louche in front of him, the sharp mixture of feeling he had for the Beast came bubbling up to the surface again. Pious smelled just like the Beast. The air in the tiny room was suddenly full of the scent that filled the night eleven years ago.

The smell was all. For Alfie it was like the smell of his mother and his killer mixed into one. Bitter and terrible and *home*. As Pious drew nearer Alfie couldn't fight. He fell to his knees in front of him, overcome with joyful terror and awe.

Pious smiled down at Alfie. Touched his face, lightly. 'I knew you'd come to us, Alfred. What took you so long? Don't you know we're your family?'

Alfie swallowed. He could feel his emotions throbbing through his body. The bitterest hatred and a tugging at his heart that almost made him want to cry. He thought of Leon. Leon who hated him so much. Leon who claimed to be out of thrall but still couldn't kill his sire. Couldn't kill the old wolf. Like father, like son.

Pious's fingers danced over Alfie's face to his neck. He touched the collar lightly then drew his fingers away. said, 'Collared? So you're getting close to the skin are you?'

Alfie was shaking. 'What?'

'Flipping. Changing outside the moon. How long has that been happening?' Pious's voice was thin and fragile. Terrifying.

'A few years.'

Pious nodded slowly, sagely. 'I suppose you're getting old. When did Tobias bite you? Eight years ago?'

'Eleven.'

'Well then. Way too old. Your time is up. Your cub needs to kill you. Have you explained?'

'Yes.' Alfie found he was shaking his head even though he was answering in the affirmative. 'I don't think they can. There are three.'

'Three cubs. And none of them wants to challenge their Alpha?'

'It's not so much they don't want to. Well, Misty died, Aurelia is far too young. Leon can't stand me, but he can't seem to defy me either. Not properly.'

Pious still had his fingers close to Alfie's collar. He drew his fingertips over it again – the silver was spelled not to sting the wearer, but it should still hurt for a werewolf to touch. But it didn't seem to bother Pious. 'Well, this is often how it goes with Beast cubs. Tricky business. That's why we try and manage the situation. Keep a close eye on them. You're an anomaly. No wonder things have got so complex for you. So what changes you now? What's your new poison? You've bitten women so I guess it was sex first, right. You bit your woman? Maybe you hadn't released in a while and as you built up a nice head of steam...' Pious's sentence ended in a dark chuckle.

'She wasn't *my* woman. She was just a girl I knew. This gorgeous crazy Japanese girl. But, yes, it was sex – the first time I changed. And I bit her. Turned her. She's dead now.' Even as he said it Alfie didn't know why he was telling this *creature* anything about Misty. He shuddered. 'I thought I was here to be punished for killing an Ancient Beast. Don't you think I'm a traitor? What is this?'

Pious laughed again. 'Oh are you really so slow that

you haven't worked it out yet, Alfred? We have no intention of killing you. That isn't what we want at all. With Tobias dead we need a replacement. His oldest living cub. And his killer. You are perfectly placed to inherit his power. In fact, you may have some of it already.'

'What?'

'We've consulted our seers, Alfred. The only way we can protect ourselves against what is coming is to reform The Silver Crown. We need a replacement for Tobias. He was your sire. We need you.'

'You want me to *join* you?'

Pious slid his hand around to Alfie's bare shoulder and then drew the backs of his fingers over the bite scar. Even through this light touch Alfie could feel a promise of ecstasy. Of claiming. 'Yes,' said Pious. 'I want you to join us, and, somehow, I don't think saying no is going to be an option.'

36

She said she'd take me with her. Make me part of the pack.

Leon felt strange. Like he was dreaming. Or like he *had* been. Like he had just woken up. Something wasn't right. He sat at the kitchen table with Zac. Pack summit. Properly. No females, no humans. 'She took them all,' Leon said. 'I thought we were in this together. That Silver Crown bitch betrayed me.'

Zac shook his head and picked up another chocolate biscuit from the plate on the table. 'Maybe she's gonna come back for you, sire,' he said through a mouthful.

'This is wrong, something's wrong. I don't know what Sabrina's game is. She'd never take Alfie without asking me unless she was doing something I didn't like. And those Vix bastards killed Misty. She knew their deaths were mine.'

The truth was Leon ached inside. Sabrina had tricked him. He knew it. Used him to get to Alfie. Then taken him away. Now she was gone he seemed to be able to think more clearly about her. 'I reckon that bitch tricked me somehow. I don't like it. She likes silver too much to be trusted. It's like she has some kind of fetish.'

'She likes silver! Woah, man. *Hurl!* That's nasty.'

Leon nodded. 'In her mouth,' he said, staring at Zac's grossed-out face. 'She just wanted Alfie. Our Alfie. He belongs to us. And if anyone's going to kill him it's going to be me.'

'So what do we do, sire?'

Leon stood up, his impressive bulk seeming to dominate the room for a second. 'We go rescue daddy. Again.'

As Zac followed Leon out of the room he said, 'Well, really last time I don't think we were so much rescuing him as ...'

In Blake's office, Iris went through every cupboard making a huge pile of weapons in the middle of the floor. Blake was sitting at his desk. Fiddling with his computer. Checking emails and sighing and typing in a terse pecky kind of way.

Iris tossed the last two silver guns on the top of the pile and turned to him. He looked up. She saw what he was thinking. Or rather, what he wasn't thinking. Her insides flipped. 'You're not coming, are you?'

Blake shook his head.

'Blake, please. I need you.'

'Really? I thought you were very keen for me to understand that you didn't need me anymore.'

'I need you to help me get Alfie back.'

Blake leaned back in his chair. It was swivelled around slightly so he was facing Iris, who was standing over by her weaponry stash in front of his bookshelves. 'He's a lyc, Iris. Look at yourself. You're going out there – with more arms than you can carry, it would seem – and risking your life to rescue a lyc.'

'It's Alfie.'

'Who is a werewolf.'

'Well that's just your problem, isn't it? You only see what you want to see. You only see the things that fit in with your view of the –'

'No, Iris, that's you. That's *your* problem. Your problem precisely. You don't get it. Everything's getting confusing around here. It used to be simple. We're the goddamn Vix. We kill lycs. We protect humans. I can't go with you Iris. I know that you have to go. You're in love. You have a destiny. It'll probably get you killed. And, actually, if you're going to die you might as well know, I love you, Iris. Actually, I still fucking love you.'

'Shut up, Blake.'

'No, Iris, there's more. I know you never really loved me. Not like you love Fido. I know you were looking for something from me. I don't know. Some kind of absolution. Survivor guilt, whatever. But it was something I couldn't give you. And it hurts to think that maybe, if I had been able to find a way to give you what you wanted, whatever that was, you'd still be with me. But if you're happy then . . . I'm glad you're happy, Iris. I just want you to be happy. Even if you are about to get yourself killed for . . .'

'I have a destiny, Blake. You just said so yourself.'

'Yeah, and how many werewolf hunters do you think have said that right before they went and got themselves killed? We don't rescue lycs. Well, I don't.'

'We used to be all about helping lycs. We *were* protecting the Beast.'

'Yes. We were. And we need to move on from that. But now the Beast is dead so let's get on with our job. Alfie is a lyc. We kill lycs. We have to. We have to be the ones that stand up and say once you're infected you're a danger to others and there is no cure so it's goodnight Vienna. It's hard sometimes, but that's our mission. Remember your vow, Iris, what you swore.'

'That's not even . . .'

'You, me and Jude, Iris. You remember. You remember each of us, one gun to each of the other's chests. You remember don't you? Putting your gun against my chest and looking me in the eye and promising that if I got bitten, if you even *thought* I'd got bitten, you'd silver me. Get to me before the moon did. You swore that Iris, to me and to Jude. I can close my eyes right now and see your face as you did it. God, you were a bloody child when we started this.' Blake leaned back even further and his eyes did close. He touched his chest with his right hand. 'I can still feel the place your gun touched me, Iris, like it's burned onto my skin.'

'That has nothing to do . . .'

Blake opened his eyes, but he didn't move from his position of rapture. 'Walk away from this Iris. It's time to choose. You've chosen not to kill him too many times. Now you need to make the other choice. Every moment you let Alfie live you are risking him infecting someone else. If you'd killed him the first time you saw him out at the parks on training he would never have bitten . . .' Blake stopped and pushed the intercom button on his phone. 'Aurelia, could you come in here, please.'

'Aurelia! What's she doing here?'

Blake stood up and walked over to the pile of guns Iris had made, took the top one and sat back down saying, 'She had nowhere else to go.'

The door opened and Aurelia walked in, smiling.

'Blake. Fuck.' Iris's eyes went wide.

'Thank you, Aurelia,' Blake said as he raised his gun and shot her between the eyes.

37

Zac knew when Leon wasn't about to stand for any debate. In fact that was the case almost all of the time.

'OK,' said Leon to Zac, standing in the hallway. 'Go upstairs and get Pearl. She can come with us.'

'You sure, sire. I wouldn't have thought you'd have wanted a female with us. And what about Pure? He's military trained.'

'He's also a bloody human. This is lycan on lycan. He stays out of it.'

'If Pearl comes he'll want to come.'

Leon put his shoulders back and puffed out his chest. 'He'll *want* to. Oh, well I'm sorry. If that's what he *wants*.'

'Don't mess with it, man, there's a weird bond between those two.'

'OK, fine. We don't need Pearl anyway. I only wanted her to come for auxiliary back up.

Leon turned and headed for the door. Zac made to grab his black leather coat from behind the door, when he heard a voice at the top of the stairs say, 'Where are you two going?'

He turned. Pearl stood at the top of the stairs with Pure just behind her.

'We're just going to get Alfie back, honey. Sabrina's taken him.'

'I thought that was the point,' said Pure. 'Aren't they going to give him his trial?'

'Yeah, look it's nothing for you two to worry about, but we're not so sure now that it was a good idea for her to take him. He's ours.'

'He's a traitor,' said Pure.

'Yeah,' said Leon, turning in the doorway, 'but he's *my* traitor.'

'Well if you're going to The Silver Crown I want to come too,' said Pearl, starting to scamper down the stairs. 'I want to see how they operate.'

Zac saw the light in her eyes. Her love of all things lycan. 'OK, babe, you can come. But Pure stays here.'

'What?' said Pure. 'Why? If Pearl's going, I'm going.'

'You're not going,' Leon snarled.

'You can't Alpha me, Leon.'

'Oh, can't I?' Leon said darkly. 'Zac, send it down The Line.'

Zac felt his stomach flip. Sending it down. Pulling a cub into line the hard way. Manually. He couldn't disobey. He turned to Pearl and using that same sire-voice he said to her, 'Tell him, Pearl.'

Pearl, her face pale, turned to Pure, 'You can't come with us, babe.'

'What, fuck this. Fuck this stupid lyc bullshit. You don't have to do what he says, Pearl.'

'I do, Pure. You don't understand.'

Pure was shaking his head. 'Damn it! This is so fucked up.'

'No it isn't,' said Leon, 'it's lycan. You wouldn't understand. You can't. You can't be part of this.'

Zac didn't know Leon had a silver blade. He'd had that one from Jin confiscated at the airport. It wasn't until he saw this one leaving Leon's hand and flying through the air that he remembered the one he'd taken from Iris. It hit Pure between the eyes. But Leon didn't have enough skill to pierce Pure's flesh. It glanced off.

And Pure had a silver blade too. He always had one. Zac knew it. So when Pure shouted out and came screaming down the stairs, Zac didn't even think. He threw himself between Pure and Leon, feeling a hot white heat in his chest as Pure barrelled into him. Pearl screamed.

Alfie heard Pious tell Sabrina to make him comfortable so he could think. She took him to another underground room. A bedroom.

No, a boudoir.

Alfie stopped in the doorway, looked at the large, pink satin-draped bed for a moment then turned and fixed Sabrina with a terse look. 'Look, I'm not going to do anything to . . . I don't want you.'

'Just get inside,' she said in a low voice.

'You can't Alpha me, Sabrina. You don't have any power.'

'I could fetch Pious. He doesn't seem to have any trouble controlling you.'

Alfie turned away and slunk into the blatant seduction den. 'No, why is that?'

'I think it's different with Ancient Beasts. Especially with your sire being dead. He sort of takes on that role. It's not like all Tobias's power went to you. It kind of split and some went to him, I guess.'

'But why would Tobias's power have gone to me?'

'You killed him. It should work the same as any cub killing his sire.'

Alfie swallowed. 'So, let me check I've got this. I mean, really got it. The Silver Crown is twelve werewolves, right?'

'Eleven now. Eleven powerful werewolves. Ancient Beasts.'

'And they all get power from each other?'

'Yeah.'

'So before the Beast – my Beast – was killed, The Silver Crown was him, Pious and ten others. You're one of them?'

Sabrina laughed. 'No. There are nine more here, the ones that met us in the car park, and there's the mother. The She Wolf. The Divine.'

Alfie felt his skin prickle. 'The She Wolf? There really is a She Wolf. The Mother of us all?'

'Of course.'

'And she's here? She's part of The Silver Crown?'

'Yes. She's what makes them so powerful.'

'The grand-sire of every werewolf in the world. God, I can't believe it.'

'You know the origin story then.'

Alfie sat down on the edge of the bed, his head swimming. 'Of course I do. When I started flipping – got close to the skin – I went all over the world. Everyone talked about the She Wolf. And Leon, once I had Leon, he always wanted to know everything. No one ever told me the She Wolf was part of The Silver Crown. That she was even real.' Alfie sat down on the cool slippery satin and looked at Sabrina. He couldn't believe what she was telling him. 'So the oldest story is true. The origin myth. A god fell in love with a wolf and made her human ...'

'But the god's wife was the moon and she was jealous. So when she came to her full power on the twenty-eighth day she changed the woman back into a wolf while the god was making love to her. And he was so disgusted with what he had done he rejected her, but she was already pregnant and the litter of cubs ...'

'Became the Ancient Beasts.'

'And now one of them is dead. His power should pass through to whoever killed them. You might end up even stronger because of the transition. Stronger than Pious.'

'So I'm ...'

'An Ancient Beast. Yes. Or you will be. There are some rites that need to be performed. That's why you don't have the power yet.'

His head spinning, Alfie let himself fall right back onto

the pink satin, which felt cold and slimy even through his jeans.

Sabrina came over and stood between his big spread legs. 'You'll need a consort. There's a mating ritual as part of the rites.'

Alfie looked up at her and all he could think about in that moment was that Iris was dead. He'd half forgotten why he felt so numb. Sabrina looked different. Suddenly Sabrina didn't look like this unattainable goddess anymore. Unearthly. She was still beautiful but in a far more achingly familiar way.

Alfie squinted at her, his breath catching in his throat. His mouth dry. He felt his eyes well up. It couldn't be. But Iris had Matthew.

'Sabrina, you look . . . oh God. Misty?'

38

Leon ran through St Clements and over Magdalene Bridge, sprinting the length of the High Street, his blood singing. He deliberately wasn't asking himself what he wanted with Alfie. Whether he wanted to kill him or save him – but the fact he was running towards him was enough.

Into The Bishop, down through the tunnels. Leon remembered most of the route, and 20 minutes in he could scent his sire – his daddy wolf – anyway.

'Hello, babe. You OK?' said Misty, pulling a pink sweater up over her head. Alfie knew the sweater was Sabrina's. Misty would never wear anything like that.

Alfie turned his head away from her. It wasn't Misty. He knew it. It was Sabrina. Just a second ago Sabrina had been standing right where Misty was now. It wasn't Misty. It wasn't. It looked just like her. 'No,' Alfie said weakly, 'don't fucking do this to me. Not her.'

'Don't do what to you, babe?' Misty said. Alfie looked up and then Sabrina was back again, unbuttoning her jeans and slipping them down, and in the next moment talking in her own voice. 'When you take the rites so you're an Ancient Beast do you know what that'll mean? The power you'll gain. You'll be fully conscious when you change. No more changing outside the moon. You could have everything. And Misty.'

'Misty? What? You're telling me Ancient Beasts can raise the dead?'

'Not exactly, Alfie.' Naked now, Sabrina climbed onto

the bed, pushing Alfie down backwards, positioning herself between his spread legs. 'But you'll be able to call up her image. Like this.' Sabrina drifted out of focus for a moment, her body shrank as she moved down towards Alfie. And then Misty was there, naked, kissing him as she dragged his shirt off. Misty. Misty who was dead. Misty who's memory was being insulted here. Misty who never let Alfie take her to his bed again after the night he bit her. Misty who wouldn't be doing this now even if she was alive. But Misty. *Misty.* Alfie opened his mouth under hers and let her in.

The tears in his eyes were for Iris. He gave the rest of his body to Misty.

She touched him. She was naked. She was the Misty he had known before the bite. Not scarred. Not scared. Sex with Misty. Familiar. Nostalgic. He was naked with her. That small delicate little body, fragile and beautiful next to Alfie's. She lay under him. Alfie felt as if he was willingly shutting down that part of his brain that wanted to give the game away. That wanted to tell him what was wrong with this picture. He was a werewolf. It was all about compartmentalising.

He curled his body and put his mouth where he would have to claim her. Where he had bitten her. But there was nothing there. Her tight little cunt was pink and pure. He ran his tongue along the closed seam of it. Opened her up with a twist. Pressed close.

He worked her. This was how it had been when he had changed and bitten her. Her little fists in his hair. Every time they tightened he felt himself get harder. That burn in his scalp. An addiction. He ran the point of his tongue in hard circles around her clit.

He felt the weight of his collar. This time it would be different. This time he wouldn't change. He slid down and pushed his tongue inside her. Fucked her like that a few times, then slid back up to her clit, replacing his tongue with a finger when she moaned at the sudden void.

He wanted to make her come so hard she pulled handfuls of his hair out by the roots. He thought about how cleansing that pain would be. He thought of Aurelia and considered, not for the first time, how wonderful it would have been if she had spat in his mouth.

Absolution. Aurelia. Misty. The women he'd bitten. Ruined. Women don't do well as wolves. Their deaths come too easy.

He curled his fingers inside Misty, jamming against her G-spot as she began to come. She screamed and pulled his hair so hard and good and clean he roared. The pain jolted through him like his own little orgasm. He rolled off her, onto his back, panting.

'So,' said Misty, as she moved down his body, about to take his cock in her perfect and perfectly beautiful mouth, 'you have a thing for tiny brunettes, huh?'

Alfie squirmed. 'Mmm?' he muttered as Misty licked the head of his cock.

'Don't think I don't know about her. About Iris.'

'Know what about her?' Alfie pulled himself up onto his elbows and looked down at Misty, curled and small between his big thighs. She smiled at him and opened her mouth wide to take his cock. Alfie moaned. *Iris*.

He imagined for a moment that the dark little head at his groin was hers. And then Sabrina/Misty shifted, turned her face just so and he saw her. Iris's sweet hot mouth on his cock. Iris's hands stroking and cupping his balls, caressing his thighs. Iris. *Iris*. He arched off the bed and came in Iris's mouth.

Sabrina was sitting between his legs. Just Sabrina. And as he looked beyond her, Alfie saw who was standing in the doorway.

'So,' said Leon, looking at Alfie and Sabrina on the bed, 'you still can't see me with a woman without taking her.

What is this fixation you've got with me, huh?' He was almost shaking with anger. So upset.

Alfie looked at him. *Was this meant to be a rescue party?*

Iris looked at Aurelia laid out on Blake's office floor. Very obviously dead. Still incredibly beautiful.

Aurelia had, along with Pure, come along when Dr Tobias had found some proper funding for their operation and they had moved to this building and employed two new werewolf hunters – their Reds – and Cate. That had been a year ago now. Iris and Blake had still been married then.

Iris was still staring blankly at Aurelia's body when Blake came back in. He'd been in his lab. He was carrying a Petri dish full of the magical turquoise and purple powder they used to dispose of the bodies of any lycs they killed during the full moon sweeps. Iris swallowed as she looked at Blake. Blake looked pale.

'I shouldn't have done that,' he said as he stopped in front of the corpse. 'I shouldn't have had to. This should have happened just after Alfie bit her,' Blake said solemnly, 'I was down, Pure was incapacitated, you or Pepper should have done it.'

'I thought she was dead,' Iris said, getting a sudden hard-edged flashback. The pack house. Aurelia lying on the floor in the hallway as Iris looked over the banisters. Blake was right. Iris blinked the image away and returned to the equally distressing one of Aurelia's body on Blake's worn carpet. 'And if I had killed her, I'd be dead. She ended up saving my life.'

'That's a what-if, Iris. You don't know what would have happened if you'd killed her there and then. Pepper would probably have ripped your head off.'

Iris felt the corners of her lips twitch into a near smile.

'Anyway,' Blake held out the dish of powder and took

a pinch, holding it high above Aurelia's body. 'You want to say a few words.'

Iris shuffled. 'Um, yeah, sure.' Iris scrambled for the right thing to say. Doctor Tobias had said something so beautiful at Jude's funeral. But Jude had died fighting. She'd had a proper funeral – not been disposed of like this. Iris swallowed. 'Aurelia Toto was a Red for a year. She killed five hounds.' Iris paused. 'It was five, right?'

'Sounds about right to me.'

'She was always professional. She worked well with Pure . . .' Iris's voice faded away.

'She fancied Pure. And Pepper fancied her. Kind of. Actually, she seemed to get over it somewhat after the bitch had grown fangs and fur.'

'*Blake*! She's dead. And she was only even a lyc for a couple of months.'

'Right, practically a fatal bite then. And they all are in the end.' Blake sprinkled the powder over Aurelia's body and they watched it waver and drift out of focus as it left one dimension and moved into another. 'She did a dangerous job and she died bravely facing down a lyc.'

'She died right here in your office.'

'No. A lyc that lived in her body died right here, Iris. Not the same.'

Iris turned away from Blake. It was like a little death between them. Once they were married. Once upon a time they looked the same and fought so similarly that neither of them ever knew who'd end up on top. But now Blake had just killed a lyc and Iris was going to save one. They weren't the same anymore.

She went over to the pile of weapons and began to tool up. Daggers on each shin and each thigh. Guns everywhere she could think of.

'You do realise that you are planning to take on eleven Ancient Beasts, don't you?'

'It doesn't matter, Blake. They could be seven hundred

nuclear-powered Ancient Beasts for all it'd stop me going to get him out of there.'

'I know,' Blake said softly as Iris finished and walked to the door. She turned on the threshold. 'Iris.'

'What.'

'If you really are going to do this I have something for you.'

Iris stood in the doorway waiting while Blake went into his office. When he emerged a moment later he was carrying a large wooden device. 'I think you should take this. It's a . . .'

'It's a crossbow,' said Iris, her voice breathy as she stared at the beautifully tooled piece of swooping wood in Blake's hands.

'Yeah. I found it in the doc's house with his papers about The Silver Crown. I looked into what it is. It's the weapon of the Warrior Wolf. I don't know how he got hold of it. But I imagine the aim was to keep it from you.' Blake crossed the room as he spoke.

As soon as he was near enough, Iris reached out and took the crossbow. It was lighter than it looked. She held it out steadily with her right arm and got the latch of Blake's high office window in her sights. 'Oh my God,' she said softly. 'It feels like . . . it feels like home.'

Somewhere in the back of his mind Leon knew he'd meant to do something when he got here. Something about Sabrina being *strange*. Something wrong about her. Was he meant to be rescuing Alfie? All he could think of was how much it hurt to see the two of them together. Alfie was saying something, something urgent sounding, but Leon wasn't listening. Sabrina could fuck with his head somehow. She confused him.

'Leon,' Sabrina said, 'why don't you come and join us?'

'No thanks,' Leon bristled. Join them? The thought of Alfie touching Sabrina made him sick. So sick he never noticed Alfie suddenly sprung off the bed and across the room, then shoved Leon up against the wall. He pinned Leon with just one tight fist in his shirt and backhanded him across the face with the other. 'You fucking cunt, Leon. She's dead because of you.'

'Who is?'

Alfie pulled back his fist and punched Leon in the gut. He knew just how to hurt him. The scar screamed. Leon went down, balling himself up on the floor as Alfie kicked him in the ribs. Shielding his face with his right forearm he looked up at Alfie, towering over him, burning with anger. Alfie was naked. After the first kick, Leon rolled onto his back and opened up his body, offering himself – defiant and submissive.

'Boys, boys,' said Sabrina behind them, her voice a soothing smoothness. 'This is no way for a cub and sire to carry on.'

Alfie kicked Leon again and turned around. He seemed to look strangely at Sabrina for a moment. Then he turned back to Leon. Leon lay still, ready for another attack, but Alfie slowly offered him his hand to pull him his feet. 'You made him do this, didn't you?' Alfie said, turning back to Sabrina. 'You tricked him or something, I don't know. It's almost like he's thralled to you.'

Sabrina laughed. 'Oh, maybe I did toy with him a little to get him to lead us to you, Alfie. But what does that matter now? You two should be happy together. Alfie's going to ascend to the level of Ancient Beast tonight. What could be better than for him to have his cub at his side?'

'What?' said Leon as he freed himself from Alfie's hands and started to walk towards Sabrina. 'I thought Alfie was a traitor. Going to die. I thought that was why you wanted me to . . .'

Alfie followed Leon across the room. As Leon's voice trailed away Alfie put a hand on his shoulder. 'They're not going to kill me. Or torture me or anything. It was all a trick, Leon. They just wanted you to lead them to me. And you did. They conned you.'

'Yeah, well, I had that figured, as it happens,' Leon said haughtily as his stomach flipped over and over, because he had known Sabrina was all wrong. He'd known it as soon as he'd woken up in Alfie's bed and found her gone. But now he was back here and looking at her, her betrayal cut through him like a silver blade.

Alfie's voice was suddenly soothing. 'Well, it's true. And whatever else she told you. That she loved you or wanted you or whatever, that was all lies too. They want to make me part of The Silver Crown. Make me an Ancient Beast and part of the circle. She never wanted you. *They* never wanted you. They wanted me.'

'Liar!' Leon pushed Alfie, barrelling him across the room and back onto the bed. Leon threw himself on Alfie's naked body, pinning Alfie down, caging him with his hard denim-clad thighs. Stared down at him with a snarl in his throat.

Sabrina laughed and clapped her hands. 'Oh yes, Leon, how wonderful. You and your sire can entertain me. You know it says in our records that he never claimed you.'

'What?' said Leon, turning his head to look at her standing by the bed.

'He never claimed you. He never came to you on your first change and put his mouth on your scar.'

Leon chuckled. 'Yeah, you're right. Stupid bastard has this thing about Lock Down. He never knew he'd bitten me. He shut himself in the cage and couldn't get out to find me. He fucked up his hands. The wolf fought all night to get to me. He still has scars.'

Sabrina moved forward and touched one of Alfie's hands – pinned in Leon's fist. She twined her fingers in his. The scars were silvery lines over his fingertips. Sabrina dipped her head and kissed them. 'There's the power of your wolf. The bond between the two of you right there.' She looked up at Leon. 'And you've never been claimed?'

'Guess not.'

'Well it's never too late. Might be the root of the problems between you two.' And Sabrina turned away and walked naked out of the room.

Leon was still holding Alfie down on the bed. He was breathing hard. Alfie said, 'What are you going to do, Leon? We've been here so many times before. What do you even want? You want to save me? You want to kill me? You want to fuck me?'

'Like you care what I want.'

'I care.' Alfie stared up at Leon. 'I don't like you saying I don't care.'

'Tough. I'll say what I like.'

Alfie reached up and drew his hand down Leon's chest until he reached the hem of his T-shirt. He pulled down the waistband of Leon's jeans a little and slid his hand inside, over Leon's abdomen. Over his scar. Leon swallowed. His dick was hard. It twitched as Alfie's hand moved lower.

Leon knew a lot about werewolves. He knew about claiming. He'd claimed Zac. But he knew that the relationship between a cub and a sire and the wound that bound them together wasn't just the ecstasy of claiming. Alfie always punished Leon with a punch in the gut. And if Alfie even touched Leon's scar in the right way he could still make it hurt. Leon's chin shook a tiny bit as Alfie's hand moved lower still, until his big fingers nudged up against the root of Leon's dick.

'You know I care about you,' Alfie said in a low voice, just a pitch away from Alpha. 'You're my cub, Leon. My sire's dead, first cub is dead, my life mate is dead. Who else is there but you?'

Leon felt it then, with Sabrina gone – what sort of hold did she have over him anyway? – he felt thrall. His thrall for Alfie. Deep and powerful. Still there. 'Yeah?' he said, trying not to let on how he felt. 'How come you never looked for me then? When I left. Every night I thought you'd come. That you'd find me. Bring me home.'

'I looked for you. Fuck, Leon, I missed you so much. I kept the pack house so you'd know where to come back to. Do you think I wanted to stay in that place full of memories? But I did. I stayed for you. I knew you'd be too proud to ever summon me.' Alfie ran his fingernails over Leon's scar again and made him gasp, blurring forwards and back over the line between pain and pleasure. While Leon was distracted by sensation, Alfie made his move. He heaved and flipped Leon off him, turning him over and reversing their positions. Leon growled. 'I know what you need, Leon,' Alfie said, pushing Leon's T-shirt up high over his hard nipples. 'Sabrina's right. I never did this when I was meant to.'

But Alfie didn't put his lips on Leon's scar, he leaned down and pressed them first to Leon's mouth, kissing him. It was gentle. It was the soft comforting kiss that Leon thought a sire ought to give his cub. Soothing. Balm. But Leon – who had imagined this moment many, many times – knew he didn't want balm. He put his hand behind Alfie's head and pulled him down. Frantic and desperate. Kissing Alfie like it was the only way he could ever be happy.

Savage and animal. Alfie's big hard bare chest was heavy and hot against Leon's. Leon moaned and Alfie pulled back, played, let his tongue tease Leon's lips. And then he laughed and moved down. Alfie ran his tongue over Leon's scar. Leon went weak. If his thrall to Alfie had ever been broken by Sabrina, ever felt in doubt, it was back now. Vivid and powerful and heartbreaking.

Without breaking the contact between his mouth and Leon's scar, Alfie unfastened Leon's jeans and worked them down. No underwear. Leon felt his cock spring out.

As Alfie moved his head, still tracing ecstasy across Leon's belly, the side of his face grazed Leon's cock. Leon sighed.

Claiming was incredible. Beyond sex. Answering a need Leon had twisted up inside himself since his very first change. But he desired Alfie in other ways too. Had done since the first time he had seen him. Before the fight in the car park that had made Alfie change and bite. Before the wolf.

Leon heard himself say something. It might have been, 'please'. And Alfie's mouth slid down and the pure bliss of claiming became the twisted confused joy of Leon's cock in the wet heat of Alfie's mouth. Apart from his feelings for Alfie, Leon had never wanted another man. Never felt like this. He bucked his hips and Alfie took him, worked him with twists and swoops, let a hand reach up and tweak a nipple here, reach down and stroke his tightening balls there. Made him want it. Made him burn. Alfie made his throat loose and light around Leon's cock until he was bucking and begging, 'Please, sire, please.'

Leon was so desperate, that he almost didn't notice Alfie pull his mouth free, kneel up, raise and splay Leon's legs and move between them. Push his dick right up against Leon's arse.

And then it was hard and brutal. Alfie's spit and precome got him inside. Leon howled and welcomed it. As Alfie thrust he reached down and found Leon's hard and still aching cock. He took it, slicked the wetness dripping from it back along its length and moved everything together.

Leon looked up at Alfie. Alfie was completely naked while Leon's clothes were still tangled around his body – shoved out of the way. Alfie, pure, naked, shining with sweat and muscularity and Alpha-power, moved over him, bore into him. Claimed him in every way possible.

When Leon bucked hard and came, Alfie fought to stay inside him then brought one of his hands up to his own mouth and licked Leon's come from his big fingers. Leon twisted, feeling the lasts pulses of his orgasm as he watched Alfie tasting him – his wolf tongue moving to not miss a drop.

And then Alfie groaned, ducked down, smashed his salty musky mouth into Leon's and fucked him hard, harder, as he came and came.

Pearl had treated Zac's wound as best she could. Pure's blade had gone right into his chest. She thought it had missed his heart, but she wasn't sure.

Pearl had tried to understand werewolf physiology – attempted to tie it in with her nursing training. One day, she had often thought to herself, when the pack got back together she could sit down with Alfie and work it all out. That was starting to look less and less likely, though.

But she'd had long conversations with Zac explaining to her that, to kill a werewolf you needed to wound them in a way that would kill a human and the weapon had to be silver. 'A silver bullet or a silver blade. In the brain. In the heart. In a vital organ. Well, you probably know better than me about that, nursey.' And he'd laughed then. Back then. He wasn't laughing now. He was grey and slick with sweat in his bed in the tiny wood-panelled room at the back of the pack house.

As Pearl mopped Zac's brow she remembered once saying to Zac, 'That doesn't make any sense though, not really.'

And Zac – still laughing – had said, 'Babe, our bodies turn into wolves once a month. Why do you expect the rest of the stuff they do to make sense?'

And that had been when Pearl had started laughing too. And they'd kissed and laughed some more and Pearl had felt so happy she thought she might explode with it.

But she wasn't happy or laughing right now, because she knew Zac was going to die.

His eyes weren't closed but they didn't seem to be seeing. He said, 'Leon', a couple of times. Pearl had told him, soft and gentle and with her heart aching, that Leon had gone to Alfie. She felt it so strongly, the thrall lines that threaded through them all. She tended Zac, who ached for Leon, who was following Alfie.

Pearl was licking her teeth, thinking about the idea Zac'd had about her taking a cub of her own, about biting Pure, but for real this time, when Zac said, 'She can't be a wolf.'

'Who?'

'Sabrina. She has too much power.'

'Zac, shush, you shouldn't be worrying about this now.' She put the back of her hand against his forehead. He was so hot. Even for a werewolf. This was delirium. And her throat ached to think that he was going to spend his last moments with her but thinking only of Leon.

'Leon is thralled to her and not Alfie. It only seems to work when she's near. But even so, that's weird. Thrall doesn't work like that. No wolf can mess with it.'

'Maybe she's really powerful,' said Pearl, 'an Ancient Beast.'

'Even a Beast couldn't. Thrall is, oh I don't know, *sacred*. Without thrall every wolf would just kill whoever sired him. Sometimes the anger at the start ... I know you wanted your bite, but that is really rare, babe.' Zac gasped in obvious pain and started to breathe heavily.

'Zac! Oh God, honey!' Pearl grabbed his hand and squeezed.

There were a few moments until Zac's breathing steadied. 'There's something very wrong here, Pearly. There's only one type of creature that could mess with thrall, mess with the type of stuff Sabrina's messing with.'

'What's that, baby?'

And he told her.

39

Iris wasn't even down the steps outside the Institute when he sprang. Someone came out of the shadows and nearly caught her in a surprise attack. But Iris had had too long a day to have her guard down even for a second.

There was a small alleyway next to the Institute and it was there that she bundled her attacker, pushing him up against the wall. He was familiar. She had a pretty good idea who it was.

'Pure.'

Pure didn't say anything. He looked at Iris, his eyes full of viciousness. He practically snarled in her face in response. 'I knew you wouldn't really be dead. I came to check. Thought the job might need finishing. Looks like I was right.'

Iris cocked her head. 'Look Pure, maybe it would be best for you if you just stayed away from me. Trying to kill me never seems to work out well for you. I don't know what your problem is but . . .'

'You don't know what my problem is?' Pure's voice was a low snarl. 'You want me to remind you? You didn't save her. You let her get bitten. And now she's with him. She does everything he says. She'll never be mine.'

'People get bitten, Pure. And they get thralled. You think I don't fucking know that better than anyone. People get killed too. This is a risky fucking business. Pearl was in the wrong place at the wrong time. Fucking tell me about it.'

Pure swallowed. Iris watched his throat move and

wondered if he understood what they had in common. Pure said, 'You're going after him, aren't you? Alfie?'

'Yes.'

'They're going to ... well I don't know exactly, but Leon said it's going to be bad.'

'I know.'

'And they'll kill you if you try and stop it.'

'I know.'

Pure's expression changed. He looked a little more sheepish. He shrugged slightly. 'You want some help?'

'Some help? From you? Weren't you part of the werewolf militia that tried to kill me?'

'So I can change my mind, can't I?'

Iris loosened her grip on him a little, 'I'd say you're something of an expert on it. Pure ...'

'Look. Iris. Are you going to kill things? If there's some killing on the cards I'm with you. I don't care how dangerous it is. I just need too ...'

'OK, OK,' said Iris, gently, 'I think I can understand that.'

Alfie stood in the middle of the bedroom staring at Leon, still lying in the bed with one knee up, casual and defiantly not interested in Alfie's explanation of the situation. 'So it's not me. It's Iris. She killed the Beast. She must have inherited his power before she died.'

'Bullshit,' said Leon.

'They seemed to think I had it because I'd killed the Beast and I was his eldest cub. But Iris killed the Beast. And didn't the prophecy call her his creation. God knows what it means.' Alfie left a single beat. 'She can claim me. *Could* claim me.'

'She could what?'

'You know what. Like I can do to you. My mouth on your scar.'

'So you were doing it with your sire then, technically. Somehow.'

Alfie gave Leon a slow withering look. 'She's the one they want. And the idiots killed her.'

'Who's the one we want?' said a voice. Alfie turned. Pious was leaning against the doorjamb. Alfie knew Pious's type very well. He'd been at university with a whole stack of Pious-types. Men that oozed smooth self-confidence, but were all broken up underneath.

Alfie smiled. 'Nothing. Pack stuff. You come to see if I've changed my mind. Ask me if I want to join you?'

Pious laughed. 'I wouldn't say "ask" exactly. Sabrina's tried simple persuasion. Do you really think it hadn't occurred to us that you might try and resist? There are other ways.'

'Magic?' said Alfie.

Pious shook his head. 'Pain.'

He snapped his fingers and five enormous human-form werewolves – all Ancient Beasts – came from behind him, through the doorway. Two of them took hold of Leon and the other three grabbed Alfie. 'Take them to the hall,' Pious said, 'it's time for the traitor to get his trial after all.'

'What?' said Alfie as the men started to drag him toward the doorway where Pious stood. 'I thought you said that was all a ruse?'

Pious smiled. 'Well, from one point of view, unless you're willing to become an Ancient Beast for us, then the law takes precedence. And you are still a traitor. From another, a bit of torture is usually the quickest way to change a stubborn mind.'

'And what about him? What are you going to do with Leon?' Alfie said, struggling.

Pious shrugged. 'Extra leverage is always useful.'

* * *

Alfie was led into the hall – the room with the table and twelve chairs – and stood up at the far end. His wrists were chained above his head. He was still naked.

He was looking at the polished table, Pious stood at its head. The three men who had held and secured Alfie sat down. The two who held Leon remained standing, gripping him fast.

'Well,' Pious said softly, 'shall I introduce you. There are six of the twelve here including myself. The minimum needed for the ritual. The others are out watching the perimeter. These are the wolves that would have you join them.'

Another of the Beasts, a small man with grey hair, stood, scraping back his chair, and began to read something aloud. It was something about Alfie and the ritual torture that was about to be performed. Alfie felt strangely detached from it. Not really involved. There were no choices here. He couldn't join The Silver Crown – he didn't kill the Beast. He didn't have the power they wanted. And so he was going to have to let them do whatever they were going to do. There was no other choice.

If they were going to torture him to death now, then so be it. He felt strangely calm.

The Ancient Beast who was speaking finished up by saying 'The Trial of Riches' and another man stood up and took a glass jar from a niche in the wall.

Pious stepped forward then and took the jar. The other man looked questioningly for a moment, then stepped back. It seemed Pious was going to do the torturing himself.

Pious moved closer and Alfie stared at him from his immobile taut position in the manacles. Pious didn't speak. The others at the table seemed to recede. It was just the two of them.

Pious had a soft smear of a smile on his lips as he

weighed the jar of silver coins in his hands, shaking it so it jingled.

He moved still closer, stopping less than a foot away from Alfie's naked vulnerable body. 'Do you know what I have here?' Pious rattled the jar again.

Alfie nodded his head. 'Silver coins. Vampire money.'

'And do you know what I'm going to do.'

Alfie swallowed and twisted a little. 'Put them on my skin.'

Pious nodded. 'Ancient Beasts aren't hurt by silver on their skin. Not like werewolves.' He smiled as another of the Ancient Beasts stood and placed another wiry silver crown on the table in front of Alfie. 'So just tell me any time you want the pain to stop.'

Iris stood in the middle of Cornmarket, Oxford's busiest pedestrian shopping street. She stared at the GPS co-ords on her coms. 'Oh, Blake,' she muttered, 'if you've been fucking with me about this.'

Pure came up and looked over her shoulder. On either side of them crowds of shoppers after January bargains streamed past them in the dusk. 'This is wrong,' said Pure.

'Well of course it's fucking wrong,' said Iris. 'Blake must've miscalculated. Alfie ought to be right here. Maybe the co-ords are just a bit off. But how can we find him in the middle of all this.'

Pure sniffed. 'Um ... you ever seen the film *Aliens*, ma'am?'

'What?'

'In *Aliens* they're tracing a signal from one of the monsters. It's getting closer and closer, but they can't understand why they can't see it. Turns out it's above them. In the ceiling.'

Iris frowned and then looked up at the darkening sky. 'Pure, I hardly think ... oh!' She looked down at the ground. The ancient cobblestones. Oxford was an old, old city – and full of secrets, full of places to hide.

'There are masses of tunnels under Oxford,' Pure said, echoing her thoughts.

'And you know a way into them, Pure boy?'

'I've lived in this city all my life, ma'am. I know a million of 'em.'

40

Alfie watched as Pious positioned the first coin halfway up the inside of his left thigh. He managed to keep silent as it pressed on his skin – glittering in the candlelight – and stared down, craning his neck to see Pious crouched on the floor, fixing the coin in place with a strip of damp white fabric like a bandage.

There was a silent pause and Pious stood and looked tight into Alfie's eyes and then he felt it. It burned. God, it hurt. He screamed and he screamed; and his wrists fought their bonds hopelessly.

He jerked and spasmed, trying hopelessly, helplessly to shake the object off his skin. He made a lot of noise, but the only intelligible word was 'No'.

And his heart turned over as he realised he *couldn't* bear it. Had no choice.

How long would it take for this to kill him? For dark to overtake him. For him to be reunited with Iris. *Iris*. He closed his eyes.

It was getting dark. Skip-running to follow Pure's long-legged pace, Iris set off with him down Cornmarket and then turned left onto the High Street. Something about the wind direction meant that it was much colder down here. The wind was sharp and vicious, bowling right at them. Iris thought about Alfie, how his big body always felt so hot-water bottle warm.

Pure stopped a short way down the High Street outside The Bishop, a huge and rambling pub, an Oxford land-mark. He pushed at the closed front door. It didn't budge. 'Locked.' He frowned. 'Why would they be closed?'

'I don't know. But we can't hang around. Do you know another entrance?'

'This is the nearest one by far,' said Pure.

'I could call Cate, get her to send some magic through.'

Pure raised a clenched fist. 'I don't think we'll need it,' he said as he knocked on the pub door.

There were a few moments of waiting. Iris didn't really expect to be let in. But, to her surprise, the big wooden door did creak open and a slightly-built blonde girl – even shorter than Iris – said, 'Yeah?'

Pure frowned. 'Is Bill around?'

'Um, hang on.' The girl's head disappeared inside the half-open door and she shouted, 'Bill! Someone to see you.'

There were another few moments of waiting – Pure and Iris looked at each other – and then a big bald man peered round the door. 'Oh, Pure. What do you want, pal?'

'Why're you closed?'

'Oh,' Bill shrugged and looked suspicious. 'Stock taking.'

'I need to come in, man. Use the tunnels.'

'Oh right,' said Bill. 'Sure.'

Bill stepped aside and Iris gave him a nod as she followed Pure into the pub. Iris had been in The Bishop before. Its traditional façade made it very popular with tourists seeking Olde Worlde Oxford. Inside – on theme – it was darkly cosy; a twisty little warren of a place. Iris darted through one small room after another, following Pure who was practically bent double to avoid catching himself on the low ceilings.

Eventually, right at the back they reached a small door. Pure opened it and revealed a set of steps. 'I used to work here when I was younger. Before I joined the army. This used to be the staff room.'

Pure went first, squeezing himself down the flight of steps. Iris followed. The floor they eventually hit at the bottom of the steps was wet. The air slightly damp. A passage twisted away in front of them, lit by flickering electric lights set into the ceiling and protected by wire. There was nowhere to go but forwards.

After a few moments of walking, Pure said, 'What do you think the mirrors are for?'

'What mirrors?' Iris turned around awkwardly in the narrow space. She looked where Pure was pointing at the tiny mirrors set into the ceiling, angled in corners, seemingly placed very deliberately. But deliberately for what?

'The ancient Egyptians did that, didn't they? Used mirrors to reflect the sunlight down into the pyramids, so that candle smoke wouldn't damage the artwork.'

'If you say so,' said Iris, 'but these ones aren't reflecting the sun now.'

'Sun's almost down. But even so, you have to adjust them all the time. Maybe they're just not set up. Anyone who used these tunnels could have fixed them up. Criminals or persecuted people or whoever hid down here.'

Iris didn't say anything. She was staring at the mirrors. 'Mirrors are a werewolf thing,' she said slowly. 'Werewolves use mirrors. Like to use mirrors. I've wondered before if it's a vampire thing. They use then because vamps can't. Like werewolves rubbing the vampire's noses in the fact they don't have reflections. Kind of the same way vampires use solid silver coins. But mirrors also have those connections to silver and to the moon. Mirrors mean werewolves. It all fits.'

'Fits what?'

'They're not for reflecting sunlight, Pure. They're too small to bring enough light in for anything useful. They're for reflecting moonlight, bringing the moon down here. You only need the tiniest glimmer to start the change.'

'So we're on the right track?'

'I'd bet on it.'

41

Leon stood by the door, pinned by two Ancient Beasts, and watched as Pious, pressed close behind Alfie, reached into the jar on the table for another coin and then wrapped his arm around Alfie's neck, pressing the burning cold metal against his collar bone. 'Shush,' he said, stroking Alfie's left hip reassuringly. Alfie stilled straight away. 'How many, Friday?' Pious cooed. 'How many can you take on your body before your self-preservation takes over?' Alfie whimpered and Leon noticed Pious sigh quietly into Alfie's ear. He bound another coin in place. Alfie screamed.

Leon shifted. He was already so hard it hurt.

Pious fixed coins around each of Alfie's wrists, fixing sparkling bracelets to still his struggles against the manacles. He pressed one squarely against each of his dark nipples. He added a neat ring of them, all around the base of Alfie's cock, while Alfie writhed and moaned incoherently.

Pious kept on adding more and more coins until they were on Alfie's thighs, his nipples, his stomach, his palms. They were the smiling dimples on his cheeks, a sprinkle of silver-grey highlights in his hair and his pretty gold-rimmed eyes, the ones that had haunted Leon's dreams for so many years, were now unseeing silver.

And around most of them, Alfie's skin had started to blister and bleed. Little puddles of his blood were gathering in the fabric strips, behind his knees and all around his groin. It ran down his legs in spiralling cobwebs, staining the sandy floor.

And Alfie just hung there, almost tranquil in his blind pain.

Throughout the process, every so often, Pious moved close to Alfie. Touched his bare flesh in a way that made Alfie jump in the expectation of more pain and whispered something. And Alfie had shaken his head every time.

Pious tilted Alfie's chin up a little and prised open Alfie's bile-smeared lips with his fingers. He took the last coin. He rubbed it slowly around Alfie's mouth, then forced Alfie's jaws rigidly apart so he could concentrate on the moist sensitive skin just beyond the tideline of his dry lips. Leon watched Pious rub the metal backwards and forwards across them, until they started to swell and blister.

When Pious seemed to grow tired of this phenomenon, he placed the coin delicately between his teeth and leaned towards Alfie, slowly tightening his grip on Alfie's frozen jaws.

And then Pious kissed him, a long perfect kiss on his abused, silver-smarting lips. Leon watched closely and saw Pious idly rolling the burning coin from his mouth into Alfie's, like a strange mockery of a sweetmeat, passed between the mouths of lovers. Leon imagined the coin rolling roughly around between his mouth and Alfie's, forced from one to another by burning tongues. He imagined it smashing against their clashing teeth and then studding their merged saliva with tiny flecks of silver, washing both their mouths in sharp keening pain.

Then the coin chinked onto the floor as Pious pulled out of the kiss to stare at Alfie's unseeing silver-covered eyes. Alfie's swollen lips began to move, wordlessly until, eventually his blistered tongue formed one soft word.

'Never,' he said and his head sank onto his chest.

Pious turned to the rest of the Beasts. 'And what do we do if he still refuses the crown?' No one answered. It wasn't a question that required an answer. Pious met Leon's eye and said, 'Bring the cub up here.'

Iris swallowed hard and straightened against the wall of the cavern. They had emerged into a small rocky chamber and, too late, realised that there were four men walking towards them. Ancient Beasts.

These were not good odds. Pure, she was pretty sure, she could rely on for some furious fighting, but could it be enough? She pulled the crossbow off her back. This mystical weapon better live up to its legend.

'You're Ancient Beasts,' Iris said, aiming the crossbow at the leader of the pack. A tall, big-built man with red hair.

'That's right. I'm Grayson, by the way.'

'Yeah, well, nice to meet you, Grayson. I'm sorry to have to tell you that I don't like Ancient Beasts very much. One of your lot killed my brother and you know where that got me? To a place where I now have to kill all the Ancient Beasts in the world. And no one will even tell me how many that is. But, it is kind of my destiny or something. And witches are pretty keen I do it so . . .' She tightened her grip on the crossbow. 'So I don't really have a lot of choice.'

'Oh, Iris. Trust you to turn up now when everyone thinks you're dead.' Iris looked up at the speaker. An extremely beautiful dark-haired women stood in the mouth of the tunnel that the Ancient Beasts had emerged through a few moments ago. 'I was wondering when I'd get to meet you. The real Warrior Wolf. I'm Sabrina.'

'I don't care who you are,' Iris said pulling out a small handgun from her pocket and aiming it at her – keeping the crossbow on the Beasts.

In retaliation, Sabrina pulled out a handgun of her own and pointed that at Iris. 'Perhaps it would make things a lot simpler if I killed you. Your boyfriend's busy right now. He's going to join The Silver Crown. That'll probably work out a lot better if he doesn't know you're still alive.'

'Yeah? Try me,' Iris said with her teeth pressed tight together, noticing for the first time that the Beasts were watching this like it was part of the show.

'Mmm, I will, naturally, but let's make this a bit more interesting first.' Sabrina threw her gun on the floor in front of her. And something about that move terrified Iris. It disarmed her more than Sabrina had disarmed herself.

For a few seconds. No one moved. Behind her, Iris could hear Pure breathing. He had a pistol in each hand pointed at the four Beasts.

Then Sabrina smiled. Iris saw a silver sparkle in her mouth. 'Come here, Iris. Let me explain something to you.'

Iris turned to Pure, shrugged and began to walk forwards. Sabrina wasn't armed. The Beasts moved back to let her pass. Pure followed her, jumping around and aiming his gun at anything that moved.

Iris walked right up to Sabrina and put the tip of the crossbow's bolt to her throat.

Alfie panted hard as Pious ripped away the coins that were covering his eyes. His head still swimming from the pain. The coins on his skin hurt like nothing he'd ever known. He couldn't think. And Leon was there. Leon was standing right in front of him. His wrists chained above his head like Alfie's. His T-shirt ripped away.

Pious stood square in front of them both. He spoke to Alfie. 'You, Friday, are so ignorant of the ways of the wolf. Not your fault of course, damn Tobias and his fear of death. The reason this is not working is your loyalty to your sire. Not Tobias, not me, your woman. She's taken your sire's power. She's too strong. Is she your mate too?'

'Iris?'

Pious came very close. He put a hand on Alfie's chest, pressing the coin bound to his left nipple harder into him. 'It was her wasn't it? She killed him not you. I knew Tobias's interpretation of the prophecy was wrong. He relied on that ratty little human to do all his translation work. 'Course I had it checked. She did it, didn't she? Your woman?'

Alfie gave a slow serious nod.

'But here's the deal. That doesn't matter. She's dead. If she did take his power it's gone. But I still want you. You're a good strong wolf. A Beast cub. If anyone can take Tobias's place you can. All you need to do is agree to take the crown. It'll make you loyal to us. Loyal to the Divine Wolf above anything. It'll sever your bonds to anyone else. Sever the pain you're feeling now. Not the coins. The other pain. The really serious stuff you're feeling. She's dead. Your mate is dead. That hurts. But I can fix that for you too. Just tell me when you want the pain to stop.' Pious twisted his hand more firmly on Alfie's smarting chest.

Alfie groaned. He could feel his loyalty to Iris burning him inside. He knew it was a power so strong it could take him through anything. He would never betray her. Even if she was dead. He simply couldn't. Even through this. He shook his head.

'Well,' said Pious, 'if you're still feeling some kind of perverted thrall to her, we have other ways. Something stronger. One of the best ways to break thrall is the downward tide. Where a wolf breaks his bond with his sire in order to protect his cub. And as we have your cub here . . .'

Pious walked over to Leon with the coins. Alfie made a bellowing noise lifting himself up weakly in his chains.

He placed a coin on Leon's stomach, right in the centre of his enormous scar, pressing it down when Leon started to buck and kick.

'No,' shouted Alfie, 'this isn't right. This has nothing to do with him.'

Pious turned and smiled at Alfie, still holding the coin onto Leon's bucking body. 'Just tell me when you want the pain to stop.'

The pain from the silver fixed to Alfie's body had receded to a low throb. Without the constant fear of more pain he was able to see things a little more rationally. He set his jaw. As Pious bound the first coin to Leon's body Alfie's eyes began to burn.

'Damn it,' Pious turned away from what he was doing. 'Get me some cold water would you?'

Leon had passed out in his chains.

'No,' Alfie shouted, finding a voice from somewhere. 'Don't. I'll do it. I'll take the crown.'

Pious smiled at Alfie. 'Oh good boy.'

Then he turned and ushered two of the Beasts forwards who unfastened Alfie's manacles.

When he was freed Alfie's legs could barely support him. Pious held him as he wrenched the silver and fabric from his body. It fell away like gossamer. Struggling with his weakened body, he reached for the crown waiting for him on the table.

Pious said. 'You need to draw forth your power as you do this or the crown will burn you. I know you can be a Beast, Alfie, take the mantle and be it.'

42

Iris bit her teeth hard together and spoke through them, 'So, Sabrina, you got any more moves or shall I just kill you now?'

'Oh, I am sorry, am I boring you? Well how about this for a little diversion.' Sabrina snapped her fingers.

Something appeared in the middle of the cavern. A huge silver orb.

'What?' said Iris. It took a second for her to realise. 'Oh. Oh God, no.'

Iris turned to Pure standing behind her. She could tell from his face that he understood too. The four Beasts before them were becoming wolves. Huge wolves. 'Oh God,' Iris whispered. All her years fighting the Beast, but suddenly all she could think of was the fact that she had never killed one of these creatures in their wolf form.

'I'll take them,' Pure said.

And before Iris could say anything he was running. Heading right into the pack of wolves. Iris stared, hesitated too long. Pure was fighting in the midst of them. Using a blade. Of course, Pure would know from his time working with her that bullets couldn't penetrate an Ancient Beast's hide. Iris didn't know what to do. The only way to help him was suicide.

You know, I so want to say 'Use the force'.

'Matthew this is not a good time.'

Matthew was standing next to her, in his ripped overcoat, with his black hair sticking up, looking casual with his weight on one hip. *Now, Iris, be nice.*

'OK, sorry, hi Matthew. How are you? Here for my death again?'

You don't die, Iris. Destiny.

'I can't kill four Beasts hand to hand. Close combat. Even with Pure's help. And bullets can't penetrate . . .'

Crossbow doesn't fire bullets, does it?

'Oh.'

It's the weapon of the Warrior Wolf, Iris. And it's called that for a reason.

Iris raised the bow and took aim. One Beast was down, it's throat slashed by Pure's blade. But Pure was on the ground, the other three Beast's surrounding him. Iris fired.

And, oh, the crossbow was amazing. If holding it had felt good, firing it was orgasmic. It seemed to respond to her will, like a lost part of her. She took one of the Beasts down with her first bolt.

Two left. One was on Pure's chest, the other was looking at her, readying itself for attack. Iris aimed. But this bolt only hit the creature's leg. It didn't flinch.

Still need a fatal shot, Iris.

The crossbow only took two bolts at a time. Iris scrambled in her pocket for more and reloaded. By the time she was ready to fire again the wolf had decided to spring. She caught it in mid-air. It crashed to the floor so hard the whole cavern seemed to shake.

As Iris whirled around to finish off the final wolf her heart stopped. Pure was on the ground beneath it. The side of his face was covered in blood. Iris screamed. She ran towards the wolf, aiming and firing as she went. The bolt slammed into it almost as Iris thought it. The wolf fell and Iris landed on her knees next to Pure.

Pure looked at her. 'It bit me,' he said.

Iris looked Pure right in the eyes. 'Yes,' she said. His face. It wasn't a fatal bite. Iris pulled the crossbow bolt out of the dead Beast lying next to them. She took Pure's hand in hers and with the other slammed the crossbow bolt right into his chest.

Sabrina screamed. Annoyance rather than fear. Iris knew all four Beasts were dead then because she felt their power smack into her – hard and nasty – and she realised she had felt that with the Beast. Power she had no place for. She wasn't a werewolf. She felt like she was going to be sick as she got to her feet, her hands sticky with Pure's blood.

'OK, Sabrina,' she said, 'I guess I only have you to kill now.' Matthew was gone. It was just Iris and Sabrina left standing.

'Take your best shot,' Sabrina sneered.

'What the fuck are you?' Iris said.

'What do you mean?'

'You didn't change. You're not a lyc. What *are* you?' Iris rooted in her pocket for one of the many guns she had on her person. This one was a teeny handgun. The smallest she had taken from Blake's office. The one he kept taped to the bottom of his wastepaper basket. 'But actually I don't care exactly what you are. All I want to know is, are silver bullets going to kill you? They do kill a lot of things, I've found. I actually killed a swan once by mistake. What do you reckon?'

'I really don't know,' said Sabrina, her eyes flicking to the gun and then back to Iris's face. She looked nervous.

Iris aimed the gun and steadied herself 'You might be thinking that I won't just shoot you like this. With you unarmed and me not really knowing exactly what you are. But I really, really will.' And as Iris said the last few words of her sentence she squeezed the trigger.

The bullet that she sent hurtling towards Sabrina should have hit her in the heart. But it didn't, it dropped right out of the air before it reached her. Iris watched it jangle onto the floor. 'Yeah, see, I kind of thought something like that might happen. So what are you? Shall we try something else? Will a silver blade kill you?'

Sabrina snorted through her nose. 'Try it.'

Behind them the huge magically-created moon had flickered and died, almost as if it couldn't sustain itself with Sabrina's attention elsewhere.

'OK,' said Iris, 'so you're what, some kind of an uber-uber-Beast.' Iris shrugged. 'Well I don't know what might kill you. But I'm sure as hell going to try a blade.' Iris drew the dagger from her shoulder holster. She dropped the gun and exploded into a run from a standing start, throwing herself into a diving kick that sent Sabrina flying over backwards with Iris on top of her.

Iris was straddling Sabrina on the floor. Sabrina's hair was sparkling. A thread of twisted wire and silver stars was wreathed through it. Iris touched it. She pulled it away. And then she raised the dagger.

But before she struck Iris noticed a small sound. A couple of stones falling from the ceiling. Then something else. A sudden rush of earth cascading down. She looked around her, still poised to strike.

There was a crashing ripping sound. The loudest sound Iris had ever heard. Up above them in the roof of the cavern was a hole. A sudden hole, bored right through the solid rock to the world outside. She could see blue sky through it. The crash had been whatever had caused that to happen.

Through the hole shot a flock of broomsticks; Cate at its head with an elegant hook-nosed woman in a business suit and high heels flying shotgun next to her, and full entourage behind them.

Iris raised her blade again.

Cate shouted, 'Iris! No!'

Iris turned again. Cate was almost on her, swooping out of the sky. She whistled past Iris, plucking the blade away. Iris screamed at her, 'No, Cate, no. I have to.'

Cate swooped through the air again, whirling around and coming to land a few feet from Iris. She dismounted with a swish of paisley skirt and walked over to Iris, the dagger in her hand. When Cate got closer she said, 'No, Iris, no. You can't.'

'I shot her with a silver bullet, but she didn't die. It didn't even hit her.'

A voice behind Iris said, 'Yeah, well that isn't surprising.'

Iris turned. The other witch, the elegant one with the suit and the nose was standing right behind her. She crouched down over Sabrina, whose eyes were closed.

Cate touched Iris's shoulder. 'She's not a werewolf,' Cate said softly, 'she's a witch. A very bad human-hating witch. I did try to warn you about them. And this is Lilith, by the way. She's one of the most powerful witches in the world. She'll fix this.'

'What?' Iris gulped. The thought that she had nearly stabbed a witch made her stomach roll with nausea. 'But she's part of The Silver Crown. What was she doing?'

Lilith was patting one of Sabrina's cheeks lightly, trying to revive her. Iris blinked – since when was Sabrina unconscious?

'Fucking up humans,' Lilith said, then started patting a little harder. 'Come on, Sab, come to mama.'

Sabrina opened her eyes and looked at Lilith. 'Aw, crap.'

Lilith laughed as Cate scampered over. 'Yeah, yeah, Sabby, who's been a bad girl? Just you wait and see what mama's got waiting for you at home.'

'What?' said Sabrina weakly.

Lilith shrugged. 'Ah, variation on a theme I guess. Witch punishments. Want to decide if you get it very hot or very wet? What about the iron shoes? We haven't done the iron shoes for ages.'

'Wet iron shoes?' Sabrina asked and Lilith gave a loud

bark of a laugh as she helped Sabrina to her feet and got her onto a spare broomstick carried by one of the other witches.

Cate said, 'OK? Sorry about all that. See you back at the office, Iris,' as she climbed over her broomstick, kicked off from the ground and was airborne.

As the flock of witches receded the ceiling of the cavern seemed to close up around them.

43

Alfie paused a moment before he set the crown down on his head. And in that moment there was a tiny sound. A delicate little *snick*. Human ears would have missed it, but all the werewolves in the room suddenly looked in the same direction.

And then a crossbow appeared around the edge of the tunnel opening and killed the two Ancient Beasts who stood at that end of the room, before Alfie even realised what he was looking at.

A voice that Alfie had thought he would never hear again followed the bow, saying, 'Oh sorry, were you waiting for me?' Iris stepped into the tunnel opening and paused for a slice of time while she took in the scene.

Alfie was in love with Iris. But never more so than in this moment. Seeing her like this. Dirty and fierce and armed. He wanted to fuck her. Right this moment. He wanted to get Iris to that room with the pink satin-draped bed. Goddamn, but she was filthy. Had she tunnelled her way down here or something? Alfie – delirious with pain, with grief, with everything – thought only about ripping off Iris's shapeless fatigues and finding pink flesh underneath. About licking her grimy cheek to leave bright tracks of cleanliness across her. His cock pulsed.

And Alfie knew that for a moment she only saw him. He was naked apart from his collar and a silver crown that he was still holding bare inches from his scalp. His body was covered in dried blood and red soreness. He saw her flinch very, very slightly when she looked at him, but then her face set hard. She said, completely coolly, 'Oh, I really wish I could kill you all twice for this.'

Behind Alfie, someone moved. Pious. He pushed the crown down onto Alfie's head. Alfie jerked and went to take it off again. But it was too late. He waited for the crown to burn him. It didn't. He took several deep breaths and turned around to Pious, just as a crossbow bolt flew threw the air and hit Pious in the chest. He fell.

Alfie turned back around. The crown on his head had dulled his senses. Every sensation. He felt as if he were underwater. Iris was alive. Iris was here. All the Beasts in the room were dead. How did she do that? When did she . . .? She was holding a crossbow. Warrior Wolf. Wolf's woman. Iris!

He felt the weight of the crown on his head. He went to take it off. He couldn't.

Iris looked over at Alfie. His skin was such a mess. Some of the red marks were blistered. Nasty. She had just killed six Beasts in this room. The crossbow had moved like magic. The adrenaline had been pumping so hard, she could barely remember doing it. And, oh god, was that Leon chained and unconscious. What was this?

Six dead Beasts. *Six? That wasn't quite right.*

'Where's the twelfth?' Iris said.

'The twelfth?' said Alfie.

'I killed four in the tunnels. Six in here. That's ten. I killed Tobias, that's eleven. There are meant to be twelve. Who's the twelfth?'

'The Divine Wolf,' said Alfie quietly. 'She's the twelfth. I'm not sure where she is. In fact, I thought maybe Sabrina, somehow might really be . . .' Alfie seemed to be acting a little strangely, although that wasn't surprising after what he must have been through.

'No, Sabrina was a bloody witch.' Iris shook her head. 'I don't know how we didn't spot it earlier.'

'Iris,' Alfie said, 'I can't get this crown off. Do you want to take a look? Maybe it's like the collar . . .'

But Iris barely heard him. She was too buzzy with adrenaline. Still on the alert for something else to kill. 'So where's this Divine Wolf?'

'I'm here.'

Iris turned around.

The woman was standing in the tunnel mouth. Ordinary. Slim and average height, short hair that was somewhere between brown and grey. Unremarkable. Apart from the fact that, as Iris looked at her, she could tell she was the most powerful lyc she had yet encountered.

'You're the mother wolf,' Iris said. She wasn't even sure how she knew. *The mother wolf.*

'Mother wolf!' the woman snapped in a voice that was low, slow and growly. 'I hate that title. There's more to me than being the mother of all werewolves you know. I prefer . . .'

'The Divine.' It was Alfie speaking. As Iris turned to look at him, he was pulling himself very straight and upright. The crown on his head was shining, his face was enraptured and his cock was hard.

Iris suddenly felt very frightened. 'Alfie, take off the crown. The crown makes you loyal. You need to take it off.'

But no one in the room was listening to Iris. The Divine said, 'Oh, this is the new pup? Come here. Let me see you.'

'Yes ma'am,' said Alfie. He marched over almost pushing Iris out of the way.

'Alfie, what are you . . .? Listen to me. Take it off.'

Alfie sank to his knees in front of the Divine. He barely looked at Iris when she spoke to him.

The Divine lifted Alfie's chin and looked into his eyes. 'Oh. Mother,' Alfie said, his words a breath.

'Alfie!' Iris shouted, but Alfie didn't react.

The Divine turned and smiled. 'I don't think he can hear you, sweetheart.'

'Of course he can hear me. Alfie! Alfie! It's me, Alfie, Iris. What's going on? Take the crown off. It's me! Iris! You broke your thrall for me, remember?'

'Oh, darling. Forget that. He would have betrayed the Beast for me too. And in a heartbeat. What he feels for me outranks anything else. There is nothing beyond this. The sensations are so strong he's barely aware of the world beyond me. I'm his mistress, his goddess, his angel. I'm everything to him right now. I'm the Beast, I'm Misty. I'm *you*.' And she bent slowly at the waist, tilted Alfie's chin and kissed him slowly on the lips.

Then without breaking the kiss, she reached down and removed his collar.

Iris just stared at them. She felt like her chest was going to burst open. 'No,' she shouted. Even though there wasn't any real need to shout in the small room.

The Divine looked at her. 'Chain her up, Alfred.'

'What?' Iris shouted. 'No!' But Alfie was already up and on her. She tried to fight but Alfie suddenly seemed so strong. Ten times stronger then usual. He dragged her across the room to where Leon was hanging and wrestled her into the other set of manacles hanging from the ceiling. He didn't make eye contact with her once.

'Good,' said the Divine. 'Now come with me, Alfred. I've really had enough of Oxford. And bring your cub.'

Alfie turned and released Leon from his manacles. He slumped into Alfie's arms and Alfie heaved him over his shoulder. They followed the Divine out of the room.

Iris screamed and screamed after Alfie, but he didn't even look back.

She was alone in the room, staring at the Silver Collar lying on the floor.

44

Blake was playing Minesweeper on his computer and thinking about how, if he hadn't killed her earlier, he could've got Aurelia to come in and suck his dick while he was doing so. That was when the entry phone buzzed.

He didn't pick up the phone. He wanted the walk. So instead he took the two flights of stairs to the foyer and opened the door himself. On the doorstep stood a tightly pulled together woman with smooth grey hair viciously clipped to her head. She was a least six inches taller than Blake.

His eyes dropped to see if she was wearing heels. She was, but only little kitten ones. Those were adding an inch and a half to her height, maximum. As a relatively short man, Blake always found tall women intimidating and brutally attractive.

She was mature, in her early fifties, but that didn't stop Blake briefly imagining taking her upstairs and bending her over his desk. He shifted a little as his dick pulsed.

'Are you Dr Malcolm Tobias?' said the woman. 'I'm Erin Cobalt. It's one year since you received your grant from us. I'm here to conduct the audit.'

To be continued

Acknowledgements and Author's note

First, I'd like to thank everyone who gave me their time, especially Ewan, my parents and Isabel for childcare. Secondly, everyone who gave me their sanity and advice especially extremely talented Black Lace author Madelynne Ellis (for loving Leon), extremely talented Black Lace author Kristina Lloyd (for loving Blake) and Elizabeth, Liz and Lizzy.

Special thanks for some significant – if oblique – inspirations also go to Naomi, Fiona, Guy, Jenni, Rebecca, Michael and Ewan who all who watched the blood moon/lunar eclipse with me in March 2007 and asked me what would happen to my werewolves during it.

Huge thanks also to everyone who assured me that Blake could keep his name the way it was and that I should stop worrying about it.

The story of Blake's encounter with Lilith can be found in 'What Witches Want' by Mathilde Madden in the Black Lace short story collection *Love on the Dark Side*.

The Silver Cage

Mathilde Madden

Iris walked over a small bridge and found herself in the botanic garden. She was looking for witches. The only people left who could help her. It was about time they took some damn responsibility for what she was going through.

Appearing as if out of the greenery a woman dressed in a pencil skirt, seamed stocking and heels fell into step with her.

'Hey, Iris right? The Warrior Wolf? Friend of Hecate?' the woman said with a brilliant smile.

Iris rolled her shoulders. They still really hurt. In fact her arms were aching all over. 'Hecate?'

'Yeah. Well, Cate. That's just kind of a joke we do. Hey, Cate! *Hecate*. My name's Lilith and I get sick of being the only witchily named one.'

Iris nodded vaguely. 'Yeah, right.'

'Your wrists are bleeding, did you know?'

Iris looked at them. Her wrists were ringed with angry red bracelets flecked with blood. She rubbed the left one with her right hand. 'Oh,' she said, 'yes. That's from trying to ... well you know.' Because of course Lilith would know. Being a witch. She would know everything.

Lilith smiled. 'Oh yeah. I know just who you are. You're the girl who was banging that ridiculously hot werewolf, aren't you? His girl Friday. Alfie, right? Hey, you know, tell me, did he ever do any modelling?'

'Modelling, no I don't think so. He probably wouldn't

want to because of what happened back with the Beast. You know he was attacked by the Beast while he was doing some modelling for my brother.'

'And that's, what, given him a phobia of taking his top off for the camera?'

'No, I think he just ... oh, I don't know. He hasn't done anything like that. Well, unless he's done it since I last saw him, anyway. That's kind of what I came to talk to you about ...'

Lilith clapped her hands, cutting off Iris's words. 'Oh, the silly boy. Probably worried about being exploited. Tell him they're very tasteful. I mean, they'll be nude but back and white. All arty. And, hey, weren't you married to Blake Tabernacle as well?'

'Um, yeah, kind of. For a bit.'

'Wow. Hard to even see him as the marrying kind,' said Lilith. 'You do have an interesting *type*. Werewolf hunters, werewolves.' Lilith gave a laughing shrug. 'What can it all mean? Are you trying for some kind of award? Weirdest back catalogue ever?'

Iris was getting increasingly confused by this conversation so she decided to ignore it. 'Please. Are you going to help me. Alfie's been taken by, uh, this *woman*,' Iris said.

'She's not a woman. She's the Divine. The divine wolf. The She Wolf. The mother of them all. She's practically the werewolf god. Or goddess, whatever. I'm not so keen on gendered words myself.'

'Well, yes, her. She has Alfie. You know, the guy you were talking about, the one you want to do some, uh, modelling? You have to help me get him back.'

Lilith stopped walking and turned to face Iris, her heels grinding in the gravel. 'I know. Thing is, doll, I think you're going to have to let her have him. I mean, he wants to be with her. I mean not *wants* want. But she's got a power over him that can't be imagined. She's it.'

'She took his collar off.'

'Well, exactly.'

'But, I love him. Is there really nothing I can do to get him back?'

Lilith wrinkled her long nose. 'Well, you know, that's not really the question. The question is what will happen if you *don't* get him back?'

'What will happen?'

'The Silver Crown have been using the Divine's power for centuries. Now the circle is truly fucked and her power is barely contained. While they had her everyone was safe. She gave them the power to keep werewolves hidden from the wider world and they kept her controlled. All of the supers agreed it was a reasonable arrangement. It's been going on forever. I know Sabrina was a little bit on the dark side, but it seemed fair enough to let her work with them. Make sure they had the Beasts they needed to keep the Divine under control. Of course, we had the prophecies, we knew you'd be along to mess it all up sooner or later.'

Iris frowned, 'The supers?'

'What?'

'You said "the supers agreed it was a reasonable arrangement". What are "the supers"?'

'Supernatural people, witches, vamps, lycs.'

'You call yourselves "the supers"?'

'Well, OK no, actually, but I figured if I did it enough it might catch on. Now, to get on with the point, the She Wolf – without The Silver Crown containing her – will probably unite all the werewolves in the world. Organise them. Bring them together. I expect she'll want to wipe humanity off the face of the earth, that's normally the way things go.'

'She can do that?'

'She's the top of the werewolf food chain. The number one sire. Every wolf answers to her.'

Iris straightened up. 'Is she an Ancient Beast?'

'I don't know. Perhaps technically. She's certainly both ancient and bestial. She is literally a wolf. It's only magic that makes her look and sound human.'

'So I could kill her. I kill Ancient Beasts.'

'Hmm,' said Lilith, letting her weight sway from foot to foot. 'You could. But that might kill every werewolf on earth.'

Iris swallowed. 'Every werewolf?'

'Well I think so. She holds it all together. Thrall. The bonds of power between werewolves that keep them all in line. Without her, without those controls, they'd just all start killing each other. You've seen how they operate. Savage creatures. They'd all die without thrall. But you could try it. I mean, it's understandable, if the alternative is watching the Divine wipe humanity off the face of the earth.'

'But Alfie. Would it kill Alfie?'

'Oh no.' Lilith smiled.

Iris's heart leapt. 'Alfie would be OK?'

'Alfie would indeed be OK, because you're not going to do it. You're not going to do anything. You're still trapped in the tunnels under Oxford, chained up, dying.'

'Oh.' Suddenly Iris's grip on where she really was felt very wobbly. 'Is this . . .?'

'A hallucination? Yes, sorry didn't you know? You're really not well at all down there.'

'Well actually, now I come to think of it, I do have no memory of how I got here.'

'Yeah. Quite. So that's the thing. I don't see how you're even going to get out of those tunnels let alone save the world.'

'I don't suppose you could do some magic and help me out.'

'Ah, well, that's the other thing. Stuff like this, we really don't like to meddle.'

'But, the wiping humanity off the face of the earth thing?'

'You know, really, if we witches intervened every time *that* was threatened . . .'

'Seriously? No chance?'

'Sorry.'

'But I'm the Warrior Wolf. It's my destiny. I'm the one who kills them all.'

'Well yes, you are, but you said it. Prophecies are never clear until the events they talk about are over. When this is played through I'm sure we'll see how to apply what is written. I'm writing this paper about that actual. Prophetic hindsight . . .'

Lilith's voice trailed off and the two women walked a little further down the gravel path together. Now she knew she was still in the tunnels the constant dull pain in Iris's arms seemed to increase until it was almost unbearable. Lilith said, 'God, this is starting to feel awkward.'

'I know. Shouldn't I have woken up screaming in the chains by now?'

'Yeah. Actually I could fix that for you. Then we could call it quits.'

'Quits?'

'Yeah. So no whining that witches never help you out.' Lilith made a gesture like she was wiping a crumb away from her bottom lip, then snapped her fingers.

Iris woke up screaming in the chains.

Visit the Black Lace website at
www.black-lace-books.com

FIND OUT THE LATEST INFORMATION AND TAKE ADVANTAGE OF OUR FANTASTIC FREE BOOK OFFER! ALSO VISIT THE SITE FOR . . .

- All Black Lace titles currently available and how to order online
- Great new offers
- Writers' guidelines
- Author interviews
- An erotica newsletter
- Features
- Cool links

BLACK LACE – THE LEADING IMPRINT OF WOMEN'S SEXY FICTION

TAKING YOUR EROTIC READING PLEASURE TO NEW HORIZONS

LOOK OUT FOR THE ALL-NEW BLACK LACE BOOKS – AVAILABLE NOW!

All books priced £7.99 in the UK. Please note publication dates apply to the UK only. For other territories, please contact your retailer.

MINX
Megan Blythe
ISBN 978 0 352 33638 5

Miss Amy Pringle is pert, spoilt and spirited when she arrives at Lancaster Hall to pursue her engagement to Lord Fitzroy, eldest son of the Earl and heir to a fortune. The Earl is not impressed with this young upstart and sets out to break her spirit through a series of painful and humiliating ordeals.

The trouble for him is that she enjoys every one of his 'punishments' and creates havoc at the Hall, provoking and infuriating the stuffy Earl at every opportunity while indulging in all manner of naughtiness below the stairs. The young Lord remains aloof, however, and, in order to win his affections, Amy sets about seducing his well-endowed but dim brother, Bubb. When she is discovered in bed with Bubb and one of the servant girls, how will father and son react?

Coming in January 2008

ONE BREATH AT A TIME
Gwen Masters
ISBN 978 0 352 34163 1

Kelley is a woman with a broken heart. She doesn't need another
complication in her life, and certainly not another man. But when she
stumbles across Tom, the things she thought she didn't want are exactly
what she needs. As they fall for each other and engage on a compelling
journey through dominance and submission, both lovers strive to shake
away their dark pasts. But is blinding passion enough to prevent them
being ripped apart?

LURED BY LUST
Tania Picarda
ISBN 978 0 352 33533 3

Clara Fox works at a prestigious art gallery. One sweltering summer's
day she receives an email from a stranger who calls himself Mr X. Clara is
curious, and begins to involve herself in a world of experimentation and
adventurous games.
   Can she juggle her kinky liaison with Mr X with all her other intense
relationships? And when her former boyfriend Paul tries to win her back,
what will he do when he finds that Clara has become a total perv?

Coming in February 2008

A GENTLEMAN'S WAGER
Madelynne Ellis
ISBN 978 0 352 33800 6

When eighteenth-century young lady Bella Rushdale finds herself fiercely attracted to handsome landowner Lucerne Marlinscar, she does not expect the rival for her affections to be another man. However, the handsome and decadent Marquis Pennerley has desired Lucerne for years and, when they are brought together at the remote Lauwine Hall for a country party on the Yorkshire Moors, he intends to claim him. This leads to a passionate struggle for dominance – at the risk of scandal – between the highly sexed Bella and the debauched aristocrat. Ultimately it will be Lucerne who will choose the outcome – and his decision is bound to upset somebody's plans.

POSSESSION
Mathilde Madden, Madelynne Ellis, Anne Tourney
ISBN 978 0 352 34164 8

Three otherworldly short novels of shape-shifters and possession:

Falling Dancer: Kelda has two jobs: full-time bartender, part-time exorcist. She meets vengeful spirits and misguided demons wherever she goes. She wishes the spirit world would leave her alone so she could have a relationship that lasted longer than twenty-four hours, but when she's contacted by a sexy musician who wants her to solve the mystery of his girlfriend's disappearance, she can't help getting involved . . .

The Silver Chains: Alfie Friday is a werewolf. For 7 years he has controlled his curse carefully by locking himself in a cage every full moon. But now he's changing when it isn't full moon. His girlfriend Misty travels to South America to try and find a way of controlling Alfie's changes, but discovers the key to the problem lies in Oxford. The place it all began for Alfie and the place he has vowed never to return to.

Broken Angel: After a stealing a copy of an ancient manuscript, Blaze Makaresh finds himself being hunted down by a gang of youkai – demons who infiltrate human society in order to satisfy their hunger for sex and flesh. When Talon, an elitist society of demon-hunters, come to his aid, he's soon enmeshed with the beautiful Asha, and the dawning of an age-old prophecy.

THE SILVER CAGE
Mathilde Madden
ISBN 978 0 352 34157 0

Iris and Alfie have been driven apart by the strongest forces in the werewolf world – the powerful thrall of the Divine Wolf – the mother of them all. Now Iris needs to win Alfie back, not just for herself, but because the fate of the world could rest upon it.

But the only way to free Alfie from the power of the Divine Wolf is to kill her. Something that could end the lives of all werewolves. Including Alfie himself – Iris's true love.

Black Lace Booklist

Information is correct at time of printing. To avoid disappointment, check availability before ordering. Go to www.black-lace-books.com. All books are priced £7.99 unless another price is given.

BLACK LACE BOOKS WITH A CONTEMPORARY SETTING

☐ ALWAYS THE BRIDEGROOM Tesni Morgan	ISBN 978 0 352 33855 6	£6.99
☐ THE ANGELS' SHARE Maya Hess	ISBN 978 0 352 34043 6	
☐ ASKING FOR TROUBLE Kristina Lloyd	ISBN 978 0 352 33362 9	
☐ BLACK LIPSTICK KISSES Monica Belle	ISBN 978 0 352 33885 3	£6.99
☐ THE BLUE GUIDE Carrie Williams	ISBN 978 0 352 34132 7	
☐ THE BOSS Monica Belle	ISBN 978 0 352 34088 7	
☐ BOUND IN BLUE Monica Belle	ISBN 978 0 352 34012 2	
☐ CAMPAIGN HEAT Gabrielle Marcola	ISBN 978 0 352 33941 6	
☐ CAT SCRATCH FEVER Sophie Mouette	ISBN 978 0 352 34021 4	
☐ CIRCUS EXCITE Nikki Magennis	ISBN 978 0 352 34033 7	
☐ CLUB CRÈME Primula Bond	ISBN 978 0 352 33907 2	£6.99
☐ COMING ROUND THE MOUNTAIN Tabitha Flyte	ISBN 978 0 352 33873 0	£6.99
☐ CONFESSIONAL Judith Roycroft	ISBN 978 0 352 33421 3	
☐ CONTINUUM Portia Da Costa	ISBN 978 0 352 33120 5	
☐ DANGEROUS CONSEQUENCES Pamela Rochford	ISBN 978 0 352 33185 4	
☐ DARK DESIGNS Madelynne Ellis	ISBN 978 0 352 34075 7	
☐ THE DEVIL INSIDE Portia Da Costa	ISBN 978 0 352 32993 6	
☐ EDEN'S FLESH Robyn Russell	ISBN 978 0 352 33923 2	£6.99
☐ EQUAL OPPORTUNITIES Mathilde Madden	ISBN 978 0 352 34070 2	
☐ FIRE AND ICE Laura Hamilton	ISBN 978 0 352 33486 2	
☐ GOING DEEP Kimberly Dean	ISBN 978 0 352 33876 1	£6.99
☐ GONE WILD Maria Eppie	ISBN 978 0 352 33670 5	
☐ HOTBED Portia Da Costa	ISBN 978 0 352 33614 9	
☐ IN PURSUIT OF ANNA Natasha Rostova	ISBN 978 0 352 34060 3	
☐ IN THE FLESH Emma Holly	ISBN 978 0 352 34117 4	
☐ LEARNING TO LOVE IT Alison Tyler	ISBN 978 0 352 33535 7	

☐ MAD ABOUT THE BOY Mathilde Madden   ISBN 978 0 352 34001 6
☐ MAKE YOU A MAN Anna Clare   ISBN 978 0 352 34006 1
☐ MAN HUNT Cathleen Ross   ISBN 978 0 352 33583 8
☐ THE MASTER OF SHILDEN Lucinda Carrington   ISBN 978 0 352 33140 3
☐ MIXED DOUBLES Zoe le Verdier   ISBN 978 0 352 33312 4   £6.99
☐ MIXED SIGNALS Anna Clare   ISBN 978 0 352 33889 1   £6.99
☐ MS BEHAVIOUR Mini Lee   ISBN 978 0 352 33962 1
☐ PACKING HEAT Karina Moore   ISBN 978 0 352 33356 8   £6.99
☐ PAGAN HEAT Monica Belle   ISBN 978 0 352 33974 4
☐ PEEP SHOW Mathilde Madden   ISBN 978 0 352 33924 9
☐ THE POWER GAME Carrera Devonshire   ISBN 978 0 352 33990 4
☐ THE PRIVATE UNDOING OF A PUBLIC SERVANT   ISBN 978 0 352 34066 5
     Leonie Martel
☐ RELEASE ME Suki Cunningham   ISBN 978 0 352 33671 2   £6.99
☐ RUDE AWAKENING Pamela Kyle   ISBN 978 0 352 33036 9
☐ SAUCE FOR THE GOOSE Mary Rose Maxwell   ISBN 978 0 352 33492 3
☐ SLAVE TO SUCCESS Kimberley Raines   ISBN 978 0 352 33687 3   £6.99
☐ STELLA DOES HOLLYWOOD Stella Black   ISBN 978 0 352 33588 3
☐ THE STRANGER Portia Da Costa   ISBN 978 0 352 33211 0
☐ SUITE SEVENTEEN Portia Da Costa   ISBN 978 0 352 34109 9
☐ SWITCHING HANDS Alaine Hood   ISBN 978 0 352 33896 9   £6.99
☐ TONGUE IN CHEEK Tabitha Flyte   ISBN 978 0 352 33484 8
☐ THE TOP OF HER GAME Emma Holly   ISBN 978 0 352 34116 7
☐ TWO WEEKS IN TANGIER Annabel Lee   ISBN 978 0 352 33599 9   £6.99
☐ UNNATURAL SELECTION Alaine Hood   ISBN 978 0 352 33963 8
☐ VELVET GLOVE Emma Holly   ISBN 978 0 352 34115 0
☐ VILLAGE OF SECRETS Mercedes Kelly   ISBN 978 0 352 33344 5
☐ WILD BY NATURE Monica Belle   ISBN 978 0 352 33915 7   £6.99
☐ WILD CARD Madeline Moore   ISBN 978 0 352 34038 2
☐ WING OF MADNESS Mae Nixon   ISBN 978 0 352 34099 3

BLACK LACE BOOKS WITH AN HISTORICAL SETTING
☐ THE AMULET Lisette Allen   ISBN 978 0 352 33019 2   £6.99
☐ THE BARBARIAN GEISHA Charlotte Royal   ISBN 978 0 352 33267 7
☐ BARBARIAN PRIZE Deanna Ashford   ISBN 978 0 352 34017 7
☐ THE CAPTIVATION Natasha Rostova   ISBN 978 0 352 33234 9

☐ DARKER THAN LOVE Kristina Lloyd	ISBN 978 0 352 33279 0
☐ DIVINE TORMENT Janine Ashbless	ISBN 978 0 352 33719 1
☐ FRENCH MANNERS Olivia Christie	ISBN 978 0 352 33214 1
☐ LORD WRAXALL'S FANCY Anna Lieff Saxby	ISBN 978 0 352 33080 2
☐ NICOLE'S REVENGE Lisette Allen	ISBN 978 0 352 29984 4
☐ THE SENSES BEJEWELLED Cleo Cordell	ISBN 978 0 352 29904 2 £6.99
☐ THE SOCIETY OF SIN Sian Lacey Taylder	ISBN 978 0 352 34080 1
☐ TEMPLAR PRIZE Deanna Ashford	ISBN 978 0 352 34137 2
☐ UNDRESSING THE DEVIL Angel Strand	ISBN 978 0 352 33938 6

BLACK LACE BOOKS WITH A PARANORMAL THEME

☐ BRIGHT FIRE Maya Hess	ISBN 978 0 352 34104 4
☐ BURNING BRIGHT Janine Ashbless	ISBN 978 0 352 34085 6
☐ CRUEL ENCHANTMENT Janine Ashbless	ISBN 978 0 352 33483 1
☐ FLOOD Anna Clare	ISBN 978 0 352 34094 8
☐ GOTHIC BLUE Portia Da Costa	ISBN 978 0 352 33075 8
☐ THE PRIDE Edie Bingham	ISBN 978 0 352 33997 3
☐ THE SILVER COLLAR Mathilde Madden	ISBN 978 0 352 34141 9
☐ THE TEN VISIONS Olivia Knight	ISBN 978 0 352 34119 8

BLACK LACE ANTHOLOGIES

☐ BLACK LACE QUICKIES 1 Various	ISBN 978 0 352 34126 6 £2.99
☐ BLACK LACE QUICKIES 2 Various	ISBN 978 0 352 34127 3 £2.99
☐ BLACK LACE QUICKIES 3 Various	ISBN 978 0 352 34128 0 £2.99
☐ BLACK LACE QUICKIES 4 Various	ISBN 978 0 352 34129 7 £2.99
☐ BLACK LACE QUICKIES 5 Various	ISBN 978 0 352 34130 3 £2.99
☐ BLACK LACE QUICKIES 6 Various	ISBN 978 0 352 34133 4 £2.99
☐ BLACK LACE QUICKIES 7 Various	ISBN 978 0 352 34146 4 £2.99
☐ BLACK LACE QUICKIES 8 Various	ISBN 978 0 352 34147 1 £2.99
☐ MORE WICKED WORDS Various	ISBN 978 0 352 33487 9 £6.99
☐ WICKED WORDS 3 Various	ISBN 978 0 352 33522 7 £6.99
☐ WICKED WORDS 4 Various	ISBN 978 0 352 33603 3 £6.99
☐ WICKED WORDS 5 Various	ISBN 978 0 352 33642 2 £6.99
☐ WICKED WORDS 6 Various	ISBN 978 0 352 33690 3 £6.99
☐ WICKED WORDS 7 Various	ISBN 978 0 352 33743 6 £6.99
☐ WICKED WORDS 8 Various	ISBN 978 0 352 33787 0 £6.99

☐ WICKED WORDS 9 Various   ISBN 978 0 352 33860 0

☐ WICKED WORDS 10 Various   ISBN 978 0 352 33893 8

☐ THE BEST OF BLACK LACE 2 Various   ISBN 978 0 352 33718 4

☐ WICKED WORDS: SEX IN THE OFFICE Various   ISBN 978 0 352 33944 7

☐ WICKED WORDS: SEX AT THE SPORTS CLUB   ISBN 978 0 352 33991 1
    Various

☐ WICKED WORDS: SEX ON HOLIDAY Various   ISBN 978 0 352 33961 4

☐ WICKED WORDS: SEX IN UNIFORM Various   ISBN 978 0 352 34002 3

☐ WICKED WORDS: SEX IN THE KITCHEN Various   ISBN 978 0 352 34018 4

☐ WICKED WORDS: SEX ON THE MOVE Various   ISBN 978 0 352 34034 4

☐ WICKED WORDS: SEX AND MUSIC Various   ISBN 978 0 352 34061 0

☐ WICKED WORDS: SEX AND SHOPPING Various   ISBN 978 0 352 34076 4

☐ SEX IN PUBLIC Various   ISBN 978 0 352 34089 4

☐ SEX WITH STRANGERS Various   ISBN 978 0 352 34105 1

☐ LOVE ON THE DARK SIDE Various   ISBN 978 0 352 34132 7

BLACK LACE NON-FICTION

☐ THE BLACK LACE BOOK OF WOMEN'S SEXUAL   ISBN 978 0 352 33793 1   £6.99
    FANTASIES Edited by Kerri Sharp

To find out the latest information about Black Lace titles, check out the website: www.black-lace-books.com or send for a booklist with complete synopses by writing to:

Black Lace Booklist, Virgin Books Ltd
Thames Wharf Studios
Rainville Road
London W6 9HA

Please include an SAE of decent size. Please note only British stamps are valid.

Our privacy policy
We will not disclose information you supply us to any other parties. We will not disclose any information which identifies you personally to any person without your express consent.

From time to time we may send out information about Black Lace books and special offers. Please tick here if you do <u>not</u> wish to receive Black Lace information. ❏

Please send me the books I have ticked above.

Name ....

Address ....

....

....

....

Post Code ....

Send to: Virgin Books Cash Sales, Thames Wharf Studios, Rainville Road, London W6 9HA.

US customers: for prices and details of how to order books for delivery by mail, call 888-330-8477.

Please enclose a cheque or postal order, made payable to Virgin Books Ltd, to the value of the books you have ordered plus postage and packing costs as follows:

UK and BFPO – £1.00 for the first book, 50p for each subsequent book.

Overseas (including Republic of Ireland) – £2.00 for the first book, £1.00 for each subsequent book.

If you would prefer to pay by VISA, ACCESS/MASTERCARD, DINERS CLUB, AMEX or SWITCH, please write your card number and expiry date here:

....

Signature ....

Please allow up to 28 days for delivery.